HALF MY AGE PLUS SEVEN

A Sinful Confession

By Cristina G.

CRISTINA G.

ISBN: 978-84-947548-1-4

First Digital Edition Kwill Books 2017

www.kwillbooks.com

To Adrian
For all the caresses and kisses
And
To all humans who love an alien
Don't settle for less than you deserve

.

Table of Contents

PROLOGUE

Tara is almost thirty-eight years old, an Eastern European woman with a very sensitive and passionate nature. She lived in Italy for ten years, and moved to England a couple of months ago to improve her English. She had no dreams, plans, or hopes other than that.

Most women are married or divorced at her age, even more than once, but not Tara, no. Because of an illness, she can't have intimate relationships, and at the time of this story she's been single for eight years. Her body has forgotten what making love feels like, or, moreover, it never knew. She is convinced that her heart is frozen until she meets Adrian and it is love at first sight.

The differences between the two are overwhelming. Sun and Moon.

Adrian is a real English boy in a relationship, twelve years younger than Tara. He's a got a troubled soul and a muddled relationship.

Dreams do come true, but be careful what you wish for.

LOVE AT FIRST SIGHT

I used to consider myself a reasonable person, quite smart actually, but this story proved me wrong. It was evident that it was going to be a disaster, even the rocks knew that, but I didn't care. All I cared was feeling Adrian's arms around my body. I needed him so badly. I thought it was an evanescent love, a caprice, but here I am, two years later, feeling for him exactly what I felt when I first saw him that day in August

I knew Adrian was not the one... for God's sake, he's twelve years younger than me! He could have never been the one for that reason only. The worst part is that I knew he was not an ordinary person, his behaviour was very off. That didn't count for my heart. Nothing did.

This is how it all started.

It was scorching hot weather, and my outfit wasn't appropriate for those temperatures. I didn't have any idea of how to dress in this country back then.

All sweaty, horrible looking, I went into a shop and there he was, a tall, young boy with beautiful green eyes and brown hair. He didn't look older than twenty-one, but my heart made a jump when our eyes met. It wasn't intentional; I simply raised my head and looked into his eyes while noticing his tall figure. I instantly knew he felt the same, but the thought of him and me was utterly ridiculous. I blushed, lowered my head, and walked by in a rush.

A week later, I went to play tennis. Play is a big word; I was starting to learn. A friend of mine offered to give me some lessons. Not that he was an instructor or anything, he just played tennis more often than me. I was early, so I sat on a bench waiting for him. A bicycle passed me by. My heart recognised him right away, and my face turned red in one instant.

He stopped and asked if we had met before. Such a cliché, right? But hey, he really believed we knew each other somehow. I said I came to England about a month ago, and it was quite impossible for us to have spoken to one another before. "Are you sure we didn't meet before? I truly have the impression I know you," he insisted.

My English wasn't great, and I am quite a shy person, although people wouldn't say that about me. "Well, I saw you in a shop a few days back, but it was just for a second," I timidly replied.

"Yes, yes! The one on the high street, right? I remember you looked hot. Sorry, feeling hot I meant," he said.

I looked down and remained silent. His phone rang, and my friend got there at the same time. I jumped to my feet, hugged and kissed my friend on the cheek, mumbling random words. The twenty-something-year-old boy looked like he had something to tell me, but changed his mind and we walked away. 'What is this? How can I meet this guy for the second time in less than seven days? It's curious. Could it be destiny?' I wondered in my head.

When my heart started dreaming about him, I told myself not even to dare to think about it. Ever, in no context. There was no way! Not in this world at least.

But destiny had a surprise for us.

A few days later, I started a computer course. My English was poor; luckily everyone was kind and patient with me.

At 1pm, the instructor gave us a break, but I had no food with me, so I went for a walk around the building. There wasn't anything that captured my attention, so I kept walking. After more or less ten minutes, I found a green area. Big trees, grass, flowers. I fell in love right away. I looked at the phone to check the time, I'd got fifteen minutes left. I made some calculations in my mind and decided that I only needed seven to get back, so I put my blue cardigan on the grass and sat on it.

There were many groups of people around, having lunch. The men were wearing dark trousers, shirts, and ties, the women were dressed a little more casual than them, but it was evident they were white-collar workers. I was a blue-collar, a cleaner, and in the future, I was sure I was going to clean their buildings too. I never dreamed of being a cleaner, so I felt a little envious.

I always liked observing people, and I tried not to be seen, but some guys spotted me, so I looked away. They must have thought I was spying on them. And I was, in a way.

I carry a book in my bag all the time, so I took it and opened it, pretending I was reading. I didn't have the courage to raise my eyes from the book again. I heard someone coming close, it was a public area, people were walking, so I didn't pay attention.

"I thought it was you! Dammit, are you stalking me?" a young voice exclaimed.

I turned my head and met the twenty-something-year-old boy, with green eyes. He was wearing black trousers, a white shirt, but no tie.

'God, are you playing with my head? What's going on? It's like we are meant to meet everywhere.' I thought, turning all red. "Hey," I said checking the time. It was time to leave. "I am sorry, but I cannot stay. My course starts in eight minutes, and I still need to get there." I walked away without waiting for a reply.

"I am here almost every day for lunch. I work in an office nearby," he shouted behind me.

The course had classes two days a week. I loved that park, and I was furious that he said he was there every day. I planned on asking my instructor if there was any way to change the break time, but then again, why would she do that? 'I will find another place to spend my break for two days a week. He's a child, for God's sake! I am thirty-eight, don't even think about it. He must be one of those young boys who look for women of my age to share minutes of intimacy without barriers. Disgusting.'

The following day, I went grocery shopping. But the second day of the course, it was raining, and I knew people don't like rain much. Therefore, I was sure the green area was going to be empty.

I always loved rain, and I was euphoric, so I took my raincoat and went directly to the park. I was right, it was empty. 'Hurray!' But I failed to consider one thing: there was no way I could sit on the grass or a bench. 'Never mind,' I thought, 'I will walk and enjoy the solitude and peace.' I had twenty minutes, so I let my feet wander the alleys and was away with the fairies. At some point, I heard some steps getting closer, and there he was again. 'What the hell?'

"Hello. I was not expecting you, or anyone else for that matter, to be here during such bad weather!" I said annoyed.

"My office windows look towards the park. I saw you from there," Adrian pointed in the direction of a building on our right.

"How did you know it was me? It's quite distant," I asked.

"I didn't, I just felt it was you. I don't know why," he confessed.

I blushed terribly, but he couldn't see because of my hoodie. He was wearing a suit and holding a huge umbrella. His trousers were quite wet already.

"Listen, you are getting wet, go inside. We'll talk another time," I concluded.

"And when would that be? I don't even know your name, your phone number, where you live, etc. Do you like cycling? Maybe we could go cycling one day?" he asked.

"My name is Tara, and here is my number," I said, handing him a business card. "You'll find all the information you want about me in there."

"What are you, a spy? Working for CIA? How come you have a business card?" he asked surprised.

"I am a blogger. I wish I was a spy, I'd earn some money," I replied.

He took the card, had a quick look at it, and said his name was Adrian, he had no business card and would call me later. I sent him inside and went back to school, then to work. Not a fun day, that's for sure.

Later in the evening, someone called me, I didn't pick up because I didn't know the number, and because I don't like speaking on the phone. I never liked it. When I went to bed, I wondered why I had given that boy my business card and didn't mention about being a cleaner, but a full-time blogger. Someone was messing around with my mind. Why was that boy so interested in me? And mostly, why was my stupid heart always starting to race when thinking of him? Not great, no. I was almost thirty-eight, living in a different country to which I moved about a month ago. Great Britain, the country of opportunities, I call it.

When I moved to this country, I had no dreams. I just wanted to learn the language, my first love is languages, and to run away... From what? Everything and everyone. But mostly myself. I didn't have great expectations, but as soon as I took my first step on this ground, I was hooked by the politeness of people, the green grass and trees, the amazing looking buildings from thousands of years ago. I lived in Italy for ten years before, but England is a different world.

It hasn't been an easy transition. I was going through a very hard period. I couldn't eat, and I couldn't sleep. I was a total mess.

One day, towards the end of the course, I felt so overwhelmed by everything that I started crying in class. I am a highly sensitive person, and I cry. I cry a lot. It's my way of coping with any type of pressure. I cry if I feel happy, I cry if I feel sad. If I didn't do it, my heart will explode, so I am happy when I cry. I am not ashamed to admit it. However, I don't like crying in public and being put centre stage.

I was furious with myself, and that made it worse. People were looking at me, and I had to run out of the class, and where else to go than my favourite place? So I went there, hid under a tree, and let my tears fall thousands on my burning cheeks. At some point, I heard steps getting closer and tried not to breathe and be discovered. Someone called my name. It was a colleague of mine. The park wasn't very big, so I could hear her calling from five metres away, "Tara, I know you're here somewhere, I brought the things you left in the class. They had to close the building for the night. Come on out."

I didn't wonder how she knew I was there because I told all my colleagues about the fact that I would stay here for twenty-four hours a day if I could. Also, the park was on my way home. I always had a walk down the paths before going home. Therefore, everyone could have found me if they wanted so I couldn't ignore her calls; besides, she'd got my stuff. 'So sweet of her.' I went to her, still sobbing, thanked her, asked for forgiveness and promised we'd talk next time in class. She wanted to speak then, but I am a private person, I do not like talking about my issues, it doesn't make me feel better, quite the contrary, so I said, "Next time." She gave me my things, and I sat on a bench, unable to walk.

Suddenly, Adrian was in front of me. I covered my face with trembling hands and asked him to leave me alone. "You don't have to say anything, just let me walk you home," he offered.

"Absolutely not!" I shouted. "I don't need anyone to take care of me, I can do that by myself. Thank you for offering though."

"All right. What about going for a drink?" he insisted.

I thought for a second, "Why not? A drink might actually do me good."

He helped me getting up as I was struggling a lot, and started walking side by side, like good old friends. "You should eat from time to time, Tara, you don't look well."

"Thanks. You sure know how to make a woman feel good about herself."

"It's not what I meant, you are very thin, it's obvious you don't feed yourself."

"I am not thin!" I cried, but then again, "Am I, really? Yeah, maybe I am. It would make sense; I don't think I have eaten much food since I arrived in England."

"What? Why? You don't like it?" he asked in shock.

"I didn't try any yet. But let's face it, England is not famous for its cuisine, or is it?"

"We do have good food here. I'll take you to dinner one day, and you'll see. What do you like to eat these days?"

"Ice cream. And I don't even like ice cream!" I confessed.

Adrian looked at me in disbelief, "If you don't like ice cream, why do you eat it then?"

"I need energy, and that's the only food my body can digest these days."

"Ice cream is not food!" Adrian exclaimed.

"Why do you think it's not food? Of course it is, everything we eat is food. Well, almost everything. You know what I mean. Ice cream is made from milk or cream. It gives me enough energy to get through a day," I explained.

"It's not healthy, Tara, and you can tell by your looks."

"I don't look healthy?" I asked.

"No, you are very pale, and you are constantly shaking. Your body is exhausted like a battery charged too many times. Earlier you weren't able to stand up. You have no energy, Tara. I am worried about you."

"I am a stranger to you. I bet you have loads of people to worry about. You shouldn't think about my life. By the way, I might give up going to the course I am doing, the computer one. I don't think it's for me. I might not take the exam."

"You will not give up, and you'll take the exam!"

"But I don't understand a word, I don't know why I am there. I am not good with exams, I panic, and my brain blanks out. I am such a loser!"

"You are not a loser. You are having a bad time, that's all. Everyone goes through periods like this. It's no shame. Oh, here we are." I raised my head to see an old black and white building.

"A pub? I don't like pubs. They are dark and gloomy," I said with disgust.

"Not all of them are gloomy. Besides, you have to get used to them, as they are quite popular here."

"What about bars?" I asked.

"There aren't many in this town."

"Coffee shops?"

"Our coffee shops don't serve alcoholic beverages. Besides, they close around seven every evening. And there isn't any nearby, we'd need to go into the city centre to find on," explained Adrian.

"That's not cool. Not cool at all." I paused and hesitated to go inside. "Never mind, I will adapt. Just give me some time," I said defeated.

"I know you will, I have faith in you. Come on, let's go and have a drink. What do you fancy?" asked Adrian.

"Fancy? What does it mean?"

"What do you want?" Adrian explained.

"Oh... whisky."

"I am sorry, did you say whisky?" he asked surprised.

"Yes," I replied genuinely.

"Could I have one whisky and a pint of ale, please?" ordered Adrian, a little confused.

"Single or double? Ice?" the barman asked.

Adrian turned over to me, and I candidly said, "Double, no ice, please!"

Both looked at me in astonishment. "Are you sure?" the barman tried to understand if I was serious about no ice thing.

"Yes, I am sure," I confirmed.

Adrian paid for the drinks, and we both went to sit down outside. The pub was in the middle of nowhere and had a beautiful view. I loved the surrounding greenery. Several birds were flying very close to the ground. Some of these birds were not shy at all and dared to land on the tables and stole food from people. I found it funny, unlike the others who shouted and cursed with rage, "Bloody thieves! Get the heck away!"

"What are these, Adrian, and why are people so upset with them? They are just birds and need food to survive. I understand it's no fun to have the food stolen, but it's not such a tragedy."

"These are not just birds, Tara, they are very noisy and dangerous predators. Many people are attacked by them daily, that's why they are upset. They are called seagulls."

"Oh, I have never seen a seagull before. I had a very poetic opinion about them. For years I dreamt of seeing these birds. Everything is ruined now. What a shame." I said with sadness. "Do you have a sea close by?"

"Yes, there is the Celtic Sea, but not in this city," replied Adrian.

"That's cool! I love walking on the beach!" I said excitedly.

"Not sure you'll love it that much here. It's very windy and cold most of the time."

"That's a pity, but you can dress warmly in case, isn't it?"

"I don't go to the sea often; I am not a beach person. By the way, you drink whisky neat? How come? It's not a typical drink for a girl."

"Whisky is my favourite drink. It took me two years to learn how to drink it. I would never drink it on the rocks or mixed with God knows what; it's blasphemy."

"What? A blasphemy? Two... two years to learn... what do you mean learn? How do you learn to drink and why would you do that in the first place?"

"It's a funny story actually. I couldn't stand drinking... not beer, wine, vodka, gin, or whisky. Nothing at all. And I was a bartender for many years. I hadn't tried any of the drinks in my bars. Until one day, when I wasn't a bartender anymore and felt I should learn to drink something for the sake of company. I didn't want to be a party pooper. After lots of thinking, I decided that whisky was the right and only choice. I bought myself a bottle of amber liquid, poured a glass and had one sip. It was so disgusting! Blah! I could not believe people said it wa good. That whisky was definitely the worst drink I had in my life. Not that I drank much anyway. I almost threw up and thought I should give up. But I didn't. I took a decision to learn to drink something, I'd chosen whisky. I didn't allow myself to capitulate. Every evening, I poured a glass of that amber liquid with a terrible smell, and had a sip, persuading myself to believe it was good. It took me four months to get used to the taste. After six months, I found myself thinking it wasn't that bad in the end. One year later, I figured it was quite good. Two years later, I couldn't believe I had so many awful thoughts about this elixir of gods. It's the only drink I like. But I could also have some wine or a beer from time to time nowadays."

"It doesn't make much sense that you can drink a double whisky and feel perfectly fine, does it?" he said.

"Adrian, I just told you that I learned to drink whisky. It's logical, my body is familiar with this drink. But I cannot drink more than one glass, and to be honest, I feel very dizzy right now. My face is all red, isn't it? God, I am such a baby!"

"You are sweet actually. I've never met anyone like you." He became all serious, and I felt my heart starting to beat incredibly fast. I blushed more and more. I felt so upset with my reaction and tried to ignore how that statement made me feel.

"When you told me your name, I thought you were Romanian. Adrian is a very common name in my country," I said, desperately trying to calm my heartbeats down.

"Is it? Hmmm. It's not hugely popular in here. Some would say it's a female's name," he replied.

"Ha! Impossible. It's definitely a male's name! Do you often go drinking with random women?" I asked, all of a sudden.

"No, not often," he said.

"How old are you, Adrian? You don't look more than twenty-one."

"I am almost twenty-six actually, but thank you for the compliment... which doesn't give me satisfaction. I don't like looking like a child. I am not that young inside."

His reply disappointed me. Despite his youthful appearance, I somehow hoped he was at least thirty. My heart was bleeding. "Yes, you have an old soul. I can see it in your eyes. What happened that made you grow up too early?"

"Oh... I am just an average person, you know, with an ordinary story. Nothing too bad or too good. It isn't worth talking about it actually."

"Every story is interesting, Adrian."

"Not mine. I bet yours is fascinating though."

"Now, why would you think that? Because I am so much older than you? I lived more years so it would make sense that my story was more exciting, right?" I was clearly annoyed.

"No, I didn't think that at all. And you are not so much older than me, are you?"

"I am... I am a lot older than you." I said with profound sadness. "But I don't want to talk about my age. I hate my wrinkles, and I hate getting old. But mostly, I despise myself for not being able to accept that ageing is unavoidable!"

"Where do you see wrinkles? I can't see any." And he stared at me to see those damn lines.

"Don't do it, Adrian. Stop, stop! I said stop staring at me! It's dark in here. You can't possibly notice my deep and horrible wrinkles!"

"I think you are overly critical of yourself. Maybe I cannot see much in here, but I saw you outside quite a few times, haven't I?" he responded.

"I think we should go, it's very late. My roommates will start to worry. I am never late. And you, your girlfriend must wonder where you are." I don't know why I said that, I had no idea he was in a relationship.

"She's fine, working late tonight, besides I live with my parents; my father and his partner, plus their daughter," he replied.

I felt a knife stab in my heart. 'Pathetic woman! What did you think that he felt the same for you? Of course he's got a girlfriend!' I wasn't shocked to find out that he lived with his parents. In Italy, every man I met lived with their parents. That was the main reason I stayed away from them. I never considered it normal. I have been living on my own since I was twenty. It was difficult for me to accept that young people don't want to be independent as soon as they start working. But who was I to judge? I come from a different background.

"Right, but you are tired and so am I," I insisted.

"I'm not tired," Adrian said. "But I can see you're exhausted. Let me take you home."

"I walk home. Every day from everywhere. It helps me clear my head."

"I like walking, and cycling," he said.

"Well, I don't have a bike. And I would be too afraid to cycle here. The streets are very narrow. I've never seen anything like that. I couldn't believe when I found out that most of your streets are two ways! I assumed they were one way only! English people are fantastic drivers, ignoring the fact you drive on the wrong side of the street."

"Who decided which side is the right one to drive on? Maybe the rest of the world drives on the wrong one. Have you ever thought about that?" he said with a weird look in his eyes.

'English pride.' "Oh, come on, you cannot possibly think that! Have you ever driven in a different country? Have you noticed that you have more visibility from every side if you sit on the left and drive on the right-hand side of the road? It's so much easier and is common sense," I responded.

"I don't drive a lot. I use my parents' car from time to time, but I prefer cycling. No, I never

drove in a different country so I can't make a comparison. But isn't all a matter of practice?" he asked in a low voice. "So, can I walk you home now? On foot?"

"Don't even think about it! I live too far," I said with conviction, although my heart wanted so much to be walked home by him, so, so very much. I was bleeding inside, but I couldn't allow my heart to start imagining impossible scenarios.

"It's dark, and you might lose your way. Please, let me walk you home. It's no trouble, I promise," he insisted.

"I said no, and no remains! Let's wait for the bus, and when it comes, I'll walk in the opposite direction. I know where I live, I won't get lost."

"I can't make you change your mind, can I?" said Adrian, defeated.

"No, I am older than you. You have to listen to me."

"Yes, Mother," he said amused.

But I wasn't laughing. Despite knowing that he wasn't mocking my age, Adrian's reply tore my heart apart. I stopped and touched my chest as I thought was about to explode from too much pain. It was my fault, though, I shouldn't have joked about being older than him.

"Are you okay? What's wrong, Tara? Are you that dizzy?

"No, I am fine. It's... Never mind."

A bus was approaching. "Look, it's your number. Hurry." I started running, but Adrian didn't. "Did you hear what I said? Can't you see that it's the bus that takes you home?"

"Yes, I heard, and I can see it's my bus. I just don't feel like running."

I knew he was doing that on purpose. If he missed the bus, I could have accepted to be walked home, but I was holding back tears. I was too upset and wasn't going to cry in front of him for a stupid word. It was pathetic. 'That boy sees me as a mother, and I am crazy about him. What am I going to do?' "People are getting off, we have time to reach it, but please hurry a little bit!" I shouted.

He didn't reply, kept walking at the same pace. The bus closed the doors and was ready to leave, but I raised my arm to make it stop. The driver looked at me for a second and pressed the button to open the doors. Adrian hugged me and got in.

EXAMS AND WHISKY

I watched the bus driving away, and I let my tears to fall freely on my burning cheeks. The pain was overwhelming; I couldn't stand it anymore, so I fell on my knees sobbing desperately. 'Why is this happening to me? I thought I had no more room for love in my heart. I thought I didn't have a heart at all! I didn't fall in love for eight or nine years, and now I fall in love with a child? What am I going to do? I'll die of a broken heart. I didn't believe it when people told me it was possible.'

"Hello, are you hurt? Should I call an ambulance?" a young male voice asked.

I raised my head to see a teenager staring at me. I tried to say something, but no sound came out of my mouth. I tried again with no luck.

"All right, I am calling an ambulance now, you are obviously in a lot of pain," said the teenager while kneeling close to me and dialling the number, "You stay calm, all right?"

"No, please, don't. I am fine. You cannot die from a broken heart, can you? Please, hang up the phone. I don't like hospitals. I'll die if an ambulance comes to take me. I promise," I murmured in despair.

The teenager hung up the phone when a voice was asking what the emergency was. "All right, all right. I will hang up. But you don't look well. Do you have someone I could call maybe? A friend, a brother, or a father perhaps?"

"No. My family lives thousands of miles away. I am alone here. Please, don't worry, I will be fine. I am just very tired and didn't have much to eat. Besides, I had a glass of whisky. I could be drunk, but I don't feel that way. It's what every drinker says, isn't it?" I tried to joke around, and he smiled. "Maybe you could help me getting up?" I asked timidly.

The boy reached a hand out to me, and I got on my feet. "Where are you from?" he asked.

"Romania," I replied in a fainted voice.

"Romania? You are a gipsy then."

"Not all Romanians are gipsies. Gipsies are a minority, as are the Chinese here. There is nothing wrong with being a gipsy, but I am 100% Romanian. Pureblood."

"I am sorry, I meant no offence."

"None taken. I am used to it. Anyway, gipsies are people just like everybody else."

"Your English is good. How long have you been living in here?"

"A little more than a month. However, I came here a few years ago and studied English for three and a half months. I should be great at it, but I am just rubbish, and it's very disappointing. Spent all that money for nothing! Thank you for being so nice about it though."

"Three months and you speak like this? Oh, come on! It's great, really!" exclaimed the teenager.

"No, it's not, but let's change the subject. Do I really look ill?" I enquired.

The teenager took a long look at me and said, "Maybe it's the light, but yes, you look ill. You should go and see a doctor." His eyes went to my knees, "Oh, you hurt yourself; there is blood everywhere. Here, let me clean you up," he offered, while opening the bottle of water he was carrying. I took some tissues from my bag, and both of us started to clean the blood. They weren't deep wounds, just small lacerations. "It doesn't hurt, I don't feel anything actually, except for this unbearable pain in my chest, but this is not something that anybody could help me with," I said.

"Hmm, curious how a few scratches made so much blood," said the boy, surprised. "Done, you're a presentable girl now."

I laughed, "I am not a girl, I am a woman. The man I love called me "mother" a few minutes ago."

"Well, he's a jerk who needs glasses then. I need to go now, my bus is coming, maybe it's going in the direction of where you live. Have a look."

"No, it's going in the opposite direction actually. I'll walk. Thank you so much for your help. You are a very sweet young boy. You might have saved a life tonight."

"It was nothing, really. But you should take more care of yourself. Are you sure you don't want me to call someone?" asked the boy, showing me the phone.

"I am sure. Besides, I have got a phone too, I could do it myself if I wanted."

"Are you going to see a doctor soon?" the teenager insisted again.

"No, no doctors. I will rather die than go to a doctor again."

The bus stopped, nobody got off. "Sure you'll be fine?"

"Yes, don't worry. Thank you again," I said with gratitude.

"Goodbye then, and take care."

"You too."

I watched another bus going away, I looked around, took a deep breath, and started walking. It was very dark, and I felt weak, but I didn't give up. The house was at least two miles away. I thought about many things, the course, my purpose in life, the time, but mostly I thought of him, Adrian. A perfect stranger that I fell in love with in one single instant.

I didn't expect to fall in love with an Englishman. The stories I heard about them were not flattering, to say the least. But isn't this stereotyping? Why was I upset about the fact that everybody thought all Romanians are gipsies if I thought all Englishmen were not very reliable? What did I know about Adrian anyway? My heart didn't ask anything, it didn't care who he lived with, if he's got a girlfriend, and so on. The heart feels, that's its job. 'He is so, so young and in a relationship, I can't possibly love him! What is wrong with me? After eight years of solitude, from all the men in the world, my heart goes for a child! Stupid, stupid heart! Why are you doing this to me? Can't you liberate yourself? Please!'

I got home very late. Everyone was already asleep. I had a quick shower and went to bed. 'It's official, I love Adrian, a boy twelve years younger than me. How very ironic and pathetic. I have no hope for a relationship, I don't even want it, but it would make me so happy to feel his arms around me. Maybe his kisses too. I shouldn't think that, I shouldn't want that, but I cannot command you, heart, can I? You love him if that's what you want. Dreaming harms none, so I'll dream, and nobody will ever know. It will be my secret. I deserve some happiness, even if it's only a dream.'

I fell asleep with Adrian in mind, and my first thought when I opened my eyes, was directed to him. As every single day since I met him. I was upset with my heart, but there was nothing I could do. I had to accept it and move on.

I took another deep breath, got dressed and went to work, then to the course. When I finished, I went to have a walk in the park. Adrian was waiting for me. He knew my schedule, I told him. I didn't know his, I never asked. We didn't use words to agree to meet, I think our hearts made a tacit pact. I was confused though because he had a girlfriend.

We said hello, he asked me if I had any real food to eat. I said I had had an English breakfast. Was a lie, of course, and he knew that. Then he complimented me on my top. I didn't understand, and I didn't even know what a "top" was. He explained it to me, and I had a look at my top then. It was nice indeed. Red and white stripes. Christmas colours. I love Christmas.

Two weeks later, I had my exam. I failed the first one by one question. I wasn't the only one.

The trainer called our names and let us know we will have a second exam in two days. My other colleagues' left, I went to her and said I wouldn't be coming that day. I was done, finished. "I can't do it. I won't pass this one either. It's no point trying. I know myself. I can't deal with exams. That's one reason I didn't go to University."

"It's not you, it's the exam, is hard. Even those who were certain will get 100%, passed by one question only. You had five errors, very unlucky. You will pass the next one, I promise."

"You have more faith in me than I do, but you don't know me at all. How can you make a promise on behalf of my actions? What if I don't pass the second one? How would I feel after that? I would never recover. Thank you for all your support. I am going home and stick with the job I have now. I don't deserve a better one anyway."

"I can see in your eyes that you're not a quitter, that's why I promised. What is that you do for a living again?" my trainer asked.

"I clean apartments," I replied with a fainted voice.

"You can do more than that, Tara. You speak Italian, there are loads of companies looking for Italian speakers. You must take the second exam. You won't blow it this time. You were very nervous during the first one, I noticed you were trembling a lot. You need to control your nerves."

"And you think I haven't tried that before? I am not twenty, unfortunately. I know when I should give up and now is a good time. Regarding the Italian-speaking skill, there are indeed companies that are looking to hire people who speak Italian, but how many Italians are living in England at the moment? And how many are coming as we speak? I am not an Italian citizen, I am Romanian. Nobody would hire a Romanian instead of an Italian. You are aware of this, right?"

"There is nothing wrong with being Romanian, Tara. Why are you so ashamed of your roots? We don't do discrimination here."

"Oh, you don't say! What about the documentary I watched the other day? *The Romanians are coming*. Did you see that? They humiliated an entire country because of a few bad subjects. You don't do discriminations, no. I have never seen anything more discriminating than that. And you are wrong, I am not ashamed of being

Romanian, I am ashamed of being human in this era." I turned on my feet, grabbed my things and walked towards the door. All the others were already gone, there was no one else but us.

"Tara, not all British people share these ideas about Romanians, please reconsider. I cannot force you to take the exam again, but without completing it, the course isn't worth anything. You've just wasted your time," she insisted.

"I wasted your time only, and I am sorry about that. I still learned a lot. I don't care about a piece of paper."

"It would look very good on your CV, Tara. You can't possibly think of being a cleaner for your entire life. You have so much potential, you could do anything! Think about it, for the love of God!" insisted the woman.

I felt touched by her efforts. She didn't even know me, she had just read my CV, still, but she wanted me to aim higher. 'These people are the best humans in the world.' I felt lucky and very guilty to disappoint her. "When I came here, I had no hope of finding any job. I am happy with that. It's more than I could have done in Romania."

"But you lived in Italy for so many years! You had better jobs there, didn't you?"

"Yes. I had great jobs in there. I am not expecting to have same sorts of jobs in here. Italian was easy to learn. English is way more complicated than I thought. I used to think I could learn any language in three months of full immersion in the country. I used to think I was a quick learner and was inclined towards languages, but I was wrong. I am so ashamed. This language drives me insane. I will never be able to talk like you do," I said with tears in my eyes.

"Why would you want to talk like me? It's a third language for you. A personal accent gives it charm. I love the sound of your English," she said with a smile on her face.

"You mean it makes you laugh. I get it. I laugh when people try to speak my language. I admit it's funny to hear someone torturing your language," I replied, trying to smile too. "Thank you for your support, I really appreciate it. I don't even know why you're doing this. You don't gain anything from pushing me to aim higher. It was really nice meeting you, and I will never forget this." Tears were rolling down my face. Nobody ever did that for me with no hidden purpose.

"Tara, you are here alone. You got here when? Less than two months ago? I put myself in your shoes, how would I feel if I were you? I would want someone to encourage me. What would I need to gain? Aren't we all humans? Please, reconsider. For your own sake. I believe in you, I really do. Go home now and have a rest. Think about it, I'll wait for you the day after tomorrow. All right?" she concluded.

I was deeply touched. I thanked her and promised I would think about it, either way I said

"Goodbye" and "Thank you. It's been very nice meeting you," just in case.

She said, "See you later."

It was dark, and Adrian was waiting for me in the park, sitting on a bench. I sat next to him and told him I didn't pass my exam, of course, and I will not go back to school. Which meant I was not going to come to the park any longer.

"Does that mean I won't be seeing you again? You don't look well, Tara. You're worrying me. What can I do to help?"

I looked into his eyes and noticed something quite disturbing. It was despair. I felt flattered and angry. 'He acts as if we are together. I wonder if his girlfriend knows about the fact he's courting another woman. How can I feel so attracted to him? He's clearly not a very faithful partner. But then again, I fell for him in one instant. I knew nothing about him.' I wanted to feel his arms around my body, and I felt guilty, filthy, and sick.

"I will be fine. As always. I have got nine lives, like a cat," I said trying to keep it together.

"How many have you lost?"

"More than one hundred." We've looked at one another and started to laugh.

"You're crazy, you know that, right?" said Adrian with sadness.

"Yes. I have to go now. Have a great evening and thank you so much for all your help."

"Can I walk you home? You don't feel well, I can see that," he insisted again.

"Thank you, but I am not going home. I will be fine, don't worry."

"I do worry though. I worry a lot," he said.

"There is no need. I am sure you have other things to worry about, all right? Goodbye, for the third time."

He didn't reply, I turned around and left, *adagio*.

AN OLD MAN IN NEED

My heart was heavy, heavier than a mountain. Not that I know what carrying a mountain feels like. I couldn't breathe from pain. That was it, I was not going to see him again. 'And I failed my exam. I am a total failure. I'll be a cleaner for whole my life. It's my destiny. I cannot escape it.' I burst into thousands of tears. Suddenly it became windy and started to rain. Absolutely typical weather in England. I wasn't surprised or annoyed. I thought it was a projection of the way I felt inside. I wrapped myself up in my raincoat and kept walking. In less than two minutes I was as wet as a badger's pocket. 'I should have taken the bus or at least an umbrella.' As I thought that, a broken umbrella flew me by. No one was chasing it, so I turned around to grab it and threw it into a bin. It was a dangerous object, it could have hurt someone.

Umbrellas are useless during such windy times. I used to carry an umbrella with me, but I gave up when two of them got broken at the first attempt to use them. I haven't carried any since then, and I don't think I will in the future either. 'No umbrella could keep you dry in England. Why have I even thought that? I have enough experience to know there is no point.'

The city was deserted when I got in. 'With a dog's weather like that, who was mad enough to walk on the streets without having a purpose like me?'

But it wasn't without purpose at all, I was going to put a senior person to bed. Charity work. I volunteered the first week I got to England. I found the advert in a local newspaper, and I volunteered right away. A complete background check was done on me, a DBS process. I heard of such things in the past, but I never needed one while I lived in Italy. Curious how countries have different policies and rules. I liked the fact they checked the history of a person, but I wondered if they believed in rehabilitation. In the fact that people can change completely if they want to.

Anyway, my DBS came out clean, but I knew that already. I always followed the rules. After three days of training, they assigned me an aged man, who was living twenty-five minutes away from my house.

This man was living alone and had issues taking care of himself. He was affected by Parkinson's disease so he couldn't feed himself because of the uncontrollable trembling of his hands, but not only this. He needed someone to help him with the most basic tasks. He was a good man, I liked him a lot. During the day, there were people sent by various medical organisations, but it was hard to find someone to put him to bed.

I stopped in front of the building and checked my pockets for the key to the entrance. I didn't find it in there, it was in my bag. I went upstairs and knocked on the door number seven.

"Come on in, Tara," a happy voice spoke up.

"How did you know it was me?"

"Who else would knock on my door, young lady?"

"Maybe your son?"

"Nah. I threw him out when he was less than eighteen. He hasn't spoken to me since. I don't know anything about him. He could be buried somewhere far away, and I am completely unaware of it. Bloody temperament I had. I should have never done that. He was my son! He needed my help."

"Stop blaming yourself, old man. He left you no choice, he was a drug addict and tried to kill his mother, remember? You took the right decision, you know that," I said with a firm voice. But I wondered if he was starting to feel his absence, "Do you miss him?"

"I can't even remember his face. I only have glimpses of him when he was a sweet child. Such a talented piano player. I must have done something wrong for him to turn out so terrible as a teenager."

"Well, I don't know the whole story, but you don't look like a bad person to me. You didn't even smoke in your life. How could a non-smoker be a bad person?!"

"Now, that's the most ridiculous logic I ever heard! Are you trying to say that all non-smokers are nice people, or are you just messing with me?" And he gave me a very long look. "You are messing with me, I knew it! You have a very weird sense of humour. It's worse than English humour, but I like it." Suddenly, the old man noticed my appearance. "Hey, look at you, you're soaking wet! You must be freezing. Young lady, there must be some women's clothes in this house. I am sure of it. Unless someone gave them to charity. Let me think... hmm." The old man put the finger on his face trying to remember where were those clothes, "Aha, I know. They are in my wardrobe, somewhere in a corner. Just a few though. I kept them so I could look at them when I miss my wife too much. I saw them last week. Yes, they are in there. Go see and put some on right away. I don't want you to get a cold. You are shaking more than my Parkinson's makes me shake. It's very disturbing."

I was shaking indeed, terribly. I had to listen to him, so I went and looked for the clothes he said. It took me more than ten minutes to find them. But the old man was right, the clothes were there. I didn't actually believe him. Hmm. I took one piece of clothing and unfolded. It was a winter dress. Velveteen! I looked at it and fell in love. It was green with small yellow flowers. Gorgeous, absolutely gorgeous it was. I checked the size, fourteen. 'Bugger, I am an eight or a ten!' I thought. 'Who cares? I need to put something dry on me or I will get a cold for sure.' I took my clothes off and put that dress on. It was very loose and long. 'There must be a belt in here somewhere.' I looked around and spotted a brown leather one on a chair. I took it and folded it twice around my waist. It was a perfect fit. I put my soaking wet clothes on the drying rack on the corridor. I then went into the bathroom and dried my hair with a clean towel. 'This is perfect.'

I wanted to make a soup, better a minestrone with meat, my personal recipe. In the kitchen, I turned the hob on and prayed that the girl remembered to buy potatoes, onions, and carrots, as I had left written two days ago.

I found everything in the storeroom. I hoped to find some meat in the fridge. No luck though. Except for milk and a lemon, there was nothing else in there. 'Maybe there is some in the freezer. That would be awesome!' I said to myself. And the first thing I saw when opening the freezer door was a bag of chicken thighs. 'Hurray! I'll make a great Romanian soup. The old man will like it very much!... I hope.' I put the thighs in a bowl and left some water running over them.

I put the kettle on, peeled one onion and three potatoes. Minced one carrot and the onion. I then washed the potatoes and diced them. 'My mother would be horrified to see me cooking the potatoes with the skin on. It was unthinkable for me too... until I got here.' I smiled and felt grateful for learning that people have different ways of cooking potatoes, and are all good.

I took a saucepan from the storeroom and place it on the hob. Dropped in three spoons of olive oil, let it heat for a minute, dumped in the minced carrot and onion. Stirred for three minutes with a wooden spoon, and added one litre of hot water from the kettle. I filled the kettle up and put it on again, took the thighs and let them slide into the saucepan, the same with the diced potatoes, and I covered the pot with a lid, regulating the heat on medium.

'Shoot, I forgot the peppers! Stupid head. My mother has never forgotten to put the peppers in a minestrone! You're just an amateur, Tara. Amateur!' I lectured myself, but I had to keep cooking without the peppers as it was too late to add them at that point. 'A can of chopped tomatoes would be great. And I hope I put the thyme into my bag this morning. It cannot be a Romanian soup without thyme.'

I heard the television on; the old man was watching something funny because he was laughing when I opened the door. He stopped though when his eyes set on me. I went and handed him a cup of tea, but he didn't move a muscle.

"Hey, old man, what's wrong? You don't want the tea?"

"Tara! For a second I thought my wife came back from the dead. But now that you are closer, I can honestly say you look nothing like my wife. It's scary how awful you can appear!"

"All right, old man, thank you. So nice of you to say that after I am brought you tea."

"That didn't come out right, did it? Hmm. Let me try this again, Tara, you look terrible!" I looked at him and burst in laughs. That wasn't much better than before, but I knew he wasn't trying to offend me, so I listened in silence.

"So, so thin! This dress is huge on you! My wife looked like a real diva in it, but you... you look like a child in her mother's dress. This is bad, very bad, Tara. You need to eat. I know that our food is not fantastic, but you're a fabulous cook! For God's sake, put something in your stomach immediately! Don't tell me you think you're fat! You are not ill, are you? *Anorethia* or something... that weird disease which affects so many young girls nowadays. They see a fat reflection in the mirror so they don't touch the food. And if they did touch it, they run into a toilet to throw up! So sad, really. You are not affected by it, right?"

He truly cared for me, I could sense that, and it touched my heart. "All right. You are the third person telling me exactly the same thing in less than a month. I don't have anorexia, I don't think I'm fat. I didn't even look in a mirror since I came here. It's true I don't eat much though. Here, a cup of tea." I said showing the mug.

"You know I cannot drink tea in the evenings. The doctor said it stops me from sleeping well."

"It's *decaf*," I replied.

"*De*... what?!"

"There is no caffeine in it. There are mechanical systems that extract it from the leaves. It's very popular these days. Coffee and tea without caffeine. You must have seen that on television."

"You're joking, right? It makes no sense at all. How can you extract the caffeine from the tea leaves or coffee beans? It destroys all the taste. I am not going to try that. It's unnatural."

"You're a funny little man, aren't you? Please, have a sip. I promise I won't make it again if you don't like it, all right? Here, it's not hot."

The old man tried to take the mug from my hands but changed his mind in a second. His hands were shaking too much that evening. Holding a mug filled with liquid was not doable. The Parkinson's was not always that bad. I felt for him.

I placed the mug on the nightstand and went to look for a straw, but I turned on my feet a second later, grabbed the mug and drew it near his mouth. "One sip."

The old man looked at the brown liquid with suspicion, but placed his lips on the border of the mug and had a sip. Held the tea inside his mouth for a few seconds, "Hmm who would have thought... It's got the same taste! Are you sure it's *decat* or whatever the hell it's called? You are not trying to mess with me again, are you?" he enquired raising his left eyebrow.

"No, I wouldn't joke about these things, you need sleep. That's great then! I am glad you are not disappointed. I'll make it every time I'll come here, all right?" I said with happiness.

"Aha... It looks disgusting though. Don't you think?" exclaimed the old man.

"Absolutely! As all the English teas in the world. Dirty water. Utterly repulsive. That's why I don't drink it. Also because it leaves spots on my teeth." I confirmed.

"But it's good for your teeth, it's got fluoride in it which makes your teeth harder," continued the old man.

"Yeah, you're right. I forgot about that. Maybe I should learn to drink it myself. As I did with the whisky. You know the story."

"Yes. You are a very resilient person, aren't you? Never giving up. Bravo!"

I grimaced, and the old man noticed, but he let it go because he knew it had to come from me. He drank the whole mug of that dirty water. He really liked tea, like a proper British person. But how can you blame him? It's a ritual, a tradition and it's actually good for you.

I was quite impressed and envious that I didn't have a similar one. I don't like drinking any sort of liquid. I am referring to water, juices, infusions. Nothing at all. Except for coffee. I love coffee, but I only drink one in the morning. That's a ritual, but it's not enough liquid for the body to properly function. I was born this way, and I am not the only one in the family, my mother, two of my sisters, my little brother, we all share the same aversion towards liquids. Such a shame really, because our body needs at least two litres of fluids. Alcohol is not included in this category. Maybe beer and cider should be though. Hmm. Never thought about it before.

I looked around the house and loved what I saw, order and personality, every object in its place. The smell was fresh, very uncommon among elderly people's homes. The dress I was wearing also had a very unique scent. 'Maybe somebody washed it recently. But who would do that and why? Curious, but I'd find that later, I need to check the soup now,' I thought and went into the kitchen. But I forgot to ask if there are any tomatoes cans in the house, so I went back to see the old man holding his wife picture he kept on the nightstand. I stopped for I didn't want to interrupt that rare moment. I didn't move a muscle but I observed every emotion on the old man face. Such a sad smile and profound love in his eyes. It was a very touching scene. The old man raised his head and spotted me, "What is it, Tara?"

"Sorry, I just wanted to ask you if there are any tomato cans in the house. I don't know where to look."

"I am sure there are. I bought a few the last time I went shopping. Nobody's used them. Let me think... hmmm. Have you looked in the storeroom? Oh, no, they are not in there. I put them where my wife stored all the cans, on top of the cupboard placed above the sink. They are definitely on there. By the way, what are you cooking? It smells delicious."

"It's a surprise, you'll find out in a minute," I said and turned to the kitchen. I was relieved that he didn't see me staring at him while having that intimate moment with his late wife.

I took a chair and climbed on it and here there were, five-tomato cans in all their splendour. So to speak. They were actually very dusty and looked like they have been in there for twenty or so years. I looked closer, and there were other jars and cans, so I took all of them down to check the expiration dates. The tomatoes cans were fine, but for the others it had been ten years since they were stored there. 'Hmm. That's something. Maybe I should throw them away. No, it's not my house, I'll ask first, or simply let them be. They don't give any trouble. Yes, I will put them back and stay quiet.' I grabbed one tomato can, and placed the others in the same location, after taking off the dust.

The soup was almost ready, so I opened the can and dumped its content inside the saucepan, add some salt and put the lid back on. 'Another ten minutes. Shoot, I forgot the thyme!' Grabbed my bag and took the small box with my favourite herb from in it. I used half of a teaspoon and the steam coming out the saucepan was inebriating.

As a matter of fact, I don't think thyme is the right name for it, that's what I found in the dictionary, but never convinced me by its truthfulness. It looks like the thyme and has similar scent and taste, except mine is much more intense. Maybe its proper name is winter savory but I am not sure. It's very much used in the Romanian cuisine, especially by elderly cooks like my mother. I wouldn't make soup without it, it wouldn't taste the same, not even close.

It's curious how I was never fond of soup or minestrone while living in Romania. I ate them because they were a tradition and I didn't want to upset my mother. She made tons of soups in her life. There was always soup in a saucepan somewhere made fresh at least three times every week, maybe even four. All different ingredients and flavours. I had one I loved, in all honesty. The minestrone made in the winter, before Christmas. With smoked pork and potatoes. It was just divine. It warmed me up entirely, body and soul. Such a great cook my mother, amazing really.

When I was living in Italy, I refused to make any soup for more than eight years with the excuse that I didn't have my favourite and irreplaceable ingredient, the thyme. I told my mother about it, and she sent me some. I made a soup right away and found it absolutely scrumptious. I missed that taste so much... and I didn't even notice. I didn't stop making soups since then. Maybe because I am getting old, or simply because I miss my country, and my mother... and my childhood. I don't really know. When I came to England, I put a full box of that special herb inside my bag. It was seeded and grown by me, on our land, so it's 100% organic. It's more valuable than gold to me. Most women carry makeup in their purses, I carry thyme, just in case I need it.

Why would I need thyme? To use it in my recipes, of course. I love cooking, and I do it often when I visit friends or people in need. I don't have anyone at home to cook for, so I am happy whenever someone appreciates a fresh homemade meal. It takes me twenty minutes or less to make seven portions of any soup. I didn't have the opportunity to make one in this house yet. It wasn't cold enough outside, not for me at least. A soup tastes much better if the weather is bad, like that evening. The ideal time for such a warm meal.

I placed on the table two spoons and two napkins. Then I took two white bowls from the cupboard and filled them with the hot liquid. I added some vegetables and a little bit of meat. I wondered if it was tender enough for this kind old man's teeth, but as it was coming off the bones, I decided it was just perfect. It was about time to have dinner, so I went to bring my guest to the table.

"Old man, it's ready. Are you hungry? But mostly, how open-minded about different cuisines are you? Hmm... Maybe I should have asked you this before preparing dinner..."

"Tara, you smell like a cook working in a restaurant, exactly like my wife. I am absolutely

49

starving and the myriads of odours coming from the kitchen, made me dream... I thought of my wife a lot. But I will tell you later. How open-minded I am?... Have I ever told you that my wife was born in Italy and her father was Polish? She made me try several flavours I didn't even imagine existed. But I cannot tell what you cooked this evening. The flavours are absolutely new to me. I must admit, I am very intrigued and famished."

I helped him to get up and put one of my arms around his waist to stabilise the trembling. He thanked me and grabbed onto the walker. Two minutes later, we were in the kitchen. He looked at the bowls with surprise, positive surprise, "It looks like a Renoir painting, Tara! A perfect colourful still-life! I have never seen anything like that. What is it? Never mind, I cannot wait to taste it!"

I was in heaven. I had always appreciated when people made so kind remarks about my food. This one was one of the best compliments I ever heard. Renoir is my favourite painter, but I never thought of my food like a still-life painting. So appropriate though!

I helped him to sit and made sure he was comfortable. I took a full spoon of that pale red liquid, blew on it and made the old man try. He wasn't suspicious, but I wasn't prepared for what happened the second he had the food in his mouth. His eyes got inundated by tears. It scared me tremendously. "Omg, I burnt your tongue, too hot, isn't it? I am so terribly sorry! I was too eager to make you try that I ignored the fact I could hurt you. I feel dreadful."

"No, Tara. It's not hot, it's... it's... I don't even find the words to describe it. It's the most divine food I have tried since my wife left me. It reminds me of something she used to make me from time to time. It didn't look the same, but there is something... a herb maybe. What spices have you put in this soup... It's a soup, right?"

"Yes, it's a soup my mother used to cook when I was a child. The only herb I used is similar to thyme..."

"Thyme! Thyme! I remember now. My wife loved this herb. However, she didn't make use of it very often. She told me that there weren't many dishes that could handle this particular flavour. I didn't know it could be added to soups. Is it your mother's recipe?"

"It's mine, actually. Based on three different typical Romanian kinds of soup. I don't know if my mother would appreciate my boldness. She is very traditional, never changed a recipe. I am exactly the opposite, although I am very attached to Romanian costumes."

"Well, Tara, I am telling you that this soup is the best I ever had in my whole life. Nothing else comes close, except, of course, for some of my wife's recipes. As a soup, it's the best. Thank you so much for going through so much trouble and cooking it for me. I will always be grateful. You made a lonely old man very happy tonight. God bless you, child. God bless you," he said with emotion.

"It was no trouble, really. I make soups since I was eight, or seven. It's very easy for me. I am thrilled you like it. I'll cook a different one next time, OK? Let me know what you'd like."

He finished the bowl and asked for another one, "but first, you eat yours, young lady. Right now," he commanded, and I listened. That was my very first real meal since I came to this country. And it was tasty, very tasty. A little too sweet maybe, but still delicious. It warmed me up, both physically and psychologically. The old man ate the second bowl, without blinking. I was tempted to give him more, but it was late, and I couldn't risk making him feel sick from too much food. He took a tissue and cleaned his mouth.

"Tara. You are a fabulous cook, you know that, right? How come I see no ring on your finger? You don't have to answer if you don't want to."

"That's OK, old man. I'll answer. I like talking to you. You are my confessor," I said with a smile on my face. "There was never a ring on any of these fingers. I am not divorced because I have never got married. I don't have any children either. I am all alone in this world... I have my siblings and my parents, of course, but you know what I mean; I don't have my own family."

"How come? You are such a beautiful and sensible young woman; I am sure men were fighting for you. Maybe you have never wanted a family?"

"No, I haven't."

"But why? It's not that you cannot feel love because there is so much sensitivity in you. What happened, Tara, to make you decide that you didn't want a family? How old were you when you've understood that you don't want children?"

"I was twelve maybe. All my friends were dreaming of getting married and having kids... I was... not. I have tried, but I couldn't, and I thought it was not my destiny. To be honest, I was convinced that I'll die at a very young age for that reason. I mean, because I couldn't see any future whatsoever, not only no kids but anything at all. I felt different somehow, and I was."

"This is a great loss for humanity, young lady. You should have children as you'd be a great mother. I am sure of it."

"That's a little excessive... *loss for humanity* don't you think? I am just an average person, not a genius. I would never consider having children without a father anyway."

"But... forgive me if I am too intrusive, you ignored my question about being able to feel love... Have you ever loved someone?"

I smiled ironically. "I have loved, many times... too many actually. My heart is the stupidest in the whole world, she goes for the most unsuitable men. And I must confess, I am in love with someone in this period, and it's killing me. Literally.

I have been single for... eight years. I didn't touch a man in eight bloody years. I was convinced my heart was dead, but suddenly she decides to fall in love with a child! Stupid, stupid heart!" I was shouting, and I didn't realise. My face was red, and I was shaking tremendously. I was filled with rage.

"Poor soul, you shouldn't be upset with your heart for falling in love. You cannot fight against it. But what do you mean when you say a child, how old is he? Fifteen?"

"Twenty-six, almost. He is a total stranger. I forgot to tell you that I didn't pass my exam and I left school. I am not going back. I am not as resilient as you think. I gave you the wrong impression. I am a massive loser." My face was covered in tears. I tried to stop them from falling, but it was impossible.

The old man was suffering for me. "Poor Tara... I am so sorry about your exam. I didn't know and didn't ask. Sorry, I assumed you've passed because you are so smart. I had no doubt about it. But it happens. It's not the end of the world, you know. Besides, there must be a second one. Some courses offer two exams in case you can't or won't pass the first."

I didn't reply, and he reached to my face and wiped it with a tissue. I blew my nose and tried to calm down. I felt very ashamed and couldn't speak, so the old man continued, "And the fact you are in love shouldn't make you suffer. Love is wonderful. Why... why do you think he's a child? At twenty-six, nobody is a child. You mean he acts like a child? How old are you? I believe it's written on your DBS, but I cannot recall now. Are you thirty yet? What's five years' difference, young lady? Nothing, when you're in love. Because he loves you back, right?"

I looked into his eyes to see if he really meant what he said about my age and I started laughing. "Oh, funny man! You know my age very well. Thank you so much for trying to cheer me up though. I really appreciate it. Women are so sensitive about their age. Your wife taught you well, I am very impressed."

"I was not trying to play nice with you, I seriously can't remember. You must be close to thirty though, because *this thirty age* sounds familiar to me. Besides, you don't look older than thirty anyway. Stop being such a child about this age difference!"

"All right... you cannot see my wrinkles clearly in these lights, I get it. I will be thirty-eight in two months. So you see, there is a huge gap between our ages."

"Thirty-eight years old! Get out of here! I know you are messing with me again. Like that time when you told me it was snowing in August. You were so convincing that I had no doubt I was about to assist at the end of the world. I won't be fooled again, young lady. No, no."

My anger dissipated, and I was in tears from laughing now. "You are the sweetest person in the whole universe, funny old man. I will always be grateful for have met you. You are making my life richer and happier, thank you," I said becoming emotional again.

"Well, Tara, we both enhance each other's lives. We are both lucky to have met. And if my wife was here, she would have adored you..."

I burst into laughter. "Yeah, yeah. I know that joke you know, 'because my wife liked everyone.'"

"My wife didn't like many people, Tara, I am not even sure she liked me! I am serious, she would have adored you. She's always wanted a girl... but after the boy... she was informed that something was wrong and another pregnancy wasn't possible. In fact, they said it was a miracle that she had a child."

I couldn't believe I misinterpreted his words, and felt guilty, but he continued on a happy note, "So, tell me about this young man. How is he? Does he exchange your feelings?"

"He is tall, smart and... in a relationship. It's weird, really weird. And to answer your question, yes, I think he feels the same for me. Which makes this bloody situation even more twisted. Moreover, he is a sombre and troubled young boy. My brain knows he is not the one, and he cannot possibly make me or any other girl happy, but that doesn't stop my heart to love him! What do you make of that? Is this bad enough for you? Do you understand now why I feel so unhappy and upset with my stupid heart?! He's got a girlfriend!"

"That's not that bad, Tara. It's not that they're married. Relationships start, relationships break up," he said with relief.

"My brain doesn't want him. It knows that he cannot make me happy. This has everything to do with my stupid heart. Even if he was single and older, I would still not be happy, because he is not the one."

"How can you possibly know that? Who told you he is not the one? Until you try, you don't know for certain. But as he is in a relationship, I cannot advise you to do so. Oh, Tara, that's so unlucky. I wish I could help you. If I had friends, I would ask them to look for someone appropriate for you. I am afraid you are alone in this."

"Yes, you said it right, I am alone in this."

I looked at the clock, it showed 10pm. "Shoot, old man! You were supposed to be in bed by 9. This is so unprofessional of me. I'll get into trouble if someone finds out about this. I'll help you put your pyjamas on after I came back from the bathroom. All right?"

The old man nodded "yes," and I rushed into the kitchen to clean the table, and put the saucepan with the remaining soup in the fridge. It was enough for two other dinners for one person.

I wasn't going to come the next two days because there was a new girl who offered to help. I put everything in place again and checked with a gaze if the hob was turned off. I went into the bathroom, then on the corridor to check if my clothes were dry. They weren't completely dried, but I had no other choice than to put them on like that. Besides, it was still heavily raining.

I took the dress off and folded back as it was. But I didn't put it inside the wardrobe where I found it. It had to be washed first. My humid clothes made me shiver, but I had to toughen up. I wasn't going to cry like a baby for some wet clothes and some heavy rain. No way.

I grabbed my bag and went into the bedroom to put the old man to bed. But he was already in it, all packed up and smiling. "I've managed to do it alone this evening, so you won't waste any more time with me, Tara. Thank you so much for the amazing soup and great company. Would you do me a favour though?"

I was really impressed by the fact he managed to get changed and even prepared his outfit for the next day. He was such an organised man! "Well done, old man, very well done! But don't ever think it's a trouble helping you, it's a pleasure. You don't waste my time; you enrich my life, so I am the one who should thank you really! What favour do you want to ask me?"

"Take the second exam, Tara. I know it's just a piece of paper and you might think it's useless, but one day it will mean something. Promise me that you will at least think about it?"

"I'll promise I'll think about it, all right? Now, tell me if you're comfortable and need something else before meeting Morpheus. Are you warm enough?"

"All is good Tara, thank you and good night."

"Good night, old man, Sleep well. By the way, I left the dress on a chair in the other room. It needs to be washed before being put back in the wardrobe. I will do the washing next time I come or could take it home and wash it in there."

"No, I'll take care of it. You think about the exam, all right? Don't be stubborn."

"All right. Night, night."

I switched off the light and left the room locking the door twice.

When I got to the street, a gust of wind turned me around... A pirouette. I found it funny, so I chuckled and kept walking. It was still raining, but the rain never bothered me, quite the contrary.

I was home in twenty-five minutes, utterly soaked, had a quick shower and decided to wear my red and white checked pyjamas that night. A gift from my mother. But I was shivering a lot, so I put the kettle on, emptied a plastic bottle of the remaining water in it, and filled it with the hot water instead. I didn't have a proper hot bottle thing, didn't like them. I took a book from the white shelf and jumped on the bed hugging the hot bottle. It was very hot, and I almost burnt myself. I laid down, placed the bottle under the duvet, and made myself comfortable, ready to read. I didn't like the book, but I needed to practise my pronunciation, so I started reading out loud. Five minutes later, my tongue was hurting like hell. It happened all the time. I went on for other ten minutes when I had to stop because the words coming out were not understandable. It had no value reading words which didn't make any sense. I closed the book and switched off the night lamp. I hugged myself tight and fell asleep thinking of Adrian.

I PASSED

Next morning at 7, I sent him a concise text, "I will take the second exam."

He replied immediately, "I knew you would."

I went to school, the class was almost empty, only the ones who failed the first exam were there. They didn't look worried or stressed. I was shaking from every fibre of my body. The trainer came in and said good morning. She was wearing a green dress which I liked very much. She looked at every each of us and said with confidence. "Everyone will pass this time. Do you hear me, Tara?"

I nodded "yes" and looked down my hands. They were trembling, worse than the first time. I was utterly terrified. I had no idea what was going to happen. I tried to calm down.

The trainer continued, "there is nothing to be worried about, take a deep breath and start. Good luck everyone."

I looked at no one and decided I was going to give my best. Fifty minutes later, everybody was gone except another male colleague and me. We were sitting at the same desk.

The trainer came to us and said, "Guys, the time is up, I need to grade the exam."

We both passed. The trainer congratulated us, and my colleague left. I heard his steps going away.

The door closed behind him. The trainer asked me to join her at the desk. She made me sit on a chair and look at my results again. "Tara, your results are the highest in your class. You've got only one wrong. You should be proud of yourself. I know I am," she said with emotion in her voice, "I told you that you've got fire within you. Resilience, such a great trait of character."

I was holding back my tears, "Yes, they are high, but that was to be expected. It's the second exam; I knew some answers, it's no big deal. I am not proud of myself, I am ashamed, and I will not take another exam again."

"Tara, why are you so hard on yourself? These results are outstanding! It doesn't matter is the second exam or that some of the questions you had already in the previous one, you remembered the correct answers. You got one wrong. Just one. I am very proud of you."

"I am not happy. I should have passed the first one. Maybe I would have been proud," I said desolated.

"Tara, you should have more consideration for yourself. You are going through an awful period, I have noticed that, and you didn't give up. I wish you could see how amazing you are. Go home and rest now. It's over. I hope we could meet again. If you need some recommendations, you can give my name. And here is my phone number," she said while hugging me.

No English person hugged me before. I fought to hold back my tears. I thanked her from the bottom of my heart. For everything. Then I grabbed my things and left. Outside, I sent a text to Adrian, "I passed."

He replied right away, "I had no doubt. I am in the park." My heart filled with joy and excitement. I couldn't wait to see him. 'I shouldn't feel so happy about it. He's an unfaithful human being. How would I feel if I was his girlfriend?' I tried to fight, stay away, walk home on a different road, but I couldn't. I really needed him. I was completely dependent on him. 'Pathetic and disgusting you are. Worse than a teenager,' I thought while walking towards the park. When he saw me, his eyes illuminated and when I got close to him, he hugged me tightly, and I left my tears rolling down my face. I so much dreamed about that hug. It was heaven.

"I'm taking you to dinner," he decided, "Celebrations are a must."

I didn't reply, and he didn't expect me to. We started walking in silence. He didn't notice my tears, so I dried my face and pretended nothing happened. He took me to a place I wouldn't know how to localise on the map if you'd asked me. A waiter accompanied us to a very small table. It made me laugh.

"Everything is completely different than in Italy," I explained. "The places are dark; the tables are tiny, the waitressing service isn't great, yet, you people are so much happier. I am so very impressed!"

"What are you trying to say, that our standards are low? Not very flattering, don't you think?" Adrian replied, a little annoyed.

"I meant that you have a great personality and are happy no matter what. You know that most people are unhappy because they have too high standards?" I tried to fix what I said previously, and I'd made it worse, by the expression Adrian had on his face. I excused myself and went to the ladies' room. I looked at my image into the mirror, and I didn't like what I saw. I was thin indeed, almost transparent I would say. My skin was pale, and my eyes seemed huge. I looked like a character from a Japanese cartoon. 'My God!' I murmured at my reflection, 'Seriously, you need to start eating. You look like a zombie. Your father would die if he saw you in this state. You know how strict he is about eating properly. You've lost too much weight. Enough!' I washed my face with cold water, gave myself another look, and left.

I ordered fish and chips. Adrian wasn't happy with my choice but didn't argue. He wanted pasta. We didn't speak much, just ate. After the tables had been cleaned, he reached one hand out and put it on top of mine. If before that I had some doubts about his intentions, that move erased all of them. He definitely wanted more from me. I pulled my hand out of his. 'Unfaithful!' I screamed in my head. 'Do you really have a girlfriend or you just said that? No man would touch another woman like that if they were in a relationship unless the love is long gone. Hmm. I didn't think of that.'

We left the restaurant in approximately one hour and started walking in silence when I realised Adrian was walking into the same direction as me. "Where are you going, Adrian? Your house is in the opposite direction."

"I am walking you home."

"I am not going home. I need to go into town. I think I will take the bus today. I don't feel well again."

"I'll take the bus too then."

We both stopped to wait for it. We didn't speak, and I kept touching my necklace.

"That's a very beautiful piece of jewellery. What does it say?" As I didn't reply he got closer to see by himself, "*Breathe*... Very interesting. Where did you buy it?"

"I wouldn't know, it's a gift from my little brother. We were living in Italy at the time. It's my favourite, but I avoid wearing it every day. It's so delicate, I am afraid it would break, and it's too valuable to me."

"What do you have to do in town, Tara? You seem to go there often after the course. Do you have a second job?"

"No. I am helping someone with... a few things."

"Tara, would you like to have another dinner, a proper dinner with me sometime soon? Maybe I can come to yours and help you cook something not too fancy?"

My heart was beating fast, and I wanted to cry from happiness; instead I coldly said, "Sure. I am free next Monday evening."

"OK. What should I bring?"

"Red wine. I will cook, I like cooking." He didn't reply. The bus came and stopped with a very big fuss. Many teenagers got off and I spotted the one who helped me a few nights ago. He didn't recognise me, so I didn't say anything. There were many empty seats; I chose two next to each other, and I sat by the window. Adrian sat next to me. I turned my head to look outside and saw that teenager again. He winked and waved a hand to me. 'He did recognise me then!' I murmured, surprised.

"What?" Adrian asked.

"Nothing, I was talking to myself." But I raised a hand to wave back. He then gave me thumbs up, and I copied the gesture. He smiled and left. I smiled too.

"Do you know that guy?"

"No," I lied.

The bus left half full. We remained silent for the whole time. My stop was next, so I pushed the button and stood up to leave. Adrian moved aside to let me pass, but a second later changed his mind and followed me. I thanked the driver and got off with a sigh. I started walking and stopped when getting close to the building where the old man was living. I turned around and said, "Thank you for dinner, it was very nice of you. Have a great evening."

"I will, my girlfriend and I are going out tonight."

My heart stopped beating, and I felt like fainting but said, "Awesome. Thank you for all your support, Adrian. I will always be grateful." I reached my right hand to him, and we shook hands like two great politicians. I then turned on my feet and left. He remained immobile, but I didn't look back.

THE BLUE DANUBE

The pain in my chest was unbearable, and my eyes were inundated with tears again. I was so upset with myself, but I shook my head and took a deep breath before opening the entrance door.

I took the stairs and knocked on the same number seven door. I got no answer, so I knocked again. Still nothing. 'Dear Lord', I prayed, 'please, don't do this to me.'

I opened the door timidly and looked around. There was no one in the living room.

"Hello? Anybody home? Old man, where are you hiding? Trying to play with me?"

I heard a voice somewhere, but it was very fainted. My hurt made a jump. "Old man!" I shouted.

"I am here Tara. Don't worry; I am fine. Just... you know." The voice came from the bathroom. I didn't want to intrude, but I had to ask, "Do you need help?"

"No, no. I almost finished."

I waited patiently trying to slow down my heart's beats. I really cared for this man, I cared for people I didn't know too. I sat on the black armchair, took my shoes off and looked around. It was extremely clean and well organised. I really loved this place. I turned my head when I heard the door opening.

"Here you are. You gave me a good scare, old man. Don't do it again, all right?"

"Sorry, I had to go to the toilet. Too much tea, decaf tea, of course."

"I didn't know you can use the toilet when you are on your own."

"I only do it when my Parkinson's is more tolerable. Today is a very good day. I feel twenty again. I wish my wife was here. We could have danced. She loved to waltz."

"Waltz is my favourite dance, old man! I can be your partner if you want."

"Oh, I would be honoured, young lady! I have got an old recorder player, still working, I tried it last week. I have some old vinyl records on that shelf." He gestured to me to look. I had noticed the recordings before, but I had no idea about how many and how interesting they were. I am not fond of old music, blues, jazz, and stuff like that. I don't understand it. I have tried so many times to study it and get the point, but it's not for me. I loved classical, opera, and classical crossover. I am no real connoisseur, of course, I just like it, and I dream of going to assist at concerts one day.

I got lost in the multitude of names and genres of those recordings. Suddenly, I saw Tchaikovsky, *The Nutcracker* and *The Waltz of the Flowers*! I couldn't believe my luck! I grabbed the recording, and was about to rush back when the old man said,

"Can you find Shostakovich? *The Second Waltz*? My wife's favourite. She absolutely loved that one. I preferred the beautiful *Blue Danube*, but we've always ended up with dancing on the second waltz.

"So let's dance on the Danube first, shall we? Then we'll see. What do you say?" I proposed.

The old man thought for a second, "Danube it is. Oh, it's going to be wonderful."

I placed the recording on the player and turned it on. No sound came out. "Hmm, how curious. Are you sure it works? Maybe it's broken. How long ago have you used it?"

"It works, I can guarantee you that. I haven't used it in a very long time, maybe years, but I tried it last week for a few minutes. Is it plugged in?"

"It is plugged in all right, but there is no light on. Very disappointing," I said.

"Did you switch the plug on?" asked the old man with hope.

"Shoot! I didn't even think about it! I always forget that part. Not sure how long it will take me to get used with this system. I've never seen it before coming to England." I switched the plug on, and the music inundated the living room.

The old man was very excited. He seemed to have rejuvenated, and I loved seeing him in that state. He was quite a happy person generally, but the loneliness could kill anyone. He missed his wife he had loved with all his heart. They were very different, the old man told me a few times, but they completed one another. The old man was the salt, and she was the pepper. Tasty and spicy.

There were very happy together, and when the old man kicked his son out, his wife was devastated, but she supported his decision. Their son needed to be treated that way, so he will learn to take care of himself and respect others. I looked at him while he took the frame and stared at his wife. "She would be happy to see me dancing; I know she would."

"I am absolutely convinced of that, old man. She loved you very much and wanted you to live your life to the fullest. Let's dance now!"

I made him wear his going-out shoes. There were clean and seemed new. It was evident he didn't use them often. I put an arm around his waist and pull him off the bed. I waited for a while so he could feel the ground under his feet and balance his weight.

"Ready, old man?" I asked.

"Ready when you are, young lady."

So, I moved, and he joined in. I was the leading person, and he felt grateful for that. It took us a few minutes to get into it, but then we smashed it. We've danced for at least twenty minutes, and I was exhausted. The old man was unstoppable.

"Old man, we need to stop. It's too much effort for too long at one time. I don't want you to feel ill after this. We'll do it again soon, all right?"

"Sure thing! Thank you, Tara."

"No, thank you, old man. You're a sensational human being and never cease to amaze me. No wonder your wife was crazy about you," I exclaimed.

"And I was crazy about her. One day you'll find someone like that too. It's the way it has to be. You deserve it."

I took his shoes off and asked what he wanted to eat.

"I am not very hungry, Tara. Could I have a yoghurt and a banana maybe?"

"Of course you can. These are great food and very healthy. I will bring them to you right away. But are you sure you don't want me to cook you something? It's no trouble, you know?"

"You are the best cook I ever met in my life, Tara, but I cannot eat much now. I am too excited. The banana will fill my stomach and provide me with enough energy for a good night's sleep." I agreed and went to bring him the banana and a jar of plain yoghurt. I put everything on a tray and came back into the living where the old man was sat down in an armchair. I stopped and looked at him because he had the eyes closed and wasn't moving. I thought he was sleeping, but he must have heard me as he opened his eyes and looked directly into mine.

"Tara, would you accept a small gift? What if I gave you the dress you wore last time? My wife's dress?"

"Why would you want to do that?"

"I want you to have it. Just in case..."

"In a case of what?" I asked with worry.

"I am old, Tara, and ill. Anything could happen, and I don't want that dress to be thrown away. It really means a lot to me. Would you please take it? I washed it yesterday. It's on the clothes-horse."

"You did what? Washed it? So it was you the last time who washed it? I thought it smelled freshly washed. And there was a very familiar perfume on it. What was it as I cannot tell precisely?"

"It's lily of the valley, my wife's favourite. And yes, I wash all my wife's clothes every month. She was very strict with hygiene."

"You must be joking! Lily of the valley is one of my favourite flowers too!"

"Really? That's another coincidence. Hmm.... Anyway, would you please take it? I know it's far too big for you now, but maybe one day, when you'll start eating like a normal person, it will fit you better."

"Old man, your wife was a size 14, I'm a 10 and have no intention of reaching a 14 in this life!"

"You are not a size 10, Tara."

"I'm not? What size am I then?"

"Maybe an 8. Or between a 4 and a 6. You have absolutely no flesh on your bones. Did you look in a mirror lately? And when you buy clothes, what size do you go for?"

"I cannot be a 6, old man. I was a 12 when I left Romania. The truth is I don't know what size I am now. I brought some clothes with me when I came, but they are way too big. I didn't think I lost that much weight though. Hmm. I don't ever remember being a size 6. Maybe when I was a child."

"Tara, will you take the dress, please?"

"But of course, old man. Why wouldn't I? I just don't want you to give it to me yet. It makes me feel sad and worried. What is going on, old man? Why do you want me to have the dress now?"

He looked at me and timidly said, "My son came to visit me yesterday."

"Your son came to see you? That's wonderful news, isn't it? Or he's still a drug addict?" I exclaimed.

"He is most definitely not a drug addict, thank God for that. He's an engineer. He lived in London until last year when he moved back here."

"He's been living in this city for a year? Did he know you were still living in here?"

"He thought I'd died. He's married, but has no children. He asked me about the flat. If it's mine or it's rented."

"Why would he ask you that?"

"I don't know. Anyway, he said that the organisation called him the other day. Not sure why. They didn't tell me anything about it."

Was he happy to see you?" I asked.

"I don't know. He was never a very enthusiastic person. Not very smiling either."

"But what did he say? Will he visit from now on? Will he stay in touch?"

"He said he'll come with his wife next time. But I don't know when."

"Are you okay with that? The fact you saw him made you happy?" I enquired.

"We felt like complete strangers, to be honest. I am not even sure he's my son. He doesn't look the same. If it wasn't for his behaviour, I would have never been able to swear he's my son."

"That is sad, old man. I am very sorry to hear that. Is he still so aggressive?"

"No, he's very laid back now. I forgot to tell you that he's an engineer. Same as his wife."

He did tell me that, but I pretended it was the first time I heard that. "That's great, old man. So, he's finished studying and graduated. That is really awesome!"

The old man looked away; his eyes were blurred with tears. I was fighting hard to hold mine back. "You don't have to wear that dress, just keep it safe, for me, all right? And visit when you want. My house is your house, all right?" said the man with sadness.

"You can count on me, old man. I will keep it safe forever. You know that the organisation assigned me another person starting with next week, right? I won't be seeing you for a while, and I've been told I cannot have friendships with my clients. It's against the policy. Maybe I will resign and come here every day. What do you say?"

"Yes, I know. I don't want you to resign, Tara. You are too valuable for the organisation. Forgive me for being so selfish and wanting to keep you for me." His eyes danced in tears, and mine were falling thousands on my cheeks. I cared for this man, and he cared for me. It was unavoidable not to feel that one for each other. We spent a lot of time together. He was my confessor and my biggest supporter. I didn't want to leave him, but I didn't have a choice. My heart was very heavy.

"You have your son now. You're not alone anymore. Maybe that's why the organisation decided to send me to a different location."

"But you're more of a daughter to me that he was ever! I don't need him."

"Don't say that, old man. Maybe he's a good person now. Maybe he cares for you."

"Maybe he does, I don't know. He's like a closed book to me. Closed books don't tell you anything. No story," he said defeated.

We remained silent, and I tried to send the sadness away. It was too thick though.

"Please, eat. I will speak with the organisation, okay? Anyway, they didn't say I won't be sent here ever again. They need me to help them with a new person. This is temporary. I will come back, I promise, even if that means I would have to resign. All right? And, no, I don't do it for you, but for me."

"How did you know I was about to say that?"

"I got to know the way you think. It was easy as we are very similar."

"Right. Tara... do you still love that young boy of yours?"

"You cannot forget someone in two days, old man. You, from all people, should know that by now."

"Of course. Forgive me, I'm not thinking straight. Does he make you happy though?"

"He makes me feel extremely miserable, to be honest. But not on purpose. He's in a relationship and twelve years younger than me. It's not something one can feel happy about. But that's okay. It was supposed to be this way. I will forget him one day. Do not worry about me; I am used to it. I know he wasn't for me... I mean, the brain knew, but the heart disapproved. Stupid heart, always in contradiction."

"You cannot command your heart, Tara. Nobody can."

"I am thirty-eight years old though (almost), I should have learned my lessons by now. I'm not fifteen anymore, but my heart acts like a teenager's. I mean, I don't even think it was ever so stupid. The older I grow, the weirdest it behaves. Pathetic, truly pathetic, don't you think?"

"All we need is love, Tara, and your heart craves for it. Don't be upset with it, embrace it and let it be. I am truly sorry you are not happy. If he feels the same for you, why can't you two be together? I know he's got a girlfriend, but he's not engaged or married. Relationships start, relationships break. I already told you this, no? It's absolutely normal. What's wrong with this guy? Can't he see how amazing you are? Wish I could talk sense to him. Age? It's just a stupid mental obstacle. Nobody can dictate who do we need to fall in love or have a story with. Don't allow society to have a say in your personal life, Tara. It's your right to choose the people you want to be with. I wish you to be happy, young girl, you deserve it!"

"Thank you, old man. Your words mean a lot to me. I know age is a mental obstacle, but I also know that he is not the one. He's got feelings for me, but it's something about him... I don't know. I guess he is too troubled. I really feel for him. Adrian doesn't know what happiness feels like, he's convinced it's just a made-up word. I wish I could prove him wrong, but he won't ever let me do that. He's a lost cause, old man, a lost cause."

"I asked you before, how do you know he is not the one?"

"What does 'the one' actually mean? Is it the one who makes you happy? The one you want to marry? The one who's good for you?"

"The one means all of these, Tara. You know that."

"I don't want to marry him, I don't want to spend all my days with him... or waiting for him to come home from God only knows where. I don't like his struggles, his way of thinking, his behaviour. I'm not sure if there is something tangible I like in him. I don't know why my heart fell for him as there aren't good reasons. That's why I'm so upset with it. It's like wanting to be in pain. Really annoying, I'm telling you. Have you ever felt something like that?"

"No, I haven't, Tara, so I cannot give you any good advice. I'm afraid you are alone in this. I'm sure you'll come out of it just great. You're a wise young woman."

"I will be fine one day. Ten years from now I might not even remember the way I'm feeling right now. So utterly miserable. I'm taking it as another lesson to learn. Fourteen or ninety, love feels the same for everyone. It doesn't matter how younger or older than you the one you love is, you'd still do anything to have them. There must be a reason for this story in my life. I am absolutely convinced of that. And one day I will find that out, and I will be cured."

"See, I told you you're wise. You'll figure it all out on your own. I believe in you."

I heard a noise in the corridor and made a jump. Somebody dropped something. Then a door was slammed with force. The whole building trembled. A door opened, and someone shouted various insults. I guessed was the same door, some neighbours were fighting. 'They must be foreign, Eastern Europeans most certainly, as I've never heard an English couple yelling that loud. Some nations are more passionate than others.' I looked at the old man and noticed he was not bothered. "Did you hear this before? Do you know these people?"

"No, never heard this before, not since I am living in this building at least... It's rather refreshing, to be honest. It makes me feel that people still have feelings. English people can be very plain. I wonder what triggered this scandal. Maybe another woman, or another man. Hmmm."

"Old man, if someone screams like a mad person doesn't always mean is from passion. It could end up in blood. Rage is an unpredictable weapon. I don't find it cool, it gives me the chills."

"Have you witnessed to this kind of fights in your country?"

"Yes, many times. Too many times. Romanians are incredibly temperamental."

"Are you temperamental, Tara?" asked the old man.

"Uncommonly! And I don't like it. I cry and shout a lot if I am frustrated or hurt."

"That happened very often, right? In your life, I mean. I can tell."

"Yes. We all have a story behind. Scars or even open wounds that we are carrying with us forever. You can forgive, but you cannot forget."

"You poor soul. I can only imagine...I'm sorry I cannot help you."

"Nobody can help me, maybe only God."

"Don't say that Tara, there are people who can heal your body and soul. In all honesty, I think you're a person who can heal not only herself but others too. Think about it."

"Old man, you have too good an opinion of me. I'm not who you think I am. I'm just an ordinary person in love with a younger boy. If this is not a clear demonstration of weakness, I don't know what it is."

"On the contrary, Tara, it is you who has too bad an opinion of yourself. There is nothing ordinary about you. You are more than I think. The fact you love a younger man is bravery. After all you've been through... to love again is just amazing." He looked at me with wonder and continued, "Your name, Tara, sounds very familiar to me, but not as a person's name... I don't know. Where does it come from?"

"*Gone With The Wind*. Tara was the name of the plantation where Scarlett was born. Have you watched the movie or read the book?"

"*Gone With The Wind*... yeah... I remember my wife dreaming about having a girl and name her Scarlett. How come your mother didn't call you Scarlett?"

"She wanted to, but the priest in my village refused to baptise me with this name due to the fact it was not on the calendar. My mother was heartbroken because she admired Scarlett's character a lot. The priest was adamant though, also because he already allowed my mother to call one of my sisters with another uncommon name."

"But Tara is not on the calendar either, or is it?"

"Nope. It is not in the calendar. However, that terrible priest had Irish ancestors and heard about this village called Tara. When my mother mentioned *Gone With The Wind*, Scarlett, and Tara, the priest said that Tara was acceptable and maybe one day my name will be included in the calendar as it happened with other weird names."

"This is an amazing story! I'm glad you were given this name, although Scarlett would have been more appropriate. I watched the movie, that character is so you! Beautiful, resilient, strong and very much courted by all men in the state."

"I do not think there are any similarities between the two of us. She was such an opportunist and played with many men's hearts. I do agree that she was a fighter though."

"Well, it is good that you are not like her then."

"But there is an expression she used that I borrowed because it helps me a lot."

"What is that? Let me guess, *'Tomorrow is another day.'* Right?"

"Such a cliché, I know! Except it's not that one, but this, *'I will think about it tomorrow.'* When I cannot sleep because of too much worry or sorrow, I repeat this phrase over and over again, until I fall asleep."

"That's very sagacious of you, Tara. You could be an excellent counsellor. You know that? Teaching people how to cope and fight against the vicissitudes of life."

"I am dreaming of becoming one actually. It's ironic though because I cannot help myself right now, how would I ever be able to help someone else?"

"Counsellors have their counsellors, Tara. It is well known. Sometimes you cannot help you, but you could help others."

We remained silent for a few minutes. I didn't want to talk anymore, and I have noticed he was tired too. It was time to go home. But my heart felt heavy. Something was keeping me from leaving, but I couldn't understand what. I looked around the house, and I was missing it already. It was a beautiful place to be in, but it wasn't the house that made me want to come here, it was the old and funny man.

The jar of yoghurt was empty, and the banana had only the skin left.

"When did you eat, old man? I must have completely blanked out as I didn't see it!"

"I don't know. We were both very distracted I guess. I don't want you to leave, Tara. I wish you'd stay with me forever... I feel very close to you," the old man confessed.

"I feel the same, old man. You are the father I never had. I promise that to speak to the organisation. All right? Maybe you could do that too. Have a little talk with your son, I believe he could be behind this decision. If that's the case, I'm glad he wants to get close to you again. It's the way it should be. He's your only son. I just hope he's a better person now."

"In just a few months you've become more of a daughter to me than he has ever been a son in all those eighteen years he lived with us. Everybody says that blood ties make you instantly love someone for no reason. Well, I now know that isn't true. I feel nothing for him. I don't recognise anything at all in him. He doesn't look like his mother or like me. He's a complete stranger. I'm not sure why that is, but it's very weird."

"If you see him these days, ask him to call me, will you? I would like to meet him soon. Maybe in here, or in town. If he's the reason that the organisation wants me to leave you, perhaps I could make him change his mind. I am known for being a very persuasive person. When I want to," I said.

"That's a brilliant idea. I'll talk to him and find out why is this happening. You have to leave now, it's extremely late and you got work tomorrow. Thank you for taking such a good care of me, Tara. I will always be grateful for every second you've spent with me. Dancing tonight was the most exciting activity I had since my wife left me. God bless you, my child."

"God bless you too, old man. Let's prepare you for bed now, all right?"

He nodded "Yes" so I brought the pyjamas and helped him putting them on. Then I accompanied him to the toilet, controlled that the heat was regulated and put him to sleep.

I gave him a small kiss on the forehead, and his eyes started dancing in tears. I became extremely emotional too, of course. I couldn't bear seeing people suffering. I always felt their pain as it was mine. 'A gift,' some say, but I think the opposite, a curse. I fought to held my tears back and walked towards the door. Before switching off the light, I stopped, turned on my feet, and had a long look at my old man. The pallor of his face made me shiver.

"Old man, are you feeling ill? You look very pale. Is there something hurting you perhaps? Should I call a doctor? Or I could call your son if you want me."

"Oh, no Tara. Don't worry, I am fine. Maybe it's the light that makes me look pale. What I am feeling is not a physical pain, there are no remedies for that, no medic could help me, especially not my son. Go home, Tara and I hope to see you soon. Good night."

"If it's not physical then you are right, there are no doctors for that. Good night. And I promise I will do everything in my power to come to see you soon. Organisation or not. All right?"

"That makes me feel better. Thank you. See you soon," he murmured.

I switched off the light and closed the door. But my feet struggled to take a step. 'This is very strange.' I thought. I've forced myself to walk away, but I was carrying an incredibly heavy burden on my shoulders. I could barely breathe. 'I'll come back, I am not leaving him. He needs me, and I need him. I'll fight if I have to. Stupid contract!' I couldn't hold my tears back any longer, so I let them fall. Thousands. I felt like an abandoned child, and I am sure the old man felt the same. How cruel is the world with all these ridiculous rules? 'The hell with them. I don't care if they fire me, I will stay by his side at any cost.'

I wiped out my face and went out on the street. A homeless man asked me if I had some spare change. I shook my head "no" and murmured "I am sorry."

"Why are you crying? Has your boyfriend broken up with you?"

I didn't expect that so I paused for a second before saying, "No, I've broken up with him."

"Why are you crying then? If you left him, it means you're not happy with him. Right?"

"It's not that simple."

"You women make everything so damn complicated! Nobody understands you. Anyway, I am sorry you are in pain. I know how that feels."

I was about to reply when another homeless man got close and started to speak with the one I was having a conversation with. I've waited for a few seconds, but they started to fight and I left. I didn't want to assist in any fight that night. I was already overwhelmed by my own existing issues, and couldn't take anything more.

Half an hour later I was in bed with my hot-water bottle. I hugged one of my pink pillows and thought of Adrian. I fell asleep and dreamed about being hugged by him. Paradise.

The next day was a very busy day. I worked in the morning and had a few interviews in the afternoon. One agency offered me a warehouse job, another one a head waiter position. All jobs in tune with my resume. I refused them both. Then another agency informed me about an office position, in a different city. They seemed very interested in my Italian language skill. I was tempted and wanted to hear more. I declined it when they've told me it was a marketing position and it involved calling people to sell stuff. "It is most definitely not something I would like to do," I confessed.

"Are you sure? It's very well paid. Think about it and let me know, all right?" said the woman in charge with the office positions.

"I am more than sure. It's one of the few jobs I wouldn't even try. No matter the pay. It's simply not for me. You'll find someone else to do it. There are loads of Italians here. It won't be difficult."

"But they've chosen your CV from the ones we sent," the agency lady insisted.

"That's rather difficult to believe. Do they know I am Romanian and just got here?"

"Maybe that's the reason they want you. You speak three languages. Very useful skill."

"Please, my English is dreadful, and I am really annoyed and ashamed."

"I think your English is good and it will get better. Please, think about it. Call me back, all right?" said the woman while standing up to leave.

I didn't want to argue, so I nodded "Yes" and left. Didn't call them back, sent an email instead. It's easier for me to write. They replied almost instantly expressing sorrow, and hoped that I would accept a different job they might have to offer in the future.

Then it was Saturday. I've worked all day for various agencies, in different locations. I got home around 11pm, utterly exhausted.

On Sunday, I met a friend and went to the church in the city centre. I didn't understand a word, and at some point, I asked my friend if the priest was preaching in English. He said amused, "No, it's Polish. The service at this hour is always in Polish. You didn't know that?"

"Of course I didn't! For the love of God, why would I want to attend a service in Polish? I don't speak Polish!" I exclaimed in the lowest tone of voice I could.

"I thought you've told me you understand it?" he whispered.

"No. I told you I understand Portuguese and all the other Romance languages. Polish is not a Romance language," I murmured.

"Romanian is not a Latin language. It makes no sense you can understand all the Romance languages. I do not get your logic."

"You are joking, right? You think Romanian is a Slavic language? What about me being a gipsy, do you believe that too?" I exclaimed again trying not to shout.

"Romania is in the middle of Russian and Slavic speaking languages, by logic, your tongue is Slavic or Russian. But I remember you telling me you can't stand Russian. Gipsy? But of course, all Romanians are gipsies, or not? I don't mind," he said with ingenuity.

"You are totally messing with me right now. Tell me it is not true you believe all these things about me and my origins!" I demanded.

"Shh..." said an old woman seated three benches ahead. She turned her head to look at us. Luckily, the church was almost empty, and we sat at the very end of it, close to the entrance. The old woman's gaze was very intimidating, so I shut up and waited for the service to finish. It took forever. If you didn't guess by now, my friend was Polish, so he understood everything that priest said. I was mad at him for making me waste so much time!

The priest gave his blessing, not that I understood a word, his gestures made it clear. Suddenly, I thought I should at least say a prayer. I knelt, closed my eyes, and tried to focus. My friend touched my arm, and I opened my eyes to stare directly at the old lady's face. I jumped, and my friend started to giggle. The old woman said something in gibberish to me, but her finger in the air was more than apparent. My friend became all serious and knelt in a rush to avoid looking at her. She sighed, made the sign of the cross, and slowly walked out of the holy place.

I finished my prayer and was preparing to leave, but my friend begged me to remain for a few more minutes. I said it was fine, thinking he wanted to pray longer. I knelt back and prayed for several minutes, losing the notion of time. I was miles away... not in front of God, but in Adrian's arms. I was feeling immensely happy when my friend poked me and grabbed me out of my piece of paradise. I looked at him like I didn't know who he was. He handed me my blue bag and we left. The church was completely empty. Outside the building not a single human being was left.

"Phew..." my friend let out a very long suspiration sound. "I thought she was going to wait to give us a lecture. My God, she scared the hell out of me."

"Language, bad boy. You've just come out of a church! What did she say? She was Polish, wasn't she?"

"She took me back to my childhood in Poland... when I used to be scolded every five minutes for talking or laughing with my friends. I felt so ashamed! Bloody religious ancient person."

"You sure are strange. Why do you go to church if you curse just in front of it? It makes no sense. Are you a believer or not?" I asked, confused.

"Oh, please. There is no God. It's just a tradition that makes me feel normal I guess."

"So you don't believe there is a greater power somewhere above us?" I tried to understand.

"No. Do you?" he asked.

"Absolutely! Some call it God, others Buddha, or Allah, Jehovah, Elohim, Krishna and so on. I don't know and don't care what's his name, or her name for that matter. I refer to him as God because that's how I learnt."

"You're full of contradictions, Tara. I do not get you at all."

"I don't get you either," I replied with sadness.

We've looked one at each other for a second and my friend lowered his head confused. "Remind me why are we friends because I seriously fail to find a reason right now. We are very different and we always end up fighting. Oh, wait, we do have something in common, the bloody Eastern European temperament!" I said with profound disappointment.

The old man came to my mind, and I realised I had no time to call as I promised. I felt dreadful and tried to ring the organisation, but no one answered. I felt the urge to go and see him, no matter the consequences, but I had a very busy schedule that day. Some people were relaxing or having fun, but I had to work in the afternoon. I didn't like it and I promised I would change that situation soon.

"My friend", I said. "I think it will be better if we spend our time with other people who are more in tune with us. This friendship is just a mascarade.

We don't know anything about one another and we fight most of the time. I don't know why we didn't think about it before. Don't you agree?"

"No, I don't agree, Tara. I helped you to get that job, remember? Then I helped you moving... That's what are friends good for, isn't it?" he replied.

"What's that supposed to mean? Are you insinuating that I only took without giving anything in return?" I asked offended.

"No. You've helped me too with those translations and resumes and stuff. I didn't mean that. I meant that we are doing stuff that friends do, so we are friends. I care about you, Tara. It doesn't matter you are a gipsy."

"Wow! It doesn't matter I'm gipsy? What is wrong with you people? Gipsies are humans too. One doesn't choose to be born English or French, Polish or Gipsy, this happens by chance! You are such an ignorant! Romanian is a Romance language and gipsies are a minority in my country. Just as they are in yours, and in many other countries," I shouted.

He looked at me very offended, tried to say something, but I turned on my feet and left saying, "Please, delete my number and so long, my friend. Thank you for all your help. I mean it."

I finished work at 9pm and went directly to bed. Hot bottle, pillow, and the same sweet thought, Adrian's arms around me. But I couldn't fall asleep. I kept thinking of my old man. I missed him, and I was feeling guilty and worried. I promised I would call in the morning, find out what was going on. It was 2 in the morning when I last looked at the time, next thing I knew the alarm went off; it was 5:30am. God, I was tired.

I jumped out of bed and started to shake like crazy, it was freezing inside the room. I didn't have time to think or feel sorry, I got changed and left the house ten minutes later. Everybody else was still asleep. I didn't have breakfast, of course.

It was still dark, but there were people on the streets already. Not many, but enough. I walked fast, not only because I was cold, but because the apartments I had to clean that day where one hour and fifteen minutes away. I got there ten minutes before, as always. The gate was still closed, so I looked around hoping there was someone somewhere. I couldn't find anyone, so I sat on the border of the pavement, praying they won't be late. I had a lot to do, even five minutes counted. Ten minutes later, still no sign. It was clear they were not going to be on time. I lost my patience because it happened all the time and I knew it. I could have come later, but every time I hoped they would start to respect the working hours one day. In vain though, as nobody checked on them. I couldn't understand this system. In Italy, one second later was unacceptable, in here you can miss a day, and you won't be fired. People were not reliable and seemed not to care about the rules. I tried to calm down, I was a guest in this country. I had no right to judge. I breathed slowly for a few seconds and thought about it with objectivity. Yes, I was too harsh on others, but I was harder on me all the time. However, I took the decision, right there and right then, that I will stop criticising everything and everyone. I felt relieved. It was about time.

I looked at the watch, 7:30 and nobody was there. I forgot about my decision not to criticise; I was furious when fifteen minutes later my team leader came with the bed sheets. She apologised, "There was heavy traffic."

'You don't say.' I thought. 'Every day is the same in here. You have been living in this town for all your life, you surely must have learned by now this is the way things go. There is traffic, leave the house earlier. To be on time!' Instead I said, "It's okay." Bloody diplomacy!

I was short fifty minutes so I rushed like a rocket through the rooms of five different apartments in four hours. Each flat had one hour allocated. But I had to finish before midday. My legs were full of bruises and I was all sweaty. I checked on all the doors, to make sure they were locked, and left. I promised I was going to quit that same day. I took the phone from my bag and all of a sudden it started ringing. I didn't recognise the number, but I answered.

"Tara? Hello. I am calling from Beeps to let you know that you have got the job you applied for a month ago."

'What job?' I wondered in my mind, but I didn't say anything. The person on the other side called my name again. "Tara, can you hear me? You still want the job, right?"

"Yes, I hear you loud and clear. I am sorry, but you've called the wrong number because I have no clue of what you are talking about."

"Aren't you a Romanian speaking Italian?"

"Yes."

"Well, you've applied for a very interesting office job. Remember? We've told you that we will let you know if you were successful. And here we are. Congratulations."

"Is this a joke? Who's speaking again? I would never apply for a marketing position." But as soon as those words came out of my mouth, I remembered. I have applied for an office type job indeed and completely forgot about it. I was convinced they will never call me. With all the Italians in town, they chose me? "I am sorry, it just went out of my head."

"Are you able to start in a week? You'll have training first," the woman asked.

"Yes. I will be there. Thank you."

"No, thank you. We are thrilled to have you in our company and looking forward to seeing you next week," said the woman with enthusiasm.

'Dear Lord!' I thought. They called me from all those applicants. It's very curious. What will they do when realising I am a complete failure? Maybe I won't even finish the training. Maybe I shouldn't present myself. I have time to think about it. Now I am going to resign from this job and apply for others.'

I went to my recruitment agency and said I was leaving. They asked me why and offered me a job in a warehouse, pick and pack or a quality check role. I said I already accepted a different job.

"What's that?" she curiously asked.

"Office job. Italian speaking."

The lady looked at me clearly not believing a word. I felt offended to death and promised I would never work with that agency again. Ever again.

"Well, in case that this office job doesn't work for you, know we are always here to take you back with open arms. All right?" she said.

I was tempted to leave without replying, but I didn't have my pay yet, so I said with a humble voice, "Thank you." Then I left and never saw that horrible woman again.

I sat on a bench in the front of the recruitment company to calm down my heart beats. It wasn't easy to resign. I breathed a few times deeply and felt like fainting.

I HATE YOU, HEART!

I had a look at my watch, it was almost 6pm. 'God, it's almost dark, and I haven't even noticed. Adrian will get to my place soon.' I started running, and ten minutes later I was home. I kindly asked my roommates not to use the kitchen for the time Adrian and I were in there. They had no problem with that. After a long shower, I turned the hob on and started to cook. In the meanwhile, I set up the table and cleaned the room.

I was going to make a risotto. One of my personal recipes. I minced a yellow onion and three cloves of garlic and tossed them into a saucepan for a few minutes.

Someone pressed the buzzer. Adrian was there, 7pm, right on time. I like punctuality.

I opened the door and told him to come upstairs. First door on the left. Number 75. My heart was racing and my mouth was dry, so I drank some water to calm my nerves. My hands were shaking terribly, more than usual, and I spilt half of the glass. 'I am thirty-eight, he's just a boy. What is wrong with you? Besides, it's just dinner, Tara. He's got a girlfriend; you know that, right? Act like an adult, woman!'

I heard steps on the stairs, so I shouted, "Come on up in the kitchen. The door is open, you'll see me."

Five seconds later he was in the room. My face was completely red. No surprise in here, but I was annoyed nevertheless. I tried to look busy, so I avoided his eyes.

"Hi, Adrian. You're right on time. It's a demonstration of respect, I love that."

"Oh, well, I am a punctual person."

"Please, make yourself at home. Do you like risotto?"

"I love risotto. Can I have a glass of water? I am very thirsty."

"You could have tea or a beer if you want," I offered.

"What type of beer?"

"I have no idea. Here, have a look," I said handing him a brown bottle.

"Ale? My favourite! How did you know?" asked Adrian, amazed.

"I didn't. There was a lot of choices, I bought the most beautiful bottle. Had no idea what was in it, except it was beer. That's the only way I can choose among this infinite range of beers."

"Well, you got the right one. What risotto are you cooking?"

"Black olives, mushrooms and smoked salmon. My personal recipe."

His face lost colour.

"What? Are you allergic to these ingredients?" I asked with worry.

He hesitated, "I...I love olives, and I can eat mushrooms, but I am allergic to fish."

I later found out that many English people don't like olives. Nothing strange about that, Great Britain is not a Mediterranean country and doesn't have olive trees. People are not used to them. But I love olives, especially the black ones. Taggiasche and Kalamata are my favourites. My British friends can't stand them. "Are so bitter, blah!"

"That's okay. I'll change the recipe in a heartbeat. Will have white risotto instead."

"What's that?" he asked confused.

"Just rice, still risotto style, with olive oil and parmesan. The most basic Italian recipe, except is always pasta instead of rice. Anyway, I was kidding. What's your relationship with bacon?"

"I normally have bacon on top of bacon. I could eat it for breakfast, lunch, and dinner. I would never get tired of it."

"Ha! Great! I am not fond of bacon much, but I eat it from time to time."

"When do you eat it if you don't eat anything whatsoever?"

"I eat it when I eat. This evening, for example. I am starving. By the way, I quit my job. We need to celebrate."

"It was about time. You can do better than that. I am sure you'll find something very soon. Have you applied for other jobs, more in line with your capacities?"

"What capacities, Adrian? I don't know how to do anything. I mean, I know how to do loads of things, but other people can do it better than me. To answer your question, no, I haven't applied for other jobs yet," I lied. I didn't want to tell him about the one I was offered and accepted already. What if I was fired in four weeks, or even before my training was finished? No way I was going to make a full of myself in his eyes again.

"Tara, you have no confidence. It's not good showing that in an interview. You have great potential and companies will be lucky to have you. I know some agencies where you can ask. Your hair looks great, by the way."

"Thank you," I said with a low voice. "Adrian, I am not sixteen anymore to be able to say I have great potential. I am a grown woman; I should be *excellent* at something by now. It's so frustrating, you've got no idea!"

"I am sure you are great at something. Speaking Italian for example. I believe in you and you should too. Let's forget about this for now, okay? Tell me, how have you been? I got used to seeing you more often and I missed that."

I had my back to him as I was cooking. I dropped the knife when I heard what he said, but I kept cooking pretending nothing happened and I didn't hear anything. My heart was running even faster than before, I thought it was about to explode.

"Are you going to join me in drinking a little bit of beer? Have a sip, I dare you!" He came close and handed me his beer. I looked at the bottle, but I didn't make a move.

"I shouldn't. My body is used with whisky, not sure what effects might the beer have on me," I said hesitating.

"Chicken," he said amused.

"Give me that bottle! But I warn you, I could be drunk in less than one minute." I grabbed the bottle and drank a long sip. It was so bitter! "Blah. This is dreadful. How can you drink something so utterly disgusting?"

"Says the girl who drinks neat whisky!" exclaims Adrian.

"Point taken," I said amused.

I wasn't kidding when I said I was going to get drunk in a few seconds. My body was weak, and my stomach was empty. I had no escape. I dangerously swayed on my feet and grabbed on the kitchen cooking border. Adrian didn't notice. I cleared my throat and informed him that the dinner was going to be ready in five minutes or so. I bent to look for something inside the fridge, and I lost balance again. This time Adrian saw it and run to help me. But I managed to avoid falling and refused his help.

I didn't want him to touch me. I would have fallen into pieces. He went to the bathroom, and I portioned the risotto and sprinkled cheese curls on top of his plate. I had no Parmigiano Reggiano or Grana Padano. I wasn't fond of strong flavoured cheese. I wasn't fond of any cheese to be entirely honest. However, I always had a great variety of it in my fridge... Another contradiction of my nature.

The food looked great, and it smelled even better. I knew it was going to be a hit. I sat and waited for him to come back.

He sat in front of me, "Thank you, Tara, this looks great. I didn't know you could cook."

"Wait until you try it to say that I can cook... Anyway, I thought I told you I cook since I was six."

"I am sure it's delicious. And, no, you haven't told me about that yet." He took a fork of risotto, blew on it, and put it in his mouth. I watched his reaction. His pupils instantly dilated. There was not a real need for words, but I craved for them so much. He said nothing so I asked, "What do you think? Do you like it?"

"It's beautiful. But you knew that already, didn't you?"

"Beautiful? Wow, what an unconventional adjective.... Food can be delicious, comestible, eatable, plain, insipid, salty, sweet, and so on, but not beautiful. Unless you speak about the look of it."

"We use this adjective to describe tasty food."

"Really? That's odd, never heard it before. In that case, thank you. I am glad you like it."

He said nothing. We ate in silence and when we finished I asked him if he needed to leave, if not, if he was okay with going into my room as the other members of the house had to cook too. He said he didn't have to be anywhere for a while, so I washed the plates, cleaned the table, and put everything back in place.

Ten minutes later, we were in my room. There were no chairs in it, just a big bed and two wardrobes. He looked confused and I felt very embarrassed.

"I am so sorry! I forgot to mention I have no chairs in my rooms; to be honest, I didn't even remember this peculiarity, got too used to it. You don't have to stay if you don't want. I understand it's a little awkward. I promised you it was not intentional. I am not trying to take you to bed."

"Oh, no? And where we will sit then?" he said smiling. "Don't worry, Tara. I trust you don't want to rape me. You're a very respectful person."

"Do I hear sarcasm in your voice?"

"Not at all. So, what do you want to do?" asked he, while sitting on the bed.

"I don't know, didn't think about this part." I looked around the room and decided to sit on the bed too. I had no other choice anyway. None of us said anything for a few minutes.

"This is not very comfortable, is it? My back hurts already. Do you mind if I lay down?" I asked timidly.

"No, no, go ahead, it's your house. I will follow."

So, I lay on the border of the left side of the bed, towards the window, as far as I could from him. He took his shoes off and lay on the right side. The bed didn't make any noise; the memory foam mattress was very soft and comfy. We didn't speak, and I did my best to regulate my breathing. My back still hurt, and I wanted to turn on a side, but I was paralysed with concern. I didn't want him to think I was looking for some physical contact. All that was surreal and the atmosphere was tense. I guess we both felt the same. But he was even better at hiding his emotions than me.

At some point, he stood up and said he needed a toilet. I felt relieved. When he came back, I was lying on a side, with the back towards him. He lay down without a word and put an arm around me. It was very unexpected, and a short groan came out of my mouth. He ignored it and murmured, "You are so thin, Tara, there is no flesh on your bones. I told you before. It was good to see you eating."

I couldn't articulate a phrase, so I kept quiet.

"Are you okay?" he murmured. "Do you want me to leave? Maybe you want to sleep, you must be tired."

"No, please don't leave. I am not going to work tomorrow. I quitted, remember?"

"Oh yeah. So, you can stay in bed until late. It will do you good, you need to charge your batteries. You've had no break since you got here."

I was fighting to keep my tears back... from happiness. He was so thoughtful, so sweet, so kind... And I so needed a little warmth in my life. Myriads of emotions overwhelmed my entire being, body, mind, and soul. My heart was racing as if I was being hunted by a dozen hungry lions. I was trembling, so he got closer and hugged me tight to his body. It was too much. My tears erupted with power and I was soon sobbing like a child.

"What's wrong, Tara? Have I done something I shouldn't have?"

"Adrian, you have a girlfriend, yet you are hugging me. I don't understand what's going on." I so hated myself for saying those words.

"We are friends, Tara. I felt like you needed a hug, nothing more. I can stop doing it if it bothers you. I am not trying to hit on you. You believe me, right?" he said with honesty.

'Who is he trying to fool, himself or me? It is so obvious we both want more.' Instead I murmured, "It doesn't bother me, Adrian. It makes me happy. I wish we could stay in this moment forever."

"Why are you crying then? Would you turn around and look at me?"

"I can't... I am too ashamed and afraid," I mumbled.

"Why are you afraid of and what have you done to feel ashamed?"

"I am afraid of what I might admit and I am ashamed because I shouldn't even think these things," I said in a trembling voice.

"What things? Just tell me," he insisted.

"So, you don't know, you don't feel that something is going on without me looking for it?"

"Would you please look at me?" he asked again.

I made myself face him. I wiped my tears off and tried to slow down my heartbeats. Impossible mission, of course. I was shaking uncontrollably. He took a blanket and covered me. It was the best feeling I had in years. Absolute bliss. My tears started to fall in cascades. He wiped them all, one by one, with infinite tenderness and care. I was convinced I'd die from too much happiness. I didn't care he was twelve years younger, and I was making a fool of myself. But the worst part was that I didn't think of him being in a relationship. No one else could have coexisted in that perfect moment. It was what I had been craving for such a long time... Adrian hugging me. But he'd done much more than I could have ever imagined or hoped for. He put his hand on both sides of my face and looked into the abyss of my eyes. I don't know what was that he was looking for, but I am sure he found infinitely more.

"What is that makes you suffer so much, Tara?" he murmured like he didn't know.

"Don't you see?"

"See what, Tara? Are you going to tell me what is that afflicts you so badly?"

I ignored the question and closed my eyes. Tears fell out quietly from them. He couldn't take his gaze away from my eyes and didn't wipe them off this time.

"You are so incredibly beautiful, Tara."

"Why are you telling me this, Adrian? What game are you playing? I warn you, I don't like games."

"It's no game, Tara, and the reason I am telling you this is because it's the truth. You are the most beautiful woman I've ever seen in real life."

"Adrian, I am twelve years older than you. If I had had sex at sixteen, I could now have a son of your age," I shouted, frustrated.

"You cannot be that old. Why are you saying these things? You look like you are thirty or something," he exclaimed.

I wanted to run away and hide, but I didn't move. "*That old*?" I asked, offended. "So, women who lived for thirty-eight years are *that old*? Nice."

"You know what I mean. I had no idea how old you are and I simply don't care. We are friends," he said, convinced.

"Friends don't say things you say. Friends don't touch each other the way you touch me. Not in my world, at least. Stop messing with my mind, English boy. You'll drive me insane."

"But you are insane... insanely beautiful."

He was most certainly playing with me, I knew it, and I had to confess, "For the love of God, Adrian, I have a crush on you. How can you not see this?"

He wasn't surprised, and he only paused for a second before saying as if it was nothing, "I have a crush on you too."

It was my turn not to feel surprised, "What are we going to do, Adrian? You are in a relationship, and there is so much age disparity between us..."

In that moment, I saw that he was as lost as I was, maybe even more. We hugged each other like it was our last day on earth, and I cried for hours until the river of my tears dried out. Then I fell asleep in his arms. Paradise.

I don't know for how long I slept, but when I opened my eyes, he was preparing to leave. I didn't check the time. "Are you coming downstairs to lock the door?" he asked with a natural voice.

"No. Just closed it. It will be fine. Goodbye, Adrian."

"See you soon," he murmured while closing the door behind him. Ten seconds later, the entrance door was closed too.

He left and took another piece of my heart with him. It hurt so much that I couldn't breathe, 'A minute ago I was in Paradise now I am in Hell. But it was worth it. *"Tis better to have loved and lost/Than never to have loved at all."* Alfred Lord Tennyson must have felt exactly like me when he wrote, *"In Memoriam A.H.H."* A beautiful poem...

What am I going to do? Will I see him again?
Should I? I hate you, heart! I hate you, destiny!'

THE OLD'S MAN SON

I closed my eyes and went back into my recent memories, for I couldn't live in the moment. I felt better there and fell asleep again.

I woke up at 10am, and the first thing I did was call the charity. The big boss answered, but when he realised it was me, his tone changed, "Tara, you are supposed to be on holiday."

"Yes, but I needed to ask you something. Could I come to see you in about one hour?"

"Two hours would be better as I am having lunch with someone in five minutes. I am glad you want to come over because I also have some things to discuss with you."

I had a quick shower, spread a layer of baby oil on my skin and put a pair of jeans on, but they were stubborn and refused to stay up, even with a belt. Only then I realised how much weight I had lost in the last three months. Those jeans were a small eight. I looked in the mirror and saw just bones. I didn't like it, but I didn't have time to think. I needed to leave soon as the organisation was outside town. I would have taken the bus if I had only one hour to get there, but I had two so I could walk. I sat on the floor for a minute to think of what I could wear that still fit me. My work trousers came to mind. They were a little big, but with a belt they were fine. The outfit was completed with a cardigan, a pair of comfortable walking shoes, a belt, and the necessary bag, all in the same non-colour, black, plus a blue jumper. The mirror reflected a smart look, the indefinite colour of my eyes borrowed the blue from the jumper, my skin was pale.

I left the house ten minutes later but I had to come back, because I forgot both my phone and watch. Couldn't go anywhere without knowing the time.

When I reached my destination, I was all sweaty and heavily breathing. I looked at my wrist to check the time, but there was no watch on it. 'How is this possible? I went back to take it and I am sure I placed it on my wrist.' I thought better and clearly remembered checking the time when crossing a highly trafficked road. I emptied the bag, and searched all my pockets (had only two) and the watch was gone. It was a beautiful watch, just two weeks old. I felt upset, I needed the watch, it wasn't a caprice. I promised I would go back the same route and hopefully find it.

I looked for my phone, which was in my bag, and thanked God I haven't lost that too. I was ten minutes earlier, so I decided to have a short walk around. I turned on my feet suddenly and ran into the man who was with my boss. I was mortified, and my face went instantly red, "I am so terribly sorry!" I said in a rush, "I didn't know there was someone behind. I hope I haven't hurt you."

"It's okay," replied the man.

"Tara, you're right on time. Well, earlier, as usual, but we are here too so it's perfect timing. Meet Drefan. Drefan, this is Tara." I reached my right hand out to him to shake hands, as every respectful Eastern European person, oops, he was left-handed. The boss continued looking at the man, "She is the girl who took care of your father for the last couple of months."

I was surprised and happy for the chance to meet my old man's son. "Nice to meet you. I've heard a lot about you."

"I'm sure you have. Nice to meet you too, Tara. Thank you for everything you've done for my father. He cared about you a lot and your name was the last he called before passing away."

My right hand went instinctively to touch my heart, as to keep it inside my body and contain the unbearable pain that overwhelmed my entire being. The light became dark, and I balanced on my feet. There was a tree on my left and reached my both hands to grab on it. It was too distant though. Someone caught me from the waist, and tried to save me from falling, but it was too late, I slid down on my knees *adagio*. My boss called my name, his voice seemed to come from infinite miles away and I went into oblivion.

I am not sure how long I'd been unconscious, most likely a couple of minutes, but when I came back into my senses, Drefan and my boss were having an animated discussion about the need for an ambulance. My boss decided to wait. "For how long? A person could die in five seconds! I am calling one right now. We could be accused of negligence and end up in prison, for the love of God!" shouted Drefan.

"You are too melodramatic. I am sure it's nothing, she doesn't eat properly. You might have noticed her gaunt figure," replied my boss in a calm voice.

Suddenly, both moved a few metres away to clarify some things. Drefan lowered his voice, but I could hear rage in it, "Why the heck didn't you tell me she was not informed about my father? What is wrong with you?"

"She was on holiday, Drefan. Besides she's just an employee, not a family member. We assigned her someone else last week. She'd said goodbye and everything. I do not understand her reaction. Maybe it's got nothing to do with your father. Let's wait and see."

"*Just an* employee? My father's..." Drefan replied, but I interrupted.

"There is no need for an ambulance," I murmured while trying to remember when was the last time I lost consciousness. The answer was never. I'd never fainted before. I was lying on the pavement. My face was wet and I had a pillow under my head. Luckily, the street wasn't very populated, and most of the employees were either working hard or having lunch. They weren't looking outside the window to watch random people fainting.

My boss and Drefan stopped when they heard my voice. "Tara, you scared the hell out of us. What's gotten into you? Are you ill or something? It's not that you're pregnant, are you?" asked my boss.

I didn't know what to say, how to explain that I was utterly devastated by what I'd heard. They would have never understood. The employees were not supposed to befriend the people they are taking care of. It was not acceptable. "I am not ill nor pregnant, boss. I am just very weak. I couldn't eat much since I am in here. Don't worry, I am fine. Sorry for giving you trouble."

"Are you sure you don't want us to call an ambulance?" intervened Drefan. "I am glad that it's not because you heard about my father. I felt guilty for bringing this news so coldly to you. I had no idea you were completely unaware of the fact he passed away. Let me help you to get inside and we'll have a little talk. Shall we?"

"No, please, no ambulance, I am more than sure," I said convinced while trying to get up, with no success though.

My boss was a physically challenged person, incapable of bending to reach for my body, but Drefan was slim and in splendid shape. He knelt next to me, put one of his strong arms around my body and asked in my ear, "Ready?"

"Ready," I replied. With a very tender movement, he helped me rise back on my feet. I stood still for a few seconds, to make sure I was strong enough to stand. He kept his arm around my waist until I took a very deep breath and decided I was fine and no other help was needed. My blouse wasn't in place so he pulled it down. I thanked him and thought it was a very kind gesture. 'I hope my old man got to know him before... Oh, God. I cannot think of it now. Please, give me strength, don't abandon me, I beg you.'

I shivered and Drefan asked for forgiveness for having dropped some cold water on my face. I ignored the words and walked towards the building.

My boss managed to take the pillow from the ground, God knows how, and came to swipe his card to open the doors. We all went inside in an Indian line, my boss was first, I followed, and Drefan closed the queue. I wasn't paying attention to anything. My mind was blank, like I was sleeping. When we got inside the office, Drefan made me sit and my boss went to make some tea. I focused my gaze in front of me. The wet pillow was on the desk. It was clear it belonged to this room. I wondered who had the idea of putting it under my head. Not that it mattered, I just needed to keep my mind busy with something.

Five minutes later, the boss brought three mugs of tea, one for each of us. I took the hot receptacle in my hands, trying to warm up a little, but they were trembling a lot and had to place it on the desk in front of me. Drefan took his jacket off and put it on my shoulders. The gesture touched my heart. I looked at him and thanked from my eyes. I couldn't help but notice how elegant and well-groomed he was.

My boss sat with a sigh and asked me what was I came to ask. I said I would listen to what he's got to say first; then I'll go with my inquiry. Truth is I was trying to come with a backup plan.

"Tara, the reason I wanted to talk to you is Drefan's father's will. He left everything to you. It wasn't much, just the flat and the things in it."

I was speechless. I looked at both in sequence; then I covered my face with both hands. A few seconds later I shouted, "What? But when, how? Someone must have helped him because he never went out of the house."

Drefan was observing me carefully. At first I thought it was because he was worried, suddenly I realised that what he was trying to see was if I had played a role in that matter. I was offended and terribly hurt, but I understood their curiosity and implied accusations. I would have thought the same if I was in Drefan's shoes.

"Well, I don't want anything, you can have it all," I said looking at Drefan. "I promise I won't fight you. Show me where to sign, and I will do it right away."

Both looked at me in disbelief. I wasn't surprised. "Are you sure?" asked Drefan timidly,

"We could share, you know? My father cared a lot for you, otherwise he wouldn't have done that."

"What are you talking about? The fact he left everything to me and not to you is because he'd had no news from you. You both lost contact years ago. He thought you were gone for good. That's the only reason he put my name on the will. I guess, he didn't have another choice."

"You're wrong, Tara. He's changed the will a week before he died. He intended to leave it all to this organisation, but for some reason, he decided to leave it to you. And that happened two days after I visited him. He had choices, but he decided that you'll be the only beneficiary of his possessions."

'Tara, pull yourself together, don't cry... don't cry, Tara. You'll think about it tomorrow. Focus, Tara, focus. They cannot understand your feelings,' I repeated all these in my mind several times, but I was utterly overwhelmed. I looked at my boss and he seemed relieved, but Drefan's expression was still puzzled. I tried to have a sip of tea, but it was disgusting. The brownish colour brought sweet memories to mind. I burst into tears.

"Take everything; I don't want it anyway! And, for your information, I cared about this man a lot. He was a fascinating person. He was good, understanding, patient and loved his wife immensely. I cannot believe you haven't called to let me know he passed away. I would have participated in his funerals. He was not a simple person in need of help, he was an extraordinary human being. He was my friend and I will miss him for eternity. It breaks my heart realising that the only thing important to you is a damn will. I cannot take this any more, I am not feeling well. I need to go home. Call me when you have the papers ready," I said looking at Drefan, then I turned to my boss and continued, "The reason I needed to talk to you, is because I was not happy about the decision you took regarding my next assignment. I wanted to ask you to let me continue helping Drefan's father, and in front of a refusal, I would have handed my resignation. But as for now, it's clearly too late for that. I wasn't simply an employee, and he was not a patient either. I am not going to work for you anymore. I am done. You may have learned not to care for people, but I am not there yet. Feelings are what make us human. Don't call me again."

My boss didn't see that coming and couldn't say a word. Drefan lowered his head to avoid looking at me. I took his jacket from my shoulders and handed it to him, then I stood up and swayed a few times. I grabbed on my chair to steady myself and both jumped to help me. "Don't you dare to touch me. None of you!" I roared.

I walked out unsure on my feet, but I haven't stopped until I got out on the street. The breeze of cold air reinvigorated me. I kept walking by inertia, completely blind, and deaf. I forgot about the watch, I cared about nothing. I wandered for several hours without a destination.

RED ROSES

It was dark when I got home. It was a miracle that I didn't get hit by a car, fall into a ravine or God knows what else. In front of my door, was a bunch of red roses. I looked at them and felt nothing. I didn't know what to make of it, so I left them there and went to bed with my clothes on. I didn't cry. My senses were petrified; I thought I was dead. I always imagined I would die without being aware of what was happening. I felt grateful somehow and felt at peace. I was free from pain, I didn't have to fight anymore, and then... it was nothing.

Someone was calling my name from thousand miles away. Then a knock, two, and another one, "Tara, please, open the door. Tara, do you hear me? I beg you say something. TARA?"

I looked around confused, 'it cannot be Heaven', too much tribulation, 'maybe it's Hell. I guess I deserve to be here.' That entity was making a lot of noise. Many other voices joined that chaos. "Maybe she's not in," a voice concluded.

"I saw her going inside the room. She looked at me in my direction as I was invisible. I thought she was tired so I didn't say anything," Lola, a roommate and friend explained.

"But she didn't pick up the flowers! Perhaps you only dreamed about seeing her," the first voice insisted.

"Don't be silly, why would I dream about Tara going into her room? It was her, I am sure! And she locked the door. I've never heard or seen her doing that. She can't stand locked doors. She said it makes her feel trapped in a cage. I should have understood right away something was wrong! Why haven't I?" Lola was blaming herself and it touched my heart.

Another voice got in, "You worry too much. What if she's with someone? Maybe a boy, or a girl. Gee. We don't even know which gender she's attracted to. Perhaps she's having fun and doesn't want to be disturbed."

"No, Tara is not that type. I have a very bad feeling about it. There was something in her eyes... Why didn't I say something? Maybe she killed herself," said Lola, alerted.

"Oh my god, don't talk like that! I could never live in this house again. I don't like dead people," another voice shouted in terror.

I decided it was Hell after hearing that discussion, but I also realised I wasn't dead and someone was worried about me. I got out of bed and unlocked the door. My four housemates, all girls, made a step back, both from fear and surprise. "I am alive, thank you for caring. I am sorry I scared you, but please let me rest. I don't feel very well," I told them in a low voice.

The girl who worried, Lola, was looking at me as if she'd seen a ghost, "Tara, are you going somewhere, or did you sleep with your clothes on? You are extremely pale. It's like your body is drained of all the blood. Do you want me to call a doctor?"

Two of my other housemates started giggling. "Tara had a close encounter with Dracula last night and she's slowly turning into a vampire," said one girl.

I looked at them and felt nothing, but I smiled to make them stop worrying. "Dracula doesn't suck the blood of women like me, I am just tired, that's all. I don't need a doctor. Doctors are not gods anyway. Please, I want some peace, I hope it's not too much to ask. I am on holiday until next week and I will be staying in my room, all right? Abstain yourselves from knocking on my door, unless the house is on fire," I said looking at them one by one. "Thank you, I know I can count on you."

I was about to close the door when a girl asked me if I was going to take the roses from the floor.

"Oh, I didn't see them when I got home yesterday. Who brought them in?" I asked trying to look pleased and surprised, truth is, I couldn't care less.

"But I watched you trying not to step on them! You surely noticed them! Tara, please, I am very worried, you look dreadful. Let me cook something for you. All right?" said Lola.

That offer triggered a feeling inside me: Horror. Lola's culinary skills were a work in progress. "I appreciate your offer, but I am not hungry, I just need to rest. Please respect my request for once," I said while bending to take the red bouquet from the carpet. Then I locked the door thanking them for the understanding.

A voice shouted that the roses were brought in by a flower shop employee and she opened the door to bring them upstairs. I sat on the bed with absolute calmness. I felt a pinch on my right hand and I raised it to see why. I was still holding the roses. The thorns pierced my skin. I didn't feel pain, but there was some blood coming out. I wiped it off with a white tissue. Then I used another one to press on the fresh tiny wound until it stopped bleeding. The flowers were wilted and in desperate need of water. 'I don't want to know who sent them. I don't care if they dry out. I just need to sleep. I am a horrible person.' I thought and laid on the bed with the roses kept tight in my right hand. I fell asleep... Only God knows for how many hours. When I opened my eyes, it was dark everywhere. I turned the light on and looked around. The roses were dead, and that reminded me of a song of the nineties, "Where the wild roses grow." It was about a beautiful girl who got killed with a stone. Not a very happy ending. Weirdly enough, it stuck in my head for all these years. I somehow loved it. I put the roses on the nightstand and went to the toilet, came back locked the door again and went under my duvet. I closed my eyes, and a lonely tear rolled out of my right eye without control. I wiped it off with a hand and let myself falling into oblivion again.

Someone knocked on my door again. 'It has to be serious if they dare to do that.' I thought and went to open the door. One of my roommates was standing in front of it and said there was a man downstairs looking for me. "He called you several times, but your phone is off. He said it's important. And he looked worried. Is he the one who sent you the flowers? Do you want me to tell him you are not home or don't feel well?"

"No, it's fine, I'll go talk to him. What day is today?"

"Friday."

"What? That's impossible, it was Wednesday yesterday."

"No, that was two days ago. You slept for more than forty-eight hours. It's 8:18pm now."

"Well, I am glad you didn't say it was 2017 at this point!"

We both laughed. "Is he the one with the flowers, Tara? Is he your boyfriend? He is very handsome and quite posh looking. Like a director or something. I saw him from the window. Great catch!"

"I have no idea from where the flowers are and also I've got no clue who the man downstairs is. What I do know though is the fact I've got no boyfriend..." I paused for a few seconds and continued in a solemn tone, "because I like girls."

My housemate was shocked but said nothing. I tried to hold back my giggling and I did a very good job as she didn't realise I was making fun of her. I went downstairs, put a pair of trainers on and went outside. There was no one in front of the entrance door. I looked to the left, right and again to the left, but no one I knew was there. 'Hmm... I thought I made fun of her and instead she is the one messing with me. My God, she's been quite convincing!' I was kind of impressed and about to go back inside when a male voice called my name, "Tara?"

I turned around and saw Drefan. "Oh, it's you. What happened? Have you prepared the papers for me to sign?"

"You look disappointed. Were you expecting someone else?" asked him.

"I was not expecting anyone actually. So, do you have the papers and a pen?"

"No, I have no papers. I just came to see how you're doing. You weren't looking well when I last saw you."

"Why is everybody so worried about me? It drives me nuts! I am fine, perfectly fine."

"Tara, when people worry about someone it usually means they care about that person," explained he in a calm voice.

I was stupefied! "Are you saying that you care about me? Why is that? You don't even know me! Is it because you're afraid I won't sign the papers?

You don't have to invent these sorts of things. I know it's hard for you to believe I am honestly intending to give it all to you without a fight, but it is the honest truth. Now please, go home and call me when you've got everything ready. I am starting a new job next Monday, it might be difficult to get me on the phone, but you could send me a text with the place and time, and I'll be there. I promise," I said raising the tone.

"Tara, I am not worried you won't sign, I don't even want that place... It is not me who's doing this..." He stopped and looked down. "Will you have a coffee with me? I know you can't stand tea."

"Of course you know I don't like tea, you saw me not being able to have a single sip in that... office," I said with sarcasm. The phrase made absolutely no sense, but it was too late to take it back.

"No, I didn't notice you didn't like tea then. My father told me. He talked a lot about you. To be honest, you were the only subject he talked about. He genuinely cared about you and was very, very worried. Before he died he asked to see you, but your phone was off. I didn't want to leave a voicemail because he said you don't listen to them. I should have sent a text... but it didn't come into my mind. I am not fond of texts. It takes too much time. When I told him your phone was off, he thought you might have lost it. Then he asked me to look out for you, because you were having a very bad time and were alone. He told me that he already said goodbye to you."

Tears were falling in cascades on my burning cheeks. All my senses were overwhelmed with pain. I couldn't bear it. It was too much. I leant against the brick wall. Two days ago, I thought there was no way I could feel more pain than that. How deadly wrong I was! 'Dear lord! He called for me and I didn't even check my mobile phone. He left this world disappointed in me. How would I ever forgive myself for that? I knew something was wrong, I had a presentiment, but I chose to ignore it. I was so selfish. I am a monster. A monster! I didn't deserve his affection. I wish to die and stop this agony. God, have mercy, I am going insane.'

"Oh, Tara. I am so sorry," said Drefan while hugging me to prevent another fall.

I didn't push him away; I didn't have the strength or the thought. There was no more room for something else than sufferance in my body, heart, and soul. I cried and cried and cried until I had no more tears. People were staring, some with curiosity, others with pity. It was almost dark and I was grateful. Drefan gave me a handkerchief to blow my nose, but I couldn't. It looked very expensive. He insisted, and as I had no other means to clean my nose I had to accept it.

Then he asked me again to go for a coffee. I nodded "Yes," and started to walk towards the high street. We went inside the first pub and looked for a lonely table. A difficult task as it was quite busy and very noisy. He ordered two cappuccinos and I went to sit down. I was too weak to stand. A few minutes later he joined me carrying a tray with some slices of cake and the two hot drinks.

I didn't say I didn't want to eat because I wasn't hungry. I just took one chocolate slice and started to chew on it absently. It was tasteless, but I finished it in a few minutes.

"Were you hungry, Tara, or you just like cakes?"

"None of the above, I just have to eat something. My body needs it, but I don't feel the desire. I don't feel anything, except desolation. And there are moments in which I am completely numb. I am not sure if it's the desperate strategy of my body to cope with all this."

"I didn't know you cared for my father that much. I am afraid I can't say the same."

"Your father was a wonderful person. I've learned a lot from him. It's such a pity you two fell out. I never met anyone like him and I would never, ever forget any moment I had the luck to spend in his company. It will take me years to get over his loss." Tears started to fall from my eyes again. Drefan put his hand on mine. I moved it. I don't like to be touched, unless I am about to faint. And I don't like to be touched by married men, or by men in a relationship. Period.

We finished our drinks and Drefan took my home. We've exchanged a short hug.

"Thank you for the flowers, you shouldn't have had."

"What flowers?"

I was confused, "Oh, so they were not from you. Sorry, I didn't check the card attached to it. Never mind."

He left and I went inside my room. The lights in the house were on. My roommates were watching a movie and laughing. Nobody noticed my presence. I heated some water, filled in my plastic bottle with it and put it in bed, covering it with the duvet so the heat won't disperse.

I had a very long, hot shower, got changed and prepared to go to bed. It was then when I noticed the flowers for the first time. They were completely dried now. 'So tragic flowers don't survive without water.' I took the small card and read, "For the most beautiful woman in the whole world." No signature. 'Drefan didn't know about them... they must be from Adrian then.'

I let the card fall and hugged my pillow thinking of him. And I cried. I wanted Adrian arms around my body. 'He'd make me feel better. A simple hug would take my pain away. But he's not mine, and I am twelve years older than him. I should be ashamed, but I am not. Maybe I should feel guilty... but for what? I haven't done anything wrong. I appreciate he's in a relationship, although I know there is no love between them. Two lonely people having a tacit understanding: we stay together to hide from loneliness, and we are friends, you can count on me, and I can count on you.' But I wanted him to be mine. I needed his arms around me. I wanted him to smile looking at me. I wanted him to feel passion and excitement. I wanted him to live. Then I fell asleep and I dreamt about falling into an abyss. I flinched and opened my eyes for a second just to close them back and fell again and again into the same black endless chasm. A recurring nightmare I had when I was a child. Many people dream the same, especially when they are down on their knees, completely defeated, with no hope and no solutions. "Bring me back to life."

On Monday morning, I went to work for my new company. It was one hour away from my place – on foot – of course. I left two hours earlier to make sure I'll be there on time. It was raining, and I couldn't remember with clarity where exactly was that place located. It took more than forty-five minutes to find the building after I found the road. I asked people, but nobody knew. I was already very stressed and soaked to the bone. Luckily, I had a clean dry outfit in my waterproof backpack. It was 8:50am when I entered the building looking for the lady's room. The receptionist pointed me into the right direction. I got changed in a flash, and at 8:55 I went inside the office. I didn't like the fact I got in so late on my first day, so I was annoyed. Someone was waiting for me so it was easy to find my location. I sat with my head lowered, I didn't know anyone in there. Two hours later, after my introduction to the job role, they gave me a ten-minute break, "Go have a coffee or tea in the kitchen."

I went outside instead, for a breath of fresh breath. It was still raining, but I didn't care. I absently walked up and down for five minutes. I was about to go inside when I saw Adrian. I thought I was hallucinating and got really scared, but when our gaze met, I knew it was real. His surprise was as big as mine. I said hello and sorry, "I need to get back to work, my break is over."

"What time do you finish?"

"5:30pm."

"I'll wait for you in here. By the way, you look very smart," he said.

I didn't have time to discuss, so I ran into the second-floor office. I imposed my mind to forget what I just saw, and focused on the job. It was easy. I always clear my mind of personal issues when I am on a job. I only allowed my mind to travel to him, just for a few seconds in every break I had that day. When my first day of work got to the end, I was afraid to leave. I didn't want to see him. It was too painful. And I stayed until I thought he left. My heart was racing. Someone came to tell me that the offices were about to be closed. I got changed into my walking outfit and took the stairs, he was not there and I sighed with relief. I told my heart to calm down, we were safe and I went outside. It was still raining. I got home in about fifty minutes, had a hot shower, and went to bed. I hugged my pillow and went to my piece of Heaven where Adrian was waiting for me. In there he was loving and... mine.

The next day, I didn't go outside until the end of the day. He was waiting for me downstairs. I couldn't hide, I couldn't run, there was no escape. We started walking.

"What are you doing here?" I asked annoyed.

"Waiting for you."

"I mean here, like *in the building*? Don't tell me you work here. It's bizarre that we meet everywhere like we have some kind of agreement."

He seemed very troubled and didn't reply. 'Someone is definitely messing with me... and him. Is it fate? Are we supposed to meet? Why? He's in a relationship, don't you think is utterly inappropriate?' I asked the God Almighty in my head. I totally believed in fate or destiny or a greater power, and I believed everything happened for a reason. But what was the reason for that? A torture?

"Where are you going, Adrian?" I asked when I realised he was walking in my home direction.

"Taking you home. I need to talk to you," he said.

"Then talk. What's going on?"

"First, why don't you reply to my texts?"

"Oh... I wasn't aware you wrote to me. I don't know where my phone is. I am using an old phone, with a Romanian SIM card just to check the time. I've lost my watch."

"All right. Secondly, what are *you* doing in here?"

"I started a new job. I had no idea you were working in the same building."

"I don't work here. I only came for two days to take care of some business for my company. It happens from time to time. Curious how they haven't sent me here for more than a year. I admit that our encounters have something of the extraordinary behind them. Why didn't you tell me you found a more suitable job?" he asked.

"Why should I, Adrian?"

"I thought we were friends?! Friends tell each other things."

"Friends? We are not friends and will never be," I shouted.

"How can you be so cruel?"

"Cruel? Me? That's ironic, don't you think? How's your girlfriend?" I asked suddenly.

"She's fine," he replied, clearly annoyed.

"I am happy to hear that. Adrian, I don't want you to take me home. I am going to meet someone in a few minutes. Oh, and I almost forgot, thank you for the flowers. You shouldn't have."

Adrian's hesitated for a few seconds then stopped, said nothing and turned back to go into town.

I pretended I didn't care and I kept walking.

A PICTURESQUE HOUSE

I was indeed going to meet someone, a landlord, to see a new house. I am a solitary person who lives alone since I can remember. But when I came to England, just a few months back, I had no job, no money and no credit history. I couldn't even think to look for a house where I could live alone. But things had changed, I had some savings and the new job seemed a done deal, it was time for me to move and live alone. The house where I was living with so many housemates was just a temporary location. I didn't enjoy my permanence there. People usually complain about solitude, I complain about the opposite, too much light and life in it. Maybe I was related to Dracula.

Although it was in the city centre, it took me a lot to find the right address for this house. I rang the bell, and the landlord came down to open the door. I was surprised to see that he was young and quite handsome. I liked him instantly and I knew he felt the same. After the introductions, we went inside the corridor, and ten seconds later I almost turned around to run away. It looked absolutely horrendous, and I wondered how the house would be, worse, or a little better? Either way, I was there, so I was going to visit it. Out of respect. The man waited for me and came downstairs to accompany me inside; he could have just pressed a button and open the door. It touched me dearly. I owed him.

The stairs in the house were incredibly steep. I wasn't bothered, the carpet was clean.

I wasn't fond of carpets, but that's how almost all interiors look in Great Britain. Very English style. I promised I would get used to it. Inside the living room was a brick wall with a fireplace, and the floor didn't have a carpet on, it was just plain wood. It looked idyllic. My eyes blurred with tears from emotion. I fell in love and bluntly said, "There is no need to show me anything else. I want this place. It's perfect."

He looked at me, smiled, and said that I should see the whole house anyway then guided me inside the bedrooms and bathroom. Each bedroom had a double bed and various pieces of furniture. One room had a beautiful wardrobe, a desk with a chair all in solid wood. The other one had another fireplace and I immediately decided that would be the room I slept in.

It did not have a wardrobe in it, but there was a cabinet drawer and a shelf cabinet, library style. Again, in solid wood. There were many pieces of furniture in the house, so I didn't have to buy anything, except for a table, some chairs, and a wardrobe for my room.

Everything was matching in colour and style. You could easily tell that the owner had exquisite taste and a heart sensitive to beauty. I liked all I saw, except for the paintings. Abstract art was not my cup of tea and I told him I preferred the Impressionist style. He then said that would take the paintings off and I was free to hang whatever I wanted instead.

The carpets were not new and there were many spots on them, although it was clear that someone had tried hard to get rid of them. It didn't seem important. The big windows were not double glazed, I didn't care. The rooms were luminous and airy. The house was right in the city centre, the best location ever. Not a great view, but I was sure I would not have time to sit and look out the window. The building was very old and there were just two apartments, so if I was getting the house, I would have had just one neighbour. It was a dream house. And I prayed God to help me get it.

We then sat on the brown leather sofa. I repeated I wanted the house. The landlord said that he'd promised to show it to other people. He didn't have a drink to offer me and invited me to go out and have one in a pub close by. I accepted with enthusiasm. He then asked how come my phone was switched off as he'd tried to call me a few times during the day and had to leave a voicemail. I replied that I was not fond of phones and it went missing for more than a week now. I also admitted that I was not going to listen to the voice mail and we should continue keeping in touch through emails if that was okay with him. The landlord nodded "yes," it was fine by him.

He took me to a very nice pub, close by. We sat outside, I had a whisky, he had a beer. We laughed a lot, for the first time in a very long time for me, and had a wonderful time. I felt very comfortable in his presence.

He didn't ask me where I was from, and I didn't say. But I intentionally guided him into believing I was Italian, as that was the only country I spoke about. The idea came from a British friend of mine. She was afraid that no landlord would rent me the house if said I was Romanian. Not after the famous documentary on BBC. And with the terrible experiences I lived in the past, I had no other choice.

He also didn't ask how long I have been working for my new company, if I had a contract and for how many months. And I didn't bring in the subject. At some point, though, he asked if I could afford to pay for the house alone. "Absolutely!" I replied with conviction. "I'll promise you'll never have any issues with me. I am the best tenant you could ever find on this earth." He smiled and didn't want to know anything else.

It was dark when I left, he offered to give me a lift, I declined and said I would walk as I needed to clear my head. He promised to let me know as soon as possible what he had decided with the house. I wasn't the only person interested in the house. Apparently, there were at least twenty people with the same intentions as mine.

I said I also had an appointment to see a house the very next day.

At 8am the landlord sent me an email telling me that he'd cancelled all the other appointments and decided to rent the flat to me if I still wanted it. I instantly replied that I was going into town right away to meet him. One hour later, I withdrew a month rent plus the deposit from my bank account, put them into an envelope and walked towards my future home. I placed the envelope on the handmade furniture and said that he saved my life.

He was very surprised, "I didn't ask you to bring me the money. You could have sent it to my bank account later, after I gave you the keys."

"That's all right. I trust you," I replied.

"When do you want to move?" he asked.

"Right away?" I said more as a joke.

The landlord laughed again and said it was fine. He was very serious about it. I couldn't believe my luck! He also offered to give me a hand with bringing my things over. I said it was not necessary, "I could ask a friend," but he insisted, and I accepted.

"I can't give you the keys now, as I only have one pair and I can't leave the house open when I come later to take you."

"That's fine. I'll have them later then."

The sun was out that day and I felt at peace. I took the bus to go back to my place and pack my stuff. I then realised that my phone was not inside my room. I promised I would check all my bags as soon as I was all settled. The clock was showing 4pm and my future landlord wasn't there yet. A very disturbing idea bore into my mind, 'I gave a stranger a lot of money without having a key to the place. I acted like the most naïve person in this entire universe.' But the other side of me retaliated, 'No. I do not act this way without a good reason. My gut told me to trust him and I know he's an honest person. He'll be here soon. Maybe there is no car park empty for him to leave the car." I checked my emails, there was just the one he sent to inform me of the time he'll be able to come and help me. I was a little worried, I must admit. I looked out the window in the street and I saw him parking. I felt guilty for having doubted him, even if only for a second. I run downstairs with my last suitcase. They were six in total. Very big and heavy. He came at the door apologising for being late, he was not able to find a car parking space. "I would have let you know but your phone is still off."

"I am terribly sorry; it must be off because of a drained battery. I looked for it today while packing, had no luck. I hope I didn't lose it. My last hope is to search inside my handbags when I unpack my stuff."

My roommates came downstairs to help me. In seven minutes, all suitcases had found a place inside my landlord's vehicle. Luckily it was quite a big one. Half an hour later, we were in town. There was no way of parking in front of the house, but it was allowed to stop and unload the car. It took only five minutes. The landlord gave me the keys to open the doors and went to leave the car somewhere else. I took a suitcase and went inside. My god, it was heavy! The corridor was narrow and I struggled immensely to climb the steep stairs with that big heavy bag, but I made it. 'Hurray!' I run outside to bring another one, then another. By the time my landlord came back, I managed to bring inside five of them. My face was red and I was out of breath, but jubilant and excited. I grabbed the last suitcase, but the landlord had already his hands on it. "Tara, seriously, let me carry this one. It is extremely heavy and you are very thin. You cannot possibly bring this upstairs by yourself."

"All of them were heavy, you know? You've already done so much for me; I don't want you to carry my bags too. It's not fair," I fought with my eyes dancing in tears.

"What I've done is nothing. We are humans, we are supposed to help one another," he said with warmth.

I was deeply touched. Most people I met in this country were extraordinary humans. "Thank you. I will never forget this," I said.

"Tara, how come you are not working today?"

"I didn't work yesterday either. When I was hired, I told my company that I might need a few days off the day I will find a house and they agreed. I am going to work two Saturdays to recuperate the hours. I love my company!"

"That's great. Glad to hear you're happy."

He brought the bag inside, washed his hands and left for a long trip. He lived more than three hundred miles away. I felt sad. There was a very good vibration between us. We could have been great friends. I was not to see him, maybe ever again, as he lived three hundred kilometres away. We kept in touch through emails. If something was broken, I let him know and he always sent someone to take care of it. A perfect landlord and tenant relationship. He trusted me and I trusted him.

I cleaned the house for a couple of hours, although it was clear that a cleaning company did that before me. However, I had to make sure it was hygienic enough for my standards.

I sat down on the corridor and compared the two bedrooms, even if as I already said, the fireplace made me instantly decide which will be the room I'd sleep in. There was no wardrobe in there, but I planned on buying one or two from a charity shop. I unpacked all my bags and started to look for the appropriate place for every single object I owned. I finished in a few of hours. I took a step back and checked the results. It was harmony everywhere. I was pleased. I felt at peace and my place back in Romania came to mind. I missed it very much, but I immediately sent away that thought. I couldn't afford to go back in a state of despair right now. 'I'll think about it tomorrow.'

There was something about this place... so cosy and positive. Great personality and resonance. It was what my heart needed. I knew I was going to be happy in there.

I prepared my outfit for the next day, a black knitted dress, tights in the same colour and a pair of rainbow stiletto shoes. And suddenly I realised that my phone hadn't showed up. I took all my bags and checked inside. No luck. 'Maybe it's in a pocket of a jacket or something.' I wasn't the type of person to keep the phone in a pocket, but I tried my luck. Nothing. There was no doubt, I lost my phone, God knows where. 'That's why I didn't pick up when Drefan called to tell me about his father. That's why I didn't see Adrian's texts and my landlord's calls. I never lost anything in my life and now I lost two important objects in less than a month. This must be some warning. I need to pay more attention; I cannot spend my money on new phones or watches.'

There were three clocks in the house, and I checked one... It was too late to go and buy one then. 'I'll do it tomorrow after work. I need a phone with an English SIM. This one is twelve years old and doesn't keep the charge.' It was decided, and I put my heart to peace.

I needed a shower and went to have one. It was cold inside the house, the heat wasn't on and had no idea of how to turn it on. I had never used this system before, but I remembered when my old man said that plugs need to be turned on for electric devices to work. So I checked the plug, it was off. I switched it on with hope, but no heat or any sound came out. I looked around and played with the two controls. No luck. I decided to leave it and ask someone about it the next day. It was clear that I needed to learn many things about English systems, methods, and habits.

I switched the kettle on, looked for a plastic bottle and filled it in with the hot water from the red kettle. I took the bottle and placed it under my duvet, as I had every night since I was in England, charged my phone and went to bed. 'I wish Adrian was here to hold me tight and keep me warm.' I hugged the pillow and fell asleep in heaven.

On Friday morning, I went to work. I had many things to catch up with and it'd been a busy morning. At midday I sent Adrian an email telling him I was going to walk through the park at the end of my shift. I didn't ask for him to wait for me, but I hoped he would. I just needed to see him.

Around 6:10pm Adrian was expecting for me on a bench. He stood up when he saw me, and without a word, we started walking towards the city centre.

"Are you going to see someone in town? Maybe the same person you saw last time?" asked Adrian.

"No. I live in the city centre now. I moved in yesterday. The person I had to meet the other day was my landlord," I said.

Adrian stopped and yelled at me, "Why didn't you tell me? I thought you had a date. I almost went insane!"

His disproportionate reaction infuriated me, "What? How dare you shouting at me? I am not required to tell you anything about my life. What is wrong with you?"

"I could have helped you moving. I know you don't know many people here."

"You're wrong. I know loads of people here, and I didn't need to ask anyone for help. The owner offered. He's an amazing person."

"How old is he?" asked Adrian in a surprisingly calm voice.

"I don't know, I didn't ask, but he looks between thirty and thirty-three. Why?"

"Curiosity. I am glad you had someone to give you a hand. How is the house? Do you like it? How many people are living inside?"

"The building is ancient, but the flat is gorgeous. It's exactly in the city centre and I am the only person inside. I'll live alone."

"Really? You're not afraid or anything?"

"Why would I be afraid? I've lived on my own since I found my first job. Actually I left my parents' house when I went to a boarding school, when I was fourteen. Cohabitation is complicated, and I need peace. I was so lucky to find this place, really lucky."

"Can I come and see it?"

"Of course. Not tonight though. I need to buy myself a phone now. Oh... I forgot to tell you that I lost the other one a few weeks back. I am not sure when, but I never read any of your texts. That's why I sent you an email instead of a text today."

"That explains everything," he said with relief.

"What do you mean?"

"I invited you to a party last week."

"Why would you invite me to a party? Where was your girlfriend?"

"Working late."

"Right. Well, Adrian, don't do it again. I am not going to be your plus one anywhere. I feel quite offended. I am not a reserve."

"I didn't think you were. I just thought some fun would do you good."

"I don't like parties, Adrian. I cannot stand them. Such a waste of time! I am not twenty anymore."

He didn't reply and we kept walking in silence until we've got into town.

"Do you want me to come with you? I know about phones, I could help you choose a good one," he offered.

"Thank you, but no thank you. I am going to buy the cheapest on the market. It seems that people are forced to stay in touch with technology nowadays. Twenty years ago, we knew a lot more about one another without these instruments. We were closer and happier. Now, we're cut out of the world without a mobile. To be honest, I wouldn't care... If I had a choice, I wouldn't buy one. But I don't."

"Who forces you?"

I thought for a second and said, "Fine, come with me, if you want and have nothing better to do." I didn't want to tell him about my problems.

Adrian gave me loads of information, and in the end, I bought a big white smartphone and a SIM. He then wanted to check if it worked and made me call his number. All was well. I thanked him and went home. Around 11pm Adrian sent me a text to see if I was receiving texts. I replied with a "goodnight" and went to bed with my usual hot water bottle. I hugged the pillow and went to Heaven where Adrian was waiting for me.

The next day I went to work as I had to make up the hours. There were just a few people in the office. Someone bought pizzas on behalf of the company. I finally got to talk with some of my colleagues. They were nice people, miles away from me, though. They asked for how long I had lived in England... I had to think as I lost track of time. It was the end of September, and I came to England in June, four months ago. So many things have happened during that short period of time. It felt like ten years, not four months ago.

They made very nice remarks about my English and all the other accomplishments. I said that my English was terrible and there was nothing extraordinary about the things I've done since I'd come to the country, but I thanked them for being so kind.

At the end of the day, three of my colleagues, all men, came to my desk and invited me to go with them in town for a drink. I accepted, against my will. I knew I had to bond with them, I felt compelled as they were really nice people. Of course, I didn't tell them what I told Adrian about parties and the time wasted statement.

We fixed a time and a place and left work. They stopped at the bus station to wait for the bus, I walked. It took me fifty minutes to get home. I had a very quick shower, rubbed my skin with baby oil and put a light make-up on, some mascara and deep red lipstick. I had issues with what to wear as I didn't have much. I sat on the bed to think about it with only fifteen minutes to go to the rendezvous; luckily, the place was three minutes away. So awesome living in the city centre!

I decided to go through my things for the last time and while doing so, I remembered I had some fancy clothing in the last drawer. A blue and white sparkly top and an elastic blue-jeans miniskirt. A gift from my sister. Italian brand. It must have cost her a fortune! A perfect outfit for a Saturday night in town. I used my hands to comb my long wavy hair and I had a quick look in a mirror. I looked young and very hot. 'Omg, I feel like Narcissus. In love with my reflection.' I smiled and sent the disturbing thought away, 'I know I am beautiful, it's a fact. There's nothing wrong with being aware of my qualities.'

I was about to go out when I realised I had no shoes on and no bag either. 'Shoot, I cannot wear the rainbow stiletto shoes or the black ones. I do have a blue and white bag though.' I ran back into my room and spotted a pair of white sandals with platforms. Not my exact cup of tea, but they were a perfect match for my outfit. I am not sure where I got those sandals from. I thought I brought them from Romania. I opened the third drawer and found the bag. I put some money in it, the phone, a pack of tissues and ran outside. Only two minutes to go. I wasn't sure where the place was so I stopped and asked a random guy. He looked at my breasts while he gave me directions. I ignored that fact, thanked him and started to run again. I was out of breath and I thought, 'I am a woman, therefore I am allowed to be a few minutes late. "*The academic quarter*" it's called in my country.' But I still hurried, as I didn't like being late. I got there two minutes after the agreed time. It was acceptable. I didn't know the place and I felt really uncomfortable in my skin. I am not fond of going out anyway, but with that outfit and not accompanied, I was just terrified. Not in my element. I never dared to dress that way before. The skirt was too short and the top very tight and sparkly.

I still hadn't learned to like these dark places called pubs, but I was glad one couldn't see much that evening. I looked for my colleagues and my eyes met some green eyes I knew well, Adrian.

My heart made a jump. 'What the heck? Is he God or Satan?!' I didn't say hello, I didn't wave my hand to him. I was annoyed. "What a small city!' Two of my co-workers came towards where I was standing looking lost, and took me with them.

Every time I raised my eyes, Adrian's gaze was on me. Hypnotised. It gave me chills. I didn't check to see who was he with, I didn't care. I didn't raise my head to meet his eyes on purpose. It was like we were the only two humans inside that building.

At some point, he started to dance with some people, probably his company, all girls. He made them spin, hugged them randomly and often, brought them drinks and seemed rather happy. I didn't feel any degree of jealousy. I didn't want to be in their place. I didn't want Adrian to dance with me or bring me drinks. It looked sad to me, like he was trying to impress everyone. I hoped I was wrong.

The time passed and my colleagues wanted to go in a different place. I declined and excused myself. "Next time," I promised and left. While I was going out, a very tall and quite handsome guy said something looking into my eyes. I lowered my head and ran away. To the day, I still don't know what he said, and I wished I had stayed to speak to him.

At 11:45pm I was home, changed into my red and white pyjamas, prepared my usual hot water bottle and made myself comfortable in bed. The phone notified me I had some texts to read. I thought they were from the bank or some spam, but I still checked. Two texts from Adrian, sent an hour ago. The first one said, "You look breathtaking. Everybody has their eyes on you. Even the girls." The second one was a question, "Would you have a drink with me?" It didn't make me feel good. I hugged the pillow and the phone rang again, another text. Still Adrian, "You left! Why?" I didn't reply, switched my phone off, hugged my pillow ready to go to my piece of paradise when I heard a click coming from the right corner of my room, where the heater was placed. I raised my head and saw the light power on. I jumped, switched the lamp on, and went to see what was going on. I played with the controls and the heat started to diffuse into the room slowly. That made me really happy. 'So that's how it works! So many new things to learn.' I didn't like the cold. I fell asleep imagining myself smiling in Adrian's arms.

On Sunday morning I went to the same church in the city centre, just at a different hour. I still didn't understand a word, even though it was English. I prayed God to free my heart from Adrian.

Then I had a walk on the outskirts of the city. It was a beautiful sunny day, although it was a little chilly. I came back in the afternoon and cooked some pasta. First time in my new flat. It was a simple recipe, olive oil and cheese - pasta in *bianco*, one of my favourites - delicious.

I didn't have an internet connection set up yet. They had fixed me an appointment for the following Tuesday. I was not going to be home, so I had to ask a friend to be there and wait for the provider's employees in my place. I took a book and read for a few hours, then I prepared my outfit office for the next day. Black stiletto shoes and tights, and a red dress. It was warm in the room, still, I needed my hot water bottle in bed. I don't know why it made me feel so comfortable having it always close. I read until 10pm, when I switched off the light, hugged my pillow and called Adrian's name in my mind. He heard me and instantly put his arms around me. I was safe, warm, and loved.

The alarm went off at 6:30am. I got out of bed, changed and left five minutes later. I still didn't have breakfast. I couldn't.

The day passed by and at 5:45pm I left the building changed in my walking outfit. Adrian was not waiting for me. Then I remembered he didn't work there.

I got into town at 6:35 and some shops were opened. Because I didn't have any clothes and shoes, I decided I should buy some. I went inside the big one in front of my flat, but I couldn't stay in more than two minutes. I have been suffering from shop phobia (only clothing and shoes) for the last fourteen years. I couldn't even look at a shop window. Only the thought of going inside, made me instantly start sweating and feeling sick. I couldn't breathe. I'd only been into a clothes shop twice in twelve years. And just for a few minutes, forced by the need of a few shirts for work. I bought four in five minutes and left without trying them. I still have some of those shirts as they didn't fit me or were too large.

My sisters did the shopping for me and I was happy with that. I used to love shopping before that and spend a lot on clothes, but I have stopped all at once because someone stole my whole wardrobe while I was moving from a house to another. I was in Italy when it happened. Fresh from a visit to my country where I did a lot of shopping. Many of my clothes were tailor-made, therefore a perfect fit. It was a huge investment, and it all disappeared in half an hour. I didn't notice their absence until we got close to the city I was moving in, five hundred kilometres away. I called to ask if some of my boxes and bags were somewhere around the house I used to live in, but I had a negative response. For the first time in my life, I felt robbed, not only of clothes but of my hard work too. I saved a lot to be able to buy that stuff, worked overtime and made loads of sacrifices. Several items reminded me of some people very dear to me. And it hurt deep down in my soul. The only pieces of clothing I had left, were those on me, a pair of sports trousers and an old top. That day I said I wouldn't spend my money on clothing again, unless I was forced to.

I told my sisters the story and they started sending me some of their clothes. I appreciated it very much and went on like this for years. But they were too far away from England, and although it was not impossible to send packs overseas, it was very expensive. I had to take care of my outfits on my own now.

For years I thought it was just a mood, but that day I had to accept it was much more than that. However, there was an easy solution to that, online shopping. Except I didn't have an internet connection in the house yet. Tomorrow was to be the day for it. I decided to wait and went home.

I was tired, but not hungry. The house had a great atmosphere in, warm and cosy. I loved that place. I had a hot shower, and prepared my outfit for the next day. I really didn't have much, and wearing the same pair of shoes or dress twice in a week, was unacceptable for me. I had to reach to an agreement with my fashionable side of personality and promised I would soon remediate.

The white sandals were looking at me from the shelf so I decided I will match them to a shirt in the same colour and a pair of black trousers. Except for the only pair of trousers that still fit me were those I used to wear on the cleaning job. The colour was a little faded but I had to live with that.

I put the kettle on and filled my plastic bottle with hot water. 'I need another bottle soon. The cap is loose and not safe. Tomorrow.'

I wanted a red scarf to go with that black and white attire, so I opened the drawer and right at the bottom of it, wrapped in yellow gift paper, was the green velvet dress. I took it out, knelt on the floor, and let myself become shrouded by pain. Teardrops fell like a summer rain on the carpet. I hugged the dress and thought of my old man. Guilt, remorse, grief, regret... I was consumed with longing to hear a word from him again. 'I miss you so much, old man. I am sorry I wasn't there when you asked for me. Please forgive me for I can't forgive myself.'

I bent down and let my body lay on the floor, completely drained of energy. I held up the dress, hugging myself, and cried rivers of tears for God knows how long. I was freezing and decided to go to bed. I wrapped the green velvet dress back in the gift paper and hid it under some pillow cases.

Then I hugged my pillow and cringed from pain again. I really wanted Adrian to hold me tight. I missed his big green eyes. 'I hope he's fine, God, please, keep him safe.' I needed to sleep so I said out loud, 'I'll think about it tomorrow.' And I went to Heaven.

The next day, in the late afternoon, my friend sent me a text to inform me that the internet was up and running. I ran home and did some online shopping. I fell asleep thinking of Adrian again and promised that I would call him soon.

DEVIANT RELATIONSHIPS

One day, I finally managed to gather the courage to send Adrian a text, "I need a friend."

He replied right away, "I'll wait for you in the same place."

My heart started to race and I wanted to cry from happiness. 'Thank God he's alive.' We walked in silence, as usual.

"Can I come and see your place?" he asked.

"Now?" I questioned.

"Yes. If you don't have other plans for tonight. I could cook for you. It's my turn anyway."

"Your turn? Who decided that? I didn't even know you can cook!"

"I am quite a good cook actually. Maybe better than you."

I laughed and remained quiet for the rest of the way. When in town, Adrian stopped to buy a few things, cheese, bacon, a bottle of red wine. Inside, he didn't even look around the house, he just made himself at home. Prepared a pan for the pasta, cut the bacon, grated the cheese.

I offered to help, but he declined so I went to have a shower. When I got out of the bathroom, the house was inundated by a very inviting aroma. I felt hungry, but I went into my room, spread baby oil on my body, and applied a night cream on my face. I dressed up casually and opened the kitchen door. 'What a mess!' I thought but didn't say it out loud. There was cheese everywhere. The pasta was boiling and the water was coming out in waves from the pan. I went and lowered the power of the hob. "Let me help with something. I cannot sit looking at how hard you work. Tell me what to do."

"All right, but I will show you instead." He placed his body behind me, grabbed my hand and guided me to take a frying pan for the bacon. His touch sent an electric shock through my body and I blanched, but he didn't let go of my hand, quite the contrary, hold it tighter. I was feeling uncomfortable and I fought to escape from him. He then hugged me from behind and I stopped breathing. I wanted to shout and kick, but I was powerless. We stayed like that for a few seconds when a thick black smoke started to spread in the house from the frying pan. We both flinched, and I grabbed the pan, warning Adrian to move aside. I let some water running into it and throw into the sink. I then dropped a lot of washing liquid into the sink pipe and let the hot water running. Adrian opened the window and started to laugh, "What a disaster!"

"My god, we were lucky that the fire alarm didn't go off. I have no idea of how to make it stop!" I exclaimed half amused, half annoyed. 'I thought he said was a great cook. Hmm.'

Adrian called to order a pizza, then opened the wine bottle and poured two glasses. I got drunk on the very first sip and I started to giggle, "Phew! So close!"

"What?" asked Adrian.

"Burning this place down! My landlord trusted me. And by the way, you didn't even notice the look of this flat. You said that you wanted to see it, that's why you're here tonight. Isn't it?"

"It's a great place, Tara. I am very happy you like it. You deserve it."

That was Adrian, almost never talked, not from his initiative at least.

We sat on the couch and waited for the pizza man to ring the bell, and when he did, Adrian went downstairs to take the pizzas and pay him. I offered to share the cost, but he declined. "It was my turn to cook and I almost destroyed your house. These pizzas are on me."

We ate in silence and drank giggling. I had one glass only and the bottle was empty which meant Adrian had had the rest of it. Both of us were completely wasted. And I asked, "Don't you have a girlfriend to go to? Maybe she's waiting for you."

"No, she's not like that."

"What do you mean she is not like that? Doesn't she worry when you don't go to see her? Doesn't she call to see where you are and if you're okay or need anything?"

"No, we have an understanding. We are free to go and do wherever we want without letting the other one know. We don't ask for permission to do anything. We don't explain our time spent with others. I don't call her; she doesn't call me unless it's something very important that cannot wait. Like a house on fire, for example."

I looked at him in total disbelief. "I have never heard of a relationship like that. For me, it is more of a convenience agreement than love. I would die with worry if you weren't home at a certain hour! But, of course, you know better. Let me ask you something, is this an open sort of relationship?"

"No, there is something we've promised each other, never sleep with another person. Everything else is allowed, but that," explained Adrian in all seriousness.

"How does that work for you?" I asked.

"Pretty well I would say. We never argue, we barely see each other."

"Exactly Adrian, you don't argue because you never see each other!"

"There is nothing wrong with that, we are both very busy people."

"Busy with what? You don't have so many friends, you don't go out every evening. What are you so busy with?"

"I have loads of friends, Tara. You shouldn't make assumptions so easily. I go out very often, in fact, I don't even know when was the last evening I was home before 3am."

"And you're happy with this arrangement you two have?"

"Yes. It is perfect, I am free, she is free. My friends have very oppressive relationships. Their girlfriends don't allow them to go anywhere without them being informed. They have to ask for permission. I could never have a relationship like that. I don' want to explain anyone what I do and why. She is not my mother, and I am not her father."

"What is she sleeping with other people and doesn't tell you about it? I asked.

"She would never do that, ever! I trust her completely."

"What if I told you I saw her kissing another guy?"

"She wouldn't do that to me," he said convinced.

"Why not? We are only humans, Adrian. There are temptations everywhere. She could get drunk one night and... puff, it happens."

"Not to us. You don't know my girlfriend. We are different."

"Adrian, forgive me, but what you're telling me is utterly ridiculous. Where is the love in here? I fail to see it. I am shocked. I could never have a relationship like this. I think it's every women's nightmare."

"My girlfriend is okay with it or are you saying that my girlfriend is not a woman?!"

"But... Are you happy, Adrian?! You two, I mean. Is she happy, are you happy?"

"Happiness is overrated; we are well together," he replied.

My limit of consternation was reached and overcame a few times during the evening, so I had no way of getting more shocked that I was already. I gave up. "Whatever you say, Adrian."

"What about you, are you happy Tara?"

"Not yet. I will be one day though. I know it, and I am working hard to get there."

"What do you mean? Either you're happy, or you're not," he insisted.

"Happiness can be learned, Adrian, as it can be taught. Most of us ignore this undeniable truth. I won't succumb to surviving. Life goes on the way we want it to go on. If we are unhappy and think happiness is overrated, then we'll never work to reach it. On the other hand, if we are unhappy, but we know that we can change that, then we can take the decision to work to get there. But it's too demanding. That's why you don't hear many people saying they are happy. We don't even know what happiness is!"

"Do you know what that is... happiness I mean?" he asked me in a low voice.

"Happiness is when you feel the arms of the loved one around you. When you kiss and make love. Happiness is when you walk under the rain and feel grateful for it. Happiness is when you share a smile to a stranger, and they imitate you. Happiness is the light, the dark, the sun, the sea, the food we eat. Happiness is giving and receiving. There is happiness everywhere and in every moment. We just don't realise it."

"If happiness is all that, how come you don't feel happy yet?"

"That's a good question, Adrian, very good question. And I could give you loads of reasons, but that will mean contradicting everything I just said. Allow me to abstain from doing that for now, but I will come back to you on this. All right?"

We remained silent for several minutes. It didn't feel awkward. Adrian was always somewhere else, and I was thinking at his question.

"Actually I withdraw what I said before, about not being happy. Truth is I am happy every day. Maybe not the whole day, but the grand part of it. It's the truth. Now Adrian, please go home, wherever that might be. I am tired and have work tomorrow."

"Are you angry with me?" he asked.

"Why would I be? No, I am not. Just tired," I replied lying, of course.

"Tara, why don't you reply to my text messages?"

"Because I have nothing to say. You are in a relationship and I am twelve years older than you. A lifetime."

"Are we friends at least?"

"Not as long as I have feelings for you. Friendship is something else for me."

He hugged me and left leaving the door unlocked. I didn't care and went to bed with a new hot water plastic bottle, hugged my pillow and shed countless tears until I fell asleep. I would have loved it if he had stayed...

***

Time went by. Adrian waited for me from time to time in the same place, and we walked in silence and separated in town. Some days I took the bus to not to be tempted to go and look for him in the park.

Every time I went out, he was in the same place as me. And we never talked about it beforehand. It was like he knew where I was going to be and got there first just to look at me when I got inside. Our hearts sensed each other's from miles away. His gaze always met mine in any place I went. A classic Bollywood movie.

One Friday night I was standing in line to order a drink when he came and offered me a glass of whisky. I didn't know he was there too and I was surprised, unsure why. As I said, he was everywhere I was. "I just got in and saw you in here so I thought I should come and say hi," he said.

"Hi and thank you for the drink," I replied.

"Who are you here with?"

"Those the people over there," I turned around and pointed into the entrance direction.

"All men," he said, smiling with sadness, I thought.

"No, there are loads of girls too," I replied.

"Would you let me take you home when this night is over?" he asked.

"I live ten minutes away. It's not necessary."

"I miss you, Tara, please let me take you home."

I looked directly into his soul and saw he was sincere. I loved him so much! So easy.

"All right. I'll send you a text later on," I agreed.

I went to join my friends and we've laughed and joked for hours. Adrian was in the middle of the dancing floor, spinning all the girls in his company, and not only. He was completely drunk as every single time I saw him out. I wished I felt jealousy or anger or anything of that sort, but all I could feel was sadness.

I understood very soon that he had a drinking problem and loved to flirt with every single woman in the room, but I knew why he was behaving like that, unhappiness, inadequacy, loneliness. I wished so much to fill the emptiness he felt inside. I wished to hug him tight and say that everything will be all right, that he was safe with me. But he was not mine, nor he will ever be, and I didn't even want that.

I knew he was not the one from the very first moment our eyes met. But I loved him anyway, and I would have done anything to see him smile.

He was the water, I was the fire.
He was the moon, I was the sun.
He was the dark, I was the light.
He was the rain, and I was the snow.

None of these duos can happen at the same time.

He was a lost cause, and I was a fighter.

***

That night, I left without saying a word. He sent me a text asking me where I was. I deleted it right away and switched the phone off. He never asked me why was I behaving that way. That was him. When he was hurt, he wouldn't say anything. He wouldn't say anything when he was happy, or afraid, or confused either. He kept everything inside, and as far as I am concerned, he hid that from his mind, body, and soul too. He didn't want to think about it, trying to understand and fix or change it... No. He was happy with being unhappy.

***

Another evening, I went to a birthday party. Adrian arrived two hours later with some friends. I stopped feeling surprised by the fact that he always found me. I was tipsy and I went to ask him how the hell he managed to be in the same place as me every time I was out. "This city has loads of places, yet, we manage to see each other in all of them. Very creepy, don't you think?"

"I have a gift to sense your presence wherever you might be," he replied winking at me.

That evening he didn't drink much and didn't dance with all the girls in his company, he just stared at me.

I was about to leave when he came to me and said he'd take me home. Except, another colleague of mine offered to do the same, but he was drunk and I tried to persuade him to let it be and allow Adrian to do it instead. My colleague was adamant, so I decided that we should all go out and walk together to my place. On our way home, there was a burger place and my drunk colleague said he was hungry and wanted to get inside.

Horrified I said, "Never!" But I saw my chance and insisted for him to go alone. He accepted and we left. When we got in front of my building, I put my arms around Adrian's neck for second, kissed him on a cheek, open the door and said, "Goodnight. Thank you for taking me home." I didn't wait for a reply, I closed the door and ran upstairs.

That night I hugged my pillow and fell asleep crying again. I wanted Adrian immensely. But that was impossible.

It is known for people to want what they cannot have... and when you are in love, you always hope... And don't know what. Torture.

***

Adrian kept sending me text messages at random hours. All very concise. I never liked people who write monosyllabic texts. We sometimes agreed to meet in the park. He waited for me there many times, but we've never talked about our real feelings. He almost never talked. Period. He used to at first, but not anymore. I couldn't stand that. I never knew what he was thinking about, what he wanted, if he was ill or happy. Nothing. A closed book.

At work, there was a guy I felt attracted to. He was single but very shy. I caught him looking at me several times. He always blushed and looked away. I thought he was sweet. I liked him a lot, and if my heart could have been free, I am sure we might have shared something big. But my stupid heart didn't allow me to act. I was furious.

One day Adrian informed me that he went to visit his mother. "I told my mother about you. I needed to tell someone."

"What do you mean you told your mother about me?! What did you tell her?"

"I told her that I have feelings for you," he said.

"Now, why would you do that? I bet she's just a few years older than me."

"Don't be silly! It wouldn't matter anyway. Tara, I am thinking of breaking up with my girlfriend. I cannot lie anymore. I am dying inside. She doesn't deserve that."

"*SHE* doesn't deserve that? What about *me*, Adrian? Do I deserve this mind playing game of yours?" I shouted, "Don't you dare leaving her! Do you think that is what I want? Well, it is not, you fool!" I couldn't hold back my tears so I ran away.

He followed me and grabbed my wrist. "Tara, please, I am going insane."

My heart literally stopped pumping blood when I heard that confession. I looked into his turbid eyes and couldn't bear the pain I was feeling. "I am so sorry, Adrian. Forgive me for being so selfish. This shouldn't hurt. I should have never said I had a crush on you... I feel so guilty now. It was such a mistake. Please, do not break up with your girlfriend. We cannot be together anyway. It is impossible, you know that well," I said defeated.

"Why would it be impossible, Tara? Are you married or tied up to someone else?"

"You know I am not... Society, Adrian. It will crucify us... only you, actually, because I don't care what people say. This is not my country, people don't know me, they can't judge me. But you..."

"Do you think I care about it?! I don't give a damn, Tara. All I care is being with you. I crave for your touch..."

"Oh, God have mercy!" I cried out in pain. "Adrian, don't split up, I beg you. I won't be able to look into your eyes again. The sense of guilt will haunt me and you forever. It will knock us down. It's too powerful. You'll lose us both."

"Tara... I need to hold you in my arms as a free man. I cannot go on like this."

"We can't have a relationship, Adrian. Do you understand that?"

"No, I don't," he said with pain.

THE PARTY

My job was going well. I was doing fine, still very much in love with Adrian. One day I realised I missed cooking a lot so I decided to throw up a party. I invited a few colleagues, some of my friends, my old roommates, and Adrian. I didn't have the heart to invite the shy guy. He and Adrian inside the same room were not a good idea. Once again I was upset with my heart.

I cooked for five hours on Friday evening and for another one on Saturday. I was very pleased with the results. After cooking, I prepared loads of glasses, cutlery, and dishes. Not the classic disposable party tableware, I couldn't stand that.

Around 5:50pm, I went to have a shower and prepare for my first party as a host. The plan was to look fantastic, of course. I spread a generous amount of baby oil on every inch of my skin and a layer of deodorant under my armpits. Then I put a sparkly shadow around my eyes, black mascara, and deep red lipstick. A black and gold bodycon dress, black underwear and black high heeled stiletto formed my attire for the evening. I was ready at 6:28, just on time. I looked in the mirror and thought I was ravishing. One minute later, my guests started to show up. All of them were incredibly impressed first with my amazing looks, then with the flat and with my cooking skills. Adrian came around 7. We said hello and I presented him to the others. I then turned my attention over to every new arrival.

He didn't bond with my mates much. He just sat in a corner holding his gaze onto me and drinking a lot all alone.

Lola, my old roommate, came to ask about him. She fell for him right away. "He's so mysterious." I told her that he wasn't single. She went to talk to him anyway. He then started to laugh, joke, and dance with her. I found it inappropriate, but it was not my business. I thought I was going to be jealous, but I was sad instead. He didn't look happy in my eyes.

Three hours later we were all dancing and having fun. Around 2am some of my guests left, I didn't insist they stayed longer. I was tired and needed to sleep. Around 3am, the ones who remained were still dancing and eating. I thought I'd crash on the floor and I swayed on my feet. One of my colleagues, quite a handsome guy, grabbed me by the waist and held me tight to his body. "Are you all right, gorgeous? Maybe a little drunk?"

"I am fine, just tired and I didn't have much to eat," I replied.

"Come and sit for a while. Your feet must hurt a lot on these high heels. And how can you not eat when this food is so incredibly delicious? You need to eat, Tara. Put some weight on."

"Do you think I am too skinny?" I asked.

"A little bit. The entire office thinks the same," my colleague confessed.

"What are you talking about? Do people speak about me in the office?" I shouted surprised.

"Of course. You brought colour into our building. Before your arrival, the office was dull and the girls were poorly dressed, but since you came, everything's changed for the better. Everybody speaks about everybody anyway," he confessed with ease.

"Get out of here! I haven't done this. Have I?"

"You have, Tara. Don't be so modest. Your high heels drive all the men crazy. And some of the girls too." And he winked at me.

"Are you saying that there are lesbians in the office? That's great news!" I exclaimed.

"You're weird, Tara, but very beautiful. How come you're still single?" he asked me without warning.

"Who would want someone like me?" I joked.

"Who wouldn't want someone like you, Tara? You're gorgeous, elegant, you have great taste, amazing cooking skills. And on top of that you are very smart. Do you want me to continue because I could go on forever? Tell me, what are you hiding? How many cadavers are in your closet?" He was hitting on me, it was clear and I was, of course, extremely flattered. I had a weakness for compliments, as many other women do. And this guy knew exactly what and how to say it. He was flirting with me and I was feeling great.

I went to change the music and met Adrian's eyes. There was thunder in them and I shivered, but ignored the feeling and went to the dance floor. Most of my guests were gone. The boy with the compliments was trying to get me drunk. I laughed and asked him to give up as it was not going to happen.

At 4am there were only three people left in the house, four with me. My old housemate, Lola, was still hitting on Adrian, and I looked at them. In that precise instant, Adrian placed one of his arms on her waist. She froze, looked into his eyes and tried to kiss him. He turned his head away and looked at me. I got his game, and I didn't like it. He was trying to make me jealous by messing with my ex-housemate. I cared about that girl and she cared about me... that's what she wanted to think at least.

"Lola?" I called her name. "Would you please help me with something?"

She hesitated for a second but walked towards me without a word. She was hurt and couldn't speak. I took her into my room, tears were falling on her cheeks. "He's playing with me."

"Yes, Lola, he is. I told you to let him be. He is not free," I said with sadness. I wasn't sure that statement was for Lola.

"But he never said anything about a girlfriend and I thought you were trying to send me away so you can have him all for yourself. But then I saw you not paying any attention to him, and I stepped in. I really like him, Tara. Tell me he's not your secret boyfriend. Oh my god!" she shouted. "He's the one who sent you those flowers, isn't he? Just remembered that."

"No, Lola. The flowers were from someone else. He's a friend, he helped me a lot. But, please, stay away from him. I don't want to see you hurt," I insisted.

In that moment my thoughts went to Drefan. He didn't call to make me sign the papers. 'Jesus! He doesn't have my new number and he doesn't know I moved! I ought to call him tomorrow. He must think I lied to him. Stupid Tara! Glad I wrote his number down though.'

"Don't mind me, Tara, I am a big girl. I can take it. He's not the only one who treated me this way. But I hoped he was not like all the others. Well, I was wrong again."

I hugged her and went inside the living room. Someone was changing the music. My compliments guy. A very slow song inundated the room and he invited me to dance. I took a glass, poured some whisky and drunk it all in one go. He looked at me smiling. I am sure his hopes got higher. I decided to live in that moment, body, and soul. I put my arms around his neck and he put his on my waist. My golden black dress was very thin, I could feel his body pulsing, and his heart racing. I felt no emotion and although I was very tipsy, I knew what I was doing. We moved slowly and he tried to kiss my neck, I pushed him away. He said he was sorry and promised not to try that again. "You are so hot," he said.

I don't know why that compliment didn't make me feel good; I kept him at a distance and blamed myself for that action. He was a man and had a lot to drink, of course he wanted me. Any other woman in my place could have been the target. And that moment I knew that I wanted Adrian to be in his place. I blushed and started to feel uncomfortable. It was a very long song and I started praying for it to stop. It went on for at least two more minutes, then it was over. The moment I was waiting for had finally come and I hurried up to switch the audio system off. "I am sorry, but I am exhausted. I need to go to sleep." I turned around to say goodnight, or good morning, to Adrian and Lola, but they were gone. I must have looked confused because my compliments guy explained, "They left a few minutes ago. When you got upset with me. That guy was furious. He didn't take his eyes off you for a second. How pathetic. You are clearly not interested in him and I thought he'd jump down my throat when I asked you to dance. Who is he, by the way?"

"He's not pathetic at all. He looks out for me and I care for him. Now please go. I shall see you on Monday."

"You're not upset with me, are you? Have I blown all my chances with you this night?"

"You are years younger than me, please, you cannot possibly hope I'd want to have anything to do with you. What, do you think it's difficult for me to find someone to sleep with?" I said with excessive fury.

"Tara, it's not like that at all. You're one of the most beautiful women I've ever seen. I am sure you could sleep with anyone in the town. I am not just trying to get you into bed, I like you a lot and I am single, so are you."

"Except I don't feel any attraction towards you. I am sorry. You need to go now," I said.

"Promise me we'll talk about this again and I'll leave."

I couldn't wait anymore, so I promised, gave him a hug and he left. I ran into my room, took my mobile and sent a text to Adrian, "Why did you leave without saying goodbye? I hoped to have a hug from you."

He replied instantly, "You were into that guy. I thought I should leave you two alone. You seemed like you were enjoying yourselves a lot."

"Well, you're wrong. I was not having any fun," I replied.

"You were hugging him," he said.

"I was hugging you," I confessed.

Five seconds' pause then he sent another text, "Are you in bed yet?"

"No. I am about to have a shower."

"I want to give you that hug then."

It was my turn to pause. My heart was about to explode. I was tired, had a glass of whisky and my body craved his arms for weeks. I took a deep breath and replied, "Then come."

Two minutes later, he sent me another text, "I am outside."

'The hell with the shower.' The button didn't open the entrance door so I ran downstairs without shoes. He was standing there with a long face. It was still dark outside and the streets were deserted. I almost bent over to hug him from the corridor, but I kept the door wide open instead. It was an invitation. He said nothing and started to climb the stairs with uncertainty. He was clearly drunk. We went inside my room. I was shaking so he made me lay on the bed and hugged me tightly. I shook even harder and murmured I was freezing. He sat on the left border of the bed, took his shoes off and lay next to me. I was terrified, didn't know what to do. 'Maybe I should run', but I looked into his eyes and I loved what I saw. There was no age disparity, no divergent opinions, no society rules. We were alone in the universe. No fears, no expectation, no tomorrow. It was just that moment. *Carpe Diem.*

He touched me in countless different ways. "Your skin is the softest I have ever felt under my palms."

I couldn't think, I couldn't breathe, just feel. Myriads of conflicting emotions. I thought my heart would burst into thousands of tiny pieces. He moved his hands up and down on my back with infinite tenderness. I never felt that way, not even in my dreams. I closed my eyes and abandoned my entire being to those loving strokes. I almost begged for mercy when he's started kissing every inch of my skin. "Why are you so damn sexy, Tara?" he murmured again. "It's impossible to resist you."

I whispered in his ear, "Adrian, do you know I am crazy about you?"

"And I am crazy about you," he whispered into mine. I groaned infinite times under his palms. He didn't stop caressing my body for hours. "Your smell is like ambrosia."

I so much craved to hear these words, and now they were real. 'Dreams do come true.' None of us was tired and I didn't ask if he needed to go home. The Paradise I used to go every night was here and didn't want to leave. I couldn't. I fell asleep into his arms. I felt his lips on my hair several times, but he didn't move a muscle to avoid waking me up.

At 11am my alarm went off. I flinched, he held me tighter. I opened my eyes and looked into his. He was in adoration so I raised my chin to reach his lips. He turned his head away and the sky crashed over my head. 'He did the same with Lola. I saw him.' My heart stopped beating, I felt my blood running out from my body. I didn't want to jump to reckless conclusions so I asked, "Why?"

"I have a girlfriend. I cannot betray her trust," he said with infinite sadness. I pushed him away. "Are you insane? What game are you playing, Adrian? You kissed every inch of my body for hours. What difference would that make? Why would a kiss on the lips be considerate a betrayal and not the millions on my other parts of the body?"

"It's not the same. You don't understand."

I couldn't believe what was going on. And I fell from the heights of heavens, into the most profound chasm, "*I* don't understand? Are you suffering from some kind of mental disease? Or you are simply messing with me?" I asked in disbelief.

"Tara, please. Don't go there."

"There where, Adrian? Asking for explanations? Well, I need to know it from you, I cannot make assumptions. It wouldn't be fair. What you say make no sense whatsoever! Are you comparing me to a whore perhaps? Whores are never kissed on the lips. Only them."

"Of course not," he replied right away.

"Then kiss me on the lips." I pretended.

He said and did nothing. My heart started bleeding. "Go home, Adrian. I have things to do. And don't call me again. Ever again. I don't want to see you, read your texts, or hear your name in my life again."

He got out of bed, put his shoes on and left. I didn't say goodbye, I didn't even look. I was in agony, so I hugged myself and cried in despair for several hours. I tried to find a reason that made sense and I got it, kissing her lips was the only thing going on between them. It felt like a betrayal to him. I despised my heart for being so stupid. 'Why is this happening, God? Why do I have to go through this? There is a purpose, right? Please, have mercy. I haven't yet recovered from my old man loss. Do you think I am strong enough to get out of this? What if I refuse to fight? What if I give up? You are challenging my sanity too often. What have I done so terrible in my life to be punished this way?' God didn't answer and I had to huddle up once more. 'Enough with this nonsense! What did you expect? He's a child in a relationship. You brought this on yourself.'

I looked into a mirror and what I saw in my eyes scared me to death. My soul was gone. I was empty inside. What a horrible discovery. But I didn't feel pain anymore so I was grateful.

I went to clean the living room. It took me four hours to wash the dishes, take the trash out, hoover and put everything in place. I then remembered I had to call Drefan, but I didn't feel like it so I sent him a text message instead, "Hello. It's Tara. I am so terribly sorry I didn't inform you before about the fact I lost my phone. If you have the papers ready, please let's arrange a meeting so I could sign and end this once and for all."

He replied two minutes later, "Tara, thank God! I thought something terrible happened to you. I am so relieved. Thank you for letting me know. I do have the papers. Is next Saturday a good day for you?"

"No, I work next Saturday, but I am free the following one."

"Great. It's a date. Where should we meet?"

"City centre. Cathedral Green. 11am?"

"Perfect. I'll speak with my lawyer. He works half day on Saturdays. Thank you, Tara. You're an amazing person."

I put the phone down and went to have a shower. I was tired and wanted to read, so I took *"Mansfield Park"* in my hands and went to bed. I read a few pages and my eyes closed. I dreamt about falling into that abyss again and I flinched several times. I heard myself grumbling and twisting in bed. I tried to open my eyes, but I couldn't. I knew I was having a bad dream, but I was not strong enough to get out of it. My heart was racing and I tried to shout... to give my body a kick. It worked. I jumped out of bed, all sweaty and heavily breathing. 'You're so pathetic, Tara. Suffering for a boy who just played with you. You should be ashamed of yourself. You make me sick.'

I washed my face with cold water. The book was completely squashed and felt guilty for that. 'Jane Austen spent time writing that book so I could enjoy it, and now it's all creased. So inconsiderate of me.'

I prepared my outfit for the next day. Some new beautiful dresses arrived the day before. The postman left them at the restaurant next door. There was a card on the corridor so I went to take the pack. It was big and heavy. I was glad I didn't have to go to the post office and carry that box for more than a mile. I'd chosen a heavy bodycon dress the colour of a clear sky in winter, black tights and a pair of navy stiletto shoes. I put them all in my backpack and went to bed. I hugged my pillow, but I couldn't sleep. My piece of Heaven was ripped apart. I had no other place to go. I forced myself to fall into Morpheus' arms, but it didn't work. After two hours of twisting, writhing and rolling from one side to another, I decided to get out of bed and walk around the living room where it was cold. I took my pyjamas off and spent half an hour reorganising the kitchen drawers. Somebody taught me this trick when I was a child, "When you cannot sleep, take your clothes off, and let your body freeze. Once you are completely frozen, go back to bed, cover yourself well and once your body starts warming up you'll fall asleep in no time. It's science," they told me. I tried it before, but it never worked. I thought I didn't do it right those times. The experiment was not successful this time either. So I thought of Scarlett, 'What would she do?' "I'll think of it tomorrow." No luck with that either, so I took a book and read until my alarm went off. I was exhausted, but I got up, put my walking outfit on, and left to work.

DREAMS DO COME TRUE

The compliment guy didn't come to say hello and I couldn't care less. The day was over, I got changed and left the building. Adrian sent me a text asking to meet in the same place because he had important news to give me. I ignored the message completely. At 6pm he sent another saying he was there waiting for me. So I went and planned to slap him in the face and leave. 'Unfaithful, selfish, disrespectful child.' I kept repeating in my head with anger. When I got there, I walked by him without stopping. He followed me without a word. I wanted to shout, but I just thought of it and kept walking faster and faster to calm me down. When there was no one on the street, he's asked me to stop for a second because he had something to say. I pretended I didn't hear. He asked me again, but I coldly replied, "I don't want to hear anything from you. I thought I told you to never search for me again. Are you deaf or just inconsiderate?"

"Tara, it's important."

"I don't care. Leave me alone," I shouted. 'Why am I here if I didn't want to speak to him? Tara, you're pathetic.'

He grabbed my hand and held me back. I tried to fight, but he was stronger. I stopped and looked away.

"Look at me, Tara," he begged.

I ignored him. He waited for a few seconds and when he understood that I would not look at him for any reason in the world, he bluntly said, "I broke up with my girlfriend. I told her everything. It's over."

I withdrew my hand from his with all the strengths I had in my body and ran away. My face was covered in tears. He came after me, forced me to stop again. There was a high brick wall behind me. I took three wobbling steps back and leant against it. My legs refused to support my weight. He put his hands on my waist to sustain me. "Look at me Tara, please."

I raised my head with my eyes closed tight. I couldn't look. I wiped some tears off with a hand and then it happened. His lips barely touched mine. "I broke up to be free to do this," he whispered and kissed my lips again, and again, and again.

My entire body was electrified and I groaned in astonishment. I pushed him away. He made a step back without fighting and looked at me with very sad eyes.

"This is terrible!" I said.

"I have feelings for another woman, I couldn't lie. I am not like that," he murmured.

"You broke up because of me! I never really wanted you to do this. I feel dreadful. You shouldn't have done it!"

Thousands of contradictory thoughts were clashing in my head, 'If you didn't want him to break up, why did you allow him to kiss you? Do you even hear yourself? What do you want, Tara? Do you want to feel his arms around you whenever you feel like it then watch him go to his official girlfriend? Do you want to have an affair with a man who's not even married? Do you want to be the other one? The reserve? Man up, Tara! Be honest with yourself! There was no other way. He loves you and you know it. That's why he left her. You should be happy.' Except I wasn't. Too much conflict inside me. I didn't want an open relationship with him, but I did want him to be mine only. What a mess!

"I had to tell her as she is important to me. She's my best friend."

"Adrian, do you realise that there can't be anything between us? There is too much age difference. We cannot be together. Besides, this is just a caprice. Next year we will have forgotten we felt this way. We'll laugh and kiss somebody else with ease.

"How do you know?" he asked and made a step closer to me. I closed my eyes again. His hands covered the sides of my face. "How do you know?"

Thousands of big warm tears were falling from my blue eyes, he wiped them off, moved a piece of my hair from my face and forced me to open my eyes. I moved my head side to side, so he kissed one eyelid, then the other one, and I still wouldn't open them so he sealed my mouth with a salty kiss. His tongue caressed my upper lip and I delicately bit his lower lip with my teeth. He groaned in pleasure and surprise. I raised my arms and hugged his neck, abandoning my soul and body to the most perfect feeling a human being can ever feel.

We explored our mouths with endless passion and I cried from happiness. We were utterly compatible in the art of kissing. Our mouths were in perfect harmony. There was no struggle, no resilience, no incertitude, no mistakes. When he brushed my upper lip, I bit on his lower one, and vice-versa. When he kissed my neck, I groaned and ran my fingers through his hair in exaltation. It was almost dark and the street was deserted. The backpack was pressing my back and it hurt a lot so I moved and he understood. "Let's go home," said Adrian.

We've walked in silence like two strangers. Home was my place. Inside the house, he took my bag off my shoulders and placed it on the floor. The he unzipped my red raincoat and I helped him taking his hoodie off. Then he slowly pushed me on the bed. I moaned. His green eyes were inundated by love and desire. I shivered and felt like fainting from pleasure. He sealed my lips with an endless tender kiss again. Our hearts were racing in unison, I was groaning, he was moaning, my head was spinning and I begged him to stop. "Adrian, you're killing me, please stop. I cannot breathe."

He looked into the depths of my eyes and his thumb lightly brushed my lower lip. My body arched I put my hands into his hair and gave him the most carnal kiss from my entire existence. His body pulsed thousands of times and we were completely drunk with love.

"You are driving me crazy," I whispered.

Adrian was a man of a few words, so he took my left hand, turned it over, and placed his soft lips onto my palm. Until that moment, I thought there was no better place than my imaginary Heaven, but the real one was much better. Hours later, we fell asleep in each other arms. Shortly after midnight, he went to the bathroom and when he came back, he looked like he was in a different dimension.

"Adrian, what happened?" I asked, alerted.

He was uncontrollably trembling, without a word he laid on the bed and placed his body in a foetal position. I got so scared that I couldn't breathe. "What's wrong? Please talk to me. Are you in pain?" I begged in tears. Completely terrified, with no idea of what was going on, I surrounded him with my body, trying to transmit some of my body heat into his. I desperately whispered hundreds of loving words. He seemed not to hear or feel anything. His body was there, but his mind was infinite miles away.

"I am calling an ambulance right away. Please, hold tight," I said and jumped off the bed to look for the phone.

He got up, took the phone out of my trembling hands without a word, gathered his things and went out of the room. In shock, I followed and begged him to stay and tell me what was going on.

I grabbed on him like a child on his mother's skirts. I hugged him tight, looked into his empty eyes, and said, "I love you, Adrian."

"I feel the same," he absently murmured.

"Then tell me what's wrong with you? I deserve to know. Right?"

"I am lost, Tara. Completely lost and I don't know what to do," he confessed.

"Adrian... Love is the most wonderful feeling in the whole universe. How can you feel lost?"

He said absolutely nothing, just turned on his feet and left. The door slammed behind him.

I slid on the floor in disbelief and sobbed for hours in despair. At 3am my body was completely frozen, but I didn't want to go to bed... not where he kissed me with infinite tenderness. I took a spare duvet from the other room, went into the living room and slept on the couch. I had nightmares in sequence. He was on top of me, exploring my mouth with avidity, and a second later he was leaving me on the floor without a word. I woke up more tired than I was a few hours ago. For a second I hoped it was just a bad dream, but I slept on the couch... 'Why would I do that if...?' A sharp pain crossed my heart and I instantly covered it with my hands. I stopped breathing, and when I tried to inhale, another sharp stab knocked me down completely. I clenched my teeth and eyes while my hands were pressing on my heart. 'Stop, God, I beg you, make it stop. It's unbearable.' I cried and prayed in my mind. For several minutes I tried to breathe as slowly as possible, enough to oxygenate my brain and make my heart pulsing blood into my veins. I was completely covered in cold sweat. 'I hope I didn't catch a cold... lying on the floor, Tara? And for what? You're thirty-eight years old, for crying out loud! Grow up already, act like an adult, woman! He's just a capricious child; he cannot give you what you need. He doesn't even know what love feels like. Stand up and shake it all off you. You'll find someone to love you the way you deserve. Keep believing. It's a new day, and a new dawn, rise and shine. You can do it!'

And the pain was gone. I jumped off the couch, dressed up in a few seconds, grabbed my backpack and left. I ran for a few minutes, but I never liked running. I checked the time; there was enough left. I thought of my capacity of recovering from such a shock. It wasn't normal. I decided that I was insane, but I liked the fact I felt no pain. I didn't worry. I got into work, put my new gorgeous dress on, tied my hair up, coloured my eyelashes in black and my lips in deep red and went into the office smiling.

Everyone's got a breaking point, I guess that was mine.

I had friends in the office so they came to ask if I was in love.

"And why would you think that?" I asked with wonder.

"You are radiating happiness," they all said.

"Do I?" I replied surprised. "How curious. In all honesty, I'm telling you that I am heartbroken."

"Liar!" They called me. I didn't argue, I preferred them to think I was happy.

My compliment colleague looked at me with sadness, and later on sent me an email, "My chances are all buried. Right?" I didn't reply, it was unprofessional to use the work email for personal issues. He didn't pressure me. There was never a point insisting with me. I am a NO or YES woman.

I didn't see Adrian that week. I sent him a text message to ask if he was fine, he didn't reply. I let it go and felt sorry for him. I knew he was suffering, but I was suffering too. "Charity begins at home."

***

A year later he confessed to me that he talked to a few people about me in that period. I said nothing to anyone. I kept it all for myself, I knew what I wanted, I knew what I needed, I knew he wouldn't give it to me. Of course, I was so many years older, presumably wiser.

He said he didn't care about what people were saying, but he asked them what to do. Inconsistency. He couldn't take a decision by himself, needed other people for that. A child who didn't know that love has all the answers. You just need to listen.

DREFAN'S REVELATION

At 11am on Saturday, I went to meet Drefan. It was chilly outside, so I was wearing a red midi coat, black jeans, stiletto open front boots, and a black blouse. As for make-up, I had my usual black mascara on, and a lipstick in the colour of my coat. I didn't have time to put my hair in a bun, as I planned to, so the waves were resting on my shoulders.

Drefan was wearing a grey coat, blue jeans, and a monochromatic blue scarf. He looked casual smart. I always loved a man who knows how to dress. He was holding a newspaper, but he wasn't reading when I got there. When he spotted me, he smiled and came towards me with open arms. It was like we were very good old friends. I liked that feeling.

"Tara, you look gorgeous! Red suits you to perfection! I am so glad to see you." He hugged me tightly, and I copied him.

"You're not too bad yourself. I love men who can wear a coat with ease."

He took a step back saying, "Let me have a closer look at you. You've gained a little colour, and maybe some weight? Have you started eating like normal people?"

"Yes, I have. Thank you for your nice words. How have you been?" I asked.

"I've been... busy, Tara, very busy. What about you? How is the job going?"

"All is well, Drefan. Now tell me, do you have the papers?"

"About that... Tara. I don't feel comfortable with taking the house away from you. My father wanted you to have it. You were a daughter to him and it is clear that you both cared one for another. I have no right to do this."

"Well, it is not compulsory, you know? Don't take it if you don't want it. Simple as that."

"Not really. I have a family," he said with sadness.

"How many children do you have?" I asked out of curiosity.

"None," he replied in a very low voice.

"Right... So it's only you and your wife in this family. Do you have jobs?"

"Yes. We are fine, financially speaking."

"Then what do you need this place for?"

He lowered his head to avoid looking at me, "It is not me, but my wife who wants it. She threatened to ask for a divorce if I don't do it."

"That's bad. Let's get this over with then. What are you waiting for? Where are the papers?"

"Wait, Tara. The papers are with my lawyer. His cabinet is ten minutes away. I just need to give him a call and he'll be ready to see us. There is something I need to tell you though."

"What's that?" I asked a little annoyed.

He looked right, then left, behind and in front of him. Clearly checking if there were people who knew him nearby. "I am thinking of getting a divorce myself. And not because of this, but because we haven't been happy in years. I am not happy. Our marriage is dull."

"I am sorry to hear that. Have you tried couple therapy?

"She doesn't want to hear about that. There is nothing wrong in our marriage she says."

"Have you told her how you feel?" I insisted.

"Not yet," he replied.

"When then? You need to speak to her. There are solutions, Drefan. Dialogue is always the way," I said more and more irritated.

"I am sorry to trouble you with my personal issues. You don't know much about me, and I already told you everything about my marriage. How pathetic. I don't have anyone else to speak with. I don't trust many people."

"But you trust me? Why?" I asked confused.

"I can't explain," he confessed.

"Do you know I am Romanian? Romanians are famous for being deceitful thieves. Your media wrote that black on white so many times. You even made documentaries who travelled the world."

"I don't believe what the media says."

"Yet, you are holding a newspaper in your hands."

"This?" he asked raising it up. "I bought it from a homeless man right down the corner."

There were many homeless people in town selling magazines and newspapers to make some many. Buying from them was a charitable gesture.

I had nothing else to say, so I stayed quiet. I thought this man was strong; I was mistaken, he was a coward. I didn't like where my mind was going, so I shut it off. 'I've never been married, I don't know how that feels. I don't know what I would do if I were in his shoes. I have no right to judge him.'

"I am really sorry you are going through such a bad time. Is there anything I can do for you?" I asked with guilt.

"Have lunch with me, perhaps? My wife is away for the weekend with her girlfriends."

I giggled, "I never understood why would you call a woman's friends girlfriends and not doing the same for the men friends."

"What? Sorry, I didn't get that. What do you mean?" he asked confused.

"Never mind, my English is a work in progress. Let's go and have lunch, shall we?"

"Is there any place you fancy?" he tried to find out.

"Not at all, I don't have a very active social life and I am not fond of restaurants anyway."

"Ha. And I thought you were a party girl," he exclaimed.

I didn't reply and he decided we should go to a very small and fancy restaurant a few metres away. It didn't make much difference to me, so I accepted and started walking.

My stiletto boots made quite a sound on the pavement and he looked at my feet.

"God, you sure have a great eye for detail. Your nail varnish matches your coat and your lipstick. You're like a photo in a fashion magazine. A model," said Drefan with admiration.

I blushed and thanked him for the compliments.

"Even the blushing matches your outfit."

"Well, that's the reason I wear red clothes, so they could match my face when somebody compliments me. It happens so often that I should wear only red all the time."

"I am not surprised that people compliment you all the time. From what my father said, you are an amazing human being. 'A very rare diamond', my father's exact words."

"It's not what I tried to say. I meant that I blush very often, sometimes without hearing a compliment. If a person looks at me, I blush. If someone talks to me, I blush. It's dreadful."

"That's a sign of a lack of confidence. But you don't look like having self-esteem issues. And why should you not think highly of you? My father was astonished by the things you've done in your life."

"I haven't accomplished anything, Drefan. Your father was a good man who didn't want to see the bad side of a person." My voice trembled and my eyes blurred with tears. Drefan's stopped and put a hand on my shoulder. I raised my head and looked at the blue sky, empty of clouds. I blinked several times to make the tears go away. I didn't want to cry.

We got inside the restaurant chosen by Drefan, and a person came to guide us to a small table in a corner. We were the only clients inside. A waitress brought the menus and asked what would we like to drink.

"Fizzy water please," I said.

"And a pint of cider for me. Thank you," Drefan stepped in.

"Wait," I asked when the waitress was leaving, "may I change my order, please?"

"Of course. What do you fancy?"

"Do you have some sweet cider? Fruity taste maybe?" I investigated.

"We have strawberry flavoured cider."

"That's great. Can I have a bottle of that instead of the fizzy water?" I asked.

"So, just the cider and not the fizzy water," said the waitress while making modifications on her notebook.

"That's right," I confirmed.

"Sure thing. Thank you. I'll be with you shortly to take your food order."

The waitress came back with the drinks five minutes later. We hadn't looked at the menus and asked for more time. She winked at Drefan and said, "Not to worry. Give me a shout when you're ready."

I decided we should make a choice right away and speak after placing the order. Drefan nodded "Yes," and we both focused our attention to the menus. I didn't like anything whatsoever. No surprise there. I didn't like fancy places, I preferred Wetherspoons. But Drefan was not a man of such locations, I didn't even dare to bring that up. Ten minutes of going through the menu and I was still unable to decide which and what. Drefan was amused, and I was annoyed and upset with myself. So I looked at him and said, "All right, Englishman, you chose for me as we don't have the whole day."

"Are you sure?" he asked with incredulity.

"Absolutely!" I said with conviction.

"You are not that type of person who asks someone to do something for her and then complain about it forever?"

"Quite the contrary, I will be forever grateful if you chose a bloody meal for me now."

"I do not know anything about what you may fancy or may not," he said defeated.

"You don't have to. I trust your judgement," I decided.

"Are you allergic or intolerant to something?"

"Nope. Thank God for that," I answered.

"Is there anything you wouldn't eat?" enquired Drefan.

"Gorgonzola."

"Italian blue cheese?"

"I am not very fond of cheese, but I can eat mozzarella and cheddar from time to time."

"All right then. I know what to order," concluded Drefan searching for the waitress. She was staring at him so came right away. "Two steaks, please, with chips."

I was drinking when he said that and choked on my drink when I heard what he asked for. I started coughing and my face turned redder than a ripe tomato.

"Hey, hey," said he tenderly, "What happened, are you okay?"

I raised my hand as to say I was fine, just needed a minute.

"You don't like the cider, ripe tomato?" he asked laughing.

I cleared my throat and shook my head with force. My wavy blonde hair covered my face, and I put my hands on top of it to hide my face forever.

"Oh, come on, take your hands off that beautiful face."

"I choked on my drink, man! That's disturbing."

"It happens to the best of us," he replied amused.

We both laughed and two random tears slid down my cheeks. I wiped them off with a hand and blew my nose. Half an hour later, the food was placed on our tiny table. The waitress served Drefan first and I thought it was extremely unprofessional. "Women always have to be served first in a restaurant." It's one of the basic rules of waitressing. I guess she didn't study much in school, or maybe she was just an amateur. Still, didn't like it. But I kept calm and acted with diplomacy. "Thank you," we both said in unison.

I looked at the plates, there were huge and covered the whole table. I found it funny, then I said, "This is farmer's food, Englishman!"

"So you've already started to complain? I knew it!"

"You run too fast, I wasn't complaining, quite the contrary, I am truly grateful. I am not fond of fancy dishes that look like a Renoir, but taste like plastic."

"And where have I heard this before... hmmm. Comparing the aspect of the food with Renoir paintings... where was that? I am sure I heard it before. It would be odd to remember something that never happened, don't you think?"

"I know where you heard it. Your father used to do that with my food, so by logic, he's done it to compliment your mother's dishes too."

"Yes, you're right! Now I remember... I found this comparison to be pathetic back then."

"What about now? Have you changed your mind?" I curiously asked.

"I think that's a compliment of the highest class. My father was a very sensitive person."

"Glad to hear that you appreciate some traits of your father's character. By the way, Renoir is my favourite painter."

"I am not surprised, you're a very profound person too."

We stopped talking and focused on eating. The steak was cooked to perfection, succulent and tender. I loved every bite. Curious enough is that I am not a meat lover at all. I never have been. I do not eat it very often, but I am not vegetarian, or vegan. I just think I ate too much meat as a child. Fifteen minutes later I finished the whole steak and almost half of my chips. I was amazed by Drefan's ability to use his left hands for all those moves that seem so difficult for us normal people. He finished all the chips and the steak too. Without asking for permission, he reached his left hand over my plate and started eating the rest of my chips. I let him do it without weird remarks. He looked like he didn't have a good meal in months.

"Do you know why I ordered a steak for you, Tara?"

"I guess it's because you think I am weak and need to accumulate strengths."

"Precisely! What are you, a mind reader?" he asked amazed.

"You don't have to be a medium to get there, Drefan. It's common sense."

"You're a very intuitive person, besides being beautiful," he decided.

I blushed again and he giggled, "You're adorable when you blush."

"This isn't blushing; this is a nightmare! So annoying!"

"Come on now, don't get angry. I was only teasing you."

I looked out the window, while the waitress took the plates away. "Anything else I could bring for you? A dessert perhaps? Our desserts are home made."

Drefan looked at me, but I wasn't sure. So he decided again, "Would you please bring us two different slices of cakes, one chocolate and one carrot cake?"

"Sorry, we don't have carrot cake today. But we have a *zuppa inglese*, an Italian delicacy."

"Omg, you have zuppa inglese? That's fantastic. Yes, please bring one of those for me," I said with enthusiasm.

"Make it two, and cancel the chocolate cake," Drefan stepped in.

"Very well, sir," the waitress replied and smiled showing all her perfect teeth. I was happy to notice she kept a very high hygiene of them.

"What's this zuppa inglese trifle? Never heard of it before."

I found my moment to make fun of him, so I said, "*Zuppa* means soup and *inglese* means English."

"What? English soup? A sweet soup?" he asked with worry.

"Blah, that's disgusting. No! You wait and see. I am sure you'll love it. Oh, I know about it because I lived in Italy for many, many years."

"You are a fascinating person, Tara. You speak Italian then."

"Yes, sir!"

"Please say something in Italian for me."

"Absolutely not!"

"So you don't speak Italian," he said trying to provoke me.

I ignored him and looked at the waitress who was coming with the trifles. She smiled at Drefan and completely ignored me. Once again, she served Drefan first, but he took the small plate from his place and put it in mine. I was taken by surprise, so the waitress who looked really confused. Drefan didn't say a word, and just stared at the plate. The waitress lost her smile, placed the other plate in front of him again, turned on her feet and left. I looked at Drefan with appreciation. "That was very nice of you, thank you. Apparently, she likes you better than she likes me. You cannot blame her though."

"She should have studied in school, ladies are always to be served first, no matter how good-looking a man is," he said smiling.

I burst into laughter and said with slight sarcasm, "Modesty, your name is Drefan!"

We didn't go to sign the papers that day. We had a walk on the riverside, my favourite part of the city. Drefan talked about many things, but I thought of Adrian. I missed him immensely and I prayed for his health. I got home in the late afternoon. Tired and melancholic. I took my plastic bottle and filled it in with hot water. Then I grabbed a book and went to bed. But I couldn't sleep.

I considered that watching a movie, a comedy, would be a great idea. I loved comedies. I found one free online and pressed go. But my thoughts went to Adrian, 'How is he feeling? Is he okay? What's he doing? With whom is he with?' I sent him a text message, "Just let me know you're all right." So he did, "I am fine." That was it. No I am sorry, no I miss you, no how are you. 'What's with this boy? Does he love me, or not? It doesn't seem so.'

I couldn't watch anymore, so I tried to sleep. It didn't work out. In the morning I was tired, luckily it was Sunday. I didn't go anywhere, I didn't eat. Just stayed in bed and read from time to time. In the evening, I prepared my outfit for the next day, a red office dress, black tights, and red shoes. I still wear this outfit to this day. Different shoes, same colour. I went to sleep with my hot water bottle, hugging the pillow, 'I will think about it tomorrow.'

BE CAREFUL WHAT YOU WISH FOR

A new week started, I went inside the office smiling and acting like I was the happiest person in the world. Some people even asked me why the heck I was so damn happy on a Monday morning. "It's a new day, a new chance to do great things."

"You're weird," they told me. I didn't mind, I knew I was. My heart was bleeding and my face was smiling. I was doing a very good job hiding how I really felt. But what would I have gained by exposing my feelings to everyone? Pity maybe. I didn't want that, we all have issues, who's got bigger, who's got smaller. The difference stands on what we decide to do, or not do. To cry or laugh. To sit on the floor defeated, or to raise our head and carry our burden. I was a fighter, I was not going to give up.

Around 6:10pm, Adrian was waiting for me in the park. He sent me a text message in the afternoon. I looked at him and felt so much pain... the boy was seriously suffering.

"Is there anything I can do to help?" I asked.

He shook his head, "No."

"Would you come to me if there was?"

He ignored my question, which meant he wouldn't.

"Tara, my ex-girlfriend is in too much pain. I don't know what to do. I feel like a jerk."

I was boiling with anger, 'You are a jerk! You left her, came to me, and now all you can do or think about is her. I wanted to shout and slap him in the face. I wanted to leave him all alone in the middle of the street and never look back. Instead, I said, "You're a good man to think of her. She's lucky to have you. Do you want me to help you with something? If not, please, go home and let me be."

He didn't fight, just left to wait for the bus. I walked in the rain and thought that she was indeed lucky to have him. I wished I had someone to care for me like he cared for her. In all honesty, I knew people cared for me that way, but I wanted Adrian to care for me like he cared for her. Him and no one else. And I cried and cried and cried. I tilted my head to the dark sky and let the water cover my skin. My tears embraced the cold raindrops and a perfect union was born. I was soaking wet and freezing, but I didn't care.

I needed a shower, so I went to the bathroom, turned the heat on, leant against the porcelain wall, slid down and let the hot water hit my naked skin with power for a very long time. The small room filled with thick waves of steam. All my sinuses were wide open, I was finally breathing properly. I didn't even know I had issues breathing. It made me feel so alive and I thanked God for the gift. Sometimes you don't treasure what you have until you lost it or you found it.

I covered my body with a soft white bathrobe, took a towel and went into the corridor. It was absolutely freezing so I started shivering. I rushed into my bedroom, thanked God it was warm in there and patted dry my skin and my hair. I took some baby oil and massaged every single inch of my body. I looked in a mirror... I was still very thin and I thought I should eat something. I put my white and red pyjamas on, went into the kitchen, dumped some cereal in a bowl, added some milk and went back to the bedroom. It was too cold in there, I didn't want to get ill. I forgot to take my hot water bottle, so I went back to prepare it when I heard the doorbell ringing. I wasn't expecting anyone. I took the door entry telephone and asked with curiosity, "Hello?!"

"It's me," he said softly. Adrian, of course.

I was surprised and didn't know what to do. Several seconds later he asked me if I was going to open the door. I said I couldn't, 'What is wrong with you? Why are you here? Are you insane?'

"Why? Do you have guests?" he asked offended.

I just didn't want to see him... A few hours ago, he was devastated because his ex was in pain, now he came to me. Why? I wanted to be alone and eat my cereal in peace, but I pressed the button and the door opened. I went to unlock the flat door and when he got in, he took me in his arms and hold me tight. He was all shivering. "I miss you so much, Tara. I don't know what to do." My heart filled with so much pain and love that my tears had to flow to release the tension. "Let me help you. I know I can," I took his hand and went inside my bedroom.

"I came with my father's car, I parked in front of your building. Do you think it's safe? I wouldn't want my father to get a fine. He will go ballistic!" he said.

"Yes. Everybody parks in here after 6pm, if they find space. Don't worry" I assured him.

I sat on the bed and watched him taking his jumper off and emptying all his pockets. Phone, headphones, keys, money... he placed them on the floor and turned over to me. He kneeled in front of me, I placed my hands on the sides of his head and looked into his eyes, "You are so troubled, I cannot suffer this. I wished you'd allow me to help you. I am older than you, unfortunately, I learned so many things in my life. I was like you once. Please, let me try at least." He didn't answer, which once again, meant he would never allow me even to try. I didn't insist. He always did whatever he wanted, when he wanted. He only did what he thought was best for him. I sighed deeply and turned my head to look at the candle I lighted on before. He followed the direction of my eyes, "I didn't know you liked candles."

"You don't know much about me, Adrian, do you?"

"You don't know much about me, either."

"That's because you don't want me to know. But I tell you things about me all the time, you just don't listen."

"I listen...." he argued.

"... But you don't hear. You're always miles away. I cannot reach you, Adrian. Why are always running away? What are you so afraid of? What happened to you that make you behave like this? You said you love me, but you act like you don't care for me at all. You come to me whenever you feel like it. You don't ask if I want to see you or I have time for you..."

He took my hands away from his face, stood up and raised his voice a little, "You're not happy seeing me? I can go away, no problem." My heart made a jump, now that he was there, I didn't want him to leave. I stood up in a hurry, placed my arms around his neck and sealed his mouth with a kiss. He remained immobile for a short second, but then he answered back with such power that overwhelmed my entire being. He switched off the light and in a second, his palms were all over my body, his tongue inside my mouth fighting against mine. I groaned in ecstasy and tilted my head back so he could kiss my neck. His lips were like burning soft rocks and every single kiss made me feel like I was in Heaven. He took off my pyjamas leaving them to fall on the floor. I didn't fight, I was completely at his disposal and I abandoned my body and soul in a perfect rhapsody of mind-blowing emotions. He was all over me... kissing, biting, licking with irrepressible avidity. I couldn't think, I couldn't move, I could barely breathe... I was flying. Paradise was far less more exciting and joyful from the place I was right then. I forgot about all the pain and sorrow, I forgot about how he's left me on the floor crying in despair. I forgot the tears, the struggle, the omissions. It was just that moment only. No past and no future, just NOW. Carpe Diem. And Carpe Diem was perfection.

"You smell like sunshine..." he murmured, and I groaned in exaltation. "Your skin is real silk..." he whispered again and I moaned incessantly. "I can't have enough of you. You're so damn sexy... Why are you so sexy, woman?"

There are no words to express what and how he made me feel. I was crazy, utterly crazy for him. He was the most amazing kisser my skin has ever met. His soft lips knew exactly where to go and how to move. I wanted to look into his eyes... to see if he was there... but he kneeled and placed his lips on my lower abdomen, and started moving lower and lower. I screamed in pleasure and fear.

I put my hands on his shirt and tried to unbutton it, but I was trembling and couldn't finish the job. He lifted it above his arms in one second. My hands took off his brown leather belt and unzipped his jeans. A few moments later, he was in underwear, and I was looking at him without seeing a thing. It was too damn dark! He gently pushed me onto the bed and covered me with his body. He was pressing against me and I was terrified. I couldn't breathe. I knew what was going to happen. I didn't have a man inside me for over eight years. 'What if it hurts? What if I bleed? What if I don't like it? He won't want to see me again. What if I fall pregnant? Jesus, no!' And I fought and pushed him away with all my force, "It's not what I want. I just wanted your kisses. I dreamed about you holding me tight... I didn't dream about this. Your arms around me are what my body craves for, your lips, and your hugs. Nothing more. I am afraid, please forgive me." Big warm tears started to fall from my cloudy eyes. I felt ashamed and completely out of the world. It made no sense, I was a thirty-eight-year-old woman. I was supposed to know everything about it. I was supposed to be confident and knowledgeable, instead, I was terrified like a teenager and I couldn't control it. He reached my face and wiped them off, one by one. "What are you afraid of?"

So I told him everything, "I was twenty-five when I had sex for the first time. He was eleven years older than me and about to become my husband, we were engaged. One night we were kissing when it happened. I didn't bleed and he accused me of lying. He humiliated me and I could not defend myself in any way. Sex has been a taboo subject for the whole of my life. I didn't know anything about it. I was not expected to have sex before marriage and it was my husband's responsibility to teach me that art. I begged and swore my body didn't know another man before him. He didn't believe me. He said he would never believe another word coming out my mouth. I never read anything about sex or the first time, but I knew I was supposed to bleed and I didn't. I thought there was something wrong with me. The date for the wedding was already set, and he moved on with it, but I found out that there were too many odd things about him and decided to leave him. He almost killed me, but that's another story. I didn't have many intimate relationships after that. I had a boyfriend who made me laugh a lot, but I couldn't love him. We had sex but it never felt good or bad. It was routine and became a burden to me in a very short time. He taught me things, but I didn't like them. I left him after two years. After many years I fell in love with someone and I wanted him so much, but my body worked against me. The first time we made love, I thought I'd die from the pain. The way I felt it was like thousands of little knives cutting my intimate area. I bled a lot and couldn't suffer to be touched with a feather. He was huge and I thought it was because of that. We thought my body would adapt and tried everything, creams, lubricants, medicines. Nothing worked and we went to a few doctors. It was so humiliating... They said it was all in my mind. I let my boyfriend inside me several times and pretended it was fine, but I was in agony. I couldn't continue like that. One day I left without saying where I was going and bought another SIM card. He found me two years later, and we made love, but it was still terribly painful. I closed my heart and body to everyone for more than eight years after that. During these years I had countless treatments, but my doctors were not very positive. I also had a surgery which made it worse. They cut away pieces of my body that will never grow back. They had no idea of what were they doing, it was an experiment..."

My voice fainted and I sobbed on Adrian's chest. He didn't say a word, what could he have said? He held me tight, and that was what I needed. I took a deep breath and continued, "They, the doctors I mean, asked me to give it another try with a man I liked, but couldn't feel any attraction to no one. I didn't even go on a single date. I was utterly terrified. The pain I used to feel was unbearable, it did not seem worth it. You are the first man my heart fell for after that. My body wants you with every fibre in it. You're deep in my heart, but I am not sure if I should take this risk again. I loved that man immensely and still couldn't do it. That's why I am single. It hurts so badly. Then... I don't want children... what if I fall pregnant? I have been told I can't have children because of an issue with my reproductive system, but nothing can be 100% certain. What will I do then with a child? My life will be over. Kaput. Done. And that poor child... with a mother like me? So sad."

He listened in silence, then quietly put his arms around my body, "You would be a great mother. I would never want to hurt you. We don't have to do it if you don't want to. I would never force anyone. As for the pregnancy, there are methods, you know. I don't want that either." And I loved him even more if that was possible. 'I love him more than yesterday. And yesterday I thought it was not possible. God, what is going on? How much love can I feel for this human being? You're too good to me. Maybe I don't deserve all this happiness. But I thank you. I could have died not knowing how Heaven feels in reality.'

I cried quietly for a few minutes while he was hugging me. Then he kissed my eyes, my neck, and my lips... "Shhhh, don't cry, beautiful creature. I could never hurt you."

I was filled with infinite desire in a few seconds. My lips were closed together, so he'd got his way in with a little fight. I lost with a tiny scream. Our bodies, hearts, and souls were pulsing in unison and then I took a very brave decision. "Do you still want me?" I whispered, out of breath.

"Always," he murmured.

"I am all yours then. Just be tender, it will feel like the first time for me."

He stopped and looked at me. The lamp was still off, but there was some light coming in from the street. I saw his eyes filled with love and desire. "Are you sure?" he timidly asked. I didn't reply, I ran my fingers through his hair and avidly kissed his lips. He caressed my back and I dug my nails into his skin again.

"You drive me so crazy... I never felt this way. I never wanted anyone this much," I murmured while his lips and hands were all over my body, in places that never seen the sun, making me feel emotions I didn't know it was humanly possible. We were lusting for each other. It hurt a little when it happened and I screamed, so he froze.

"It's my mind's reaction. My body is fine. I am sorry," I said.

"Don't be, I wouldn't want to hurt you," he murmured.

I was breathing heavily and he was too. I pulled his hair with one hand and guided his mouth on mine. The other hand was rubbing his back and my nails were leaving scratches on his clean skin, but he said nothing. I was gasping, he was groaning. After a while, I realised he was exactly my size, and I relaxed my body allowing it to feel every single move. It was perfect. I raised my head to look at him inside me. No tiny knives. I reached down there to check if it was blood what I was feeling, it wasn't, and I felt relieved. Our hearts were racing in unison. It was a little painful, but the pleasure was beyond words. His hands were caressing my skin and his lips were kissing my neck. I was biting his ears, pulling his hair, my body arched to feel him deeper.

"Are you okay?" he murmured. I was speechless. It was the first time when I was enjoying feeling a man inside me. It was heaven and I moaned in ecstasy. There was no need for words, he understood. We were all sweaty and heavily breathing. The ending was glorious, like an explosion of a faraway star. We cuddled and he held me tight. He was the boy and I was the woman, but I felt like a teenager in her older boyfriend's arms. It was safe there.

'He didn't hurt me, he would never hurt me. He is my size and I really want him. He is not fond of weird positions. He's much more than I ever dreamed for.'

I couldn't hold back my tears. They were falling thousands on my red cheeks, like tiny drops of a summer rain. He tried to wipe them off.

"No, let them fall. My mind cannot contain all this happiness inside. These are happiness tears."

"You are such a crier," he joked.

"I am extremely passionate, Adrian, and sensitive. I feel too much. It's overwhelming. I'd go insane if I were not able to cry. I am sorry if it bothers you."

"It doesn't bother me, silly. I just don't want to see you suffering."

"Suffering is good... it makes you feel alive. Don't you think?"

He didn't reply and my tears kept falling for a while. My head was lying on his chest. He kissed my eyes thousands of times. There was no other thing in the whole universe, besides us two and our emotions. "Making love to you is like magic becoming a reality," he murmured. "I didn't know it can feel this way. Your passion is overwhelming."

"Is it too much for you? I could try being less passionate if you don't like it. I know it's a lot. I have Latin blood in my veins."

"No, don't ever change. You're perfect."

I knew he meant every word and I was grateful. It's what my mind craved for... Someone to see me the way I was, beyond the words, the tears, the etiquette, and the masks we wear every day.

I fell asleep only to wake up to watch him leaving, "Do you really have to go?"

"Yes. It's 2am and I need to finish some things. I'll see you tomorrow, all right? Sleep tight."

I didn't answer, and even if I wanted him to stay, I was already sleeping when he closed the door.

The next morning, I went to work happier than ever before and hoped to see him after work. But he didn't reply to my text messages. I walked alone thinking of him. He didn't give me any sign for days.

On Friday evening I was out with some friends. I stepped into a pub, and our hearts acknowledged one another. As every time before. No matter where I went if Adrian was inside, the first person my eyes saw, was him. If I was the one to be sat down, if he came in, he would see me first out of everybody else. He came close to me and I introduced him to my friends. Nobody seemed to know him, which was good. He sat next to me and rested his hand on my leg. I took it from there and moved it onto his leg instead. He understood that I didn't like to be touched in public. It was not true, I was craving for a kiss from him, right there and right then. But we were not into a relationship, nobody knew a thing and I wanted to remain like that.

He took me home and we made love for hours. We both felt the same devastating emotions. After that I asked him never to touch me in public again, "Nobody has to know about this. It's our secret."

"But why? Why do you want this to be a secret? What do you have to lose?" he asked.

"I have nothing to lose, but I told you before, you have everything to lose."

"I disagree. It's not illegal to love. You are free, and I am free. There is nothing to hide."

"Are you? Free, I mean. Are you? Have you told your ex about me?" I asked. He looked at me and didn't reply, which clearly meant he hasn't. 'Liar.' "Do you see why I want this to be a secret? It is for you and you don't even realise. I beg you, respect my wishes. One day you'll thank me."

"Says the woman with experience..." he replied.

I didn't like it and I pushed him away, "Don't ever joke about my age. It's my sensitive spot. I am trying to learn to accept it, but I am not there yet. Please show some consideration."

"Tara, you do not look your age. Nobody will notice that you're older than me if that's what you fear. You are extremely good-looking, that cannot be missed, your age yes."

"I know I look like thirty-two or something, but you look like twenty-one, dammit!"

"People won't ask for an ID. I really don't get why you want this to be a secret."

I didn't want to discuss it anymore. He sighed and hugged me tightly and we fell asleep into each other arms. He stayed that night and I was over the moon. I didn't sleep at all... I could never sleep with another person in my bed. In the morning I made him breakfast, eggs, beans, and bacon. I only had a coffee. His phone rang, he looked at the number, grabbed his things and left. I wasn't happy, but I had no right to say anything.

Later in the evening, I sent him a text message, "I want to cook for you, I want to hold you tight when you feel alone, I want to make you feel safe. I have no right, but please know that I will always be here for you." He replied hours later, "I know."

I went to bed hugging my pillow and I couldn't go to my piece of Heaven. It was gone. I struggled, but I manage to close my eyes for a few hours. The next day I went for a walk and met some friends for a coffee.

At 10pm he sent me a text, "Are you okay?" I didn't reply. I wasn't okay at all.

The next day he said he'd wait for me on Monday, but I told him I was in a rush as I was meeting someone on the other side of the city. And I did the same for the whole week.

On Friday evening I met him in town, by pure chance again. "You look gorgeous," he said. "May I take you home when you've finished?"

"I have finished, I don't feel like staying out anymore," I replied.

"Let me say goodbye to my friends and I am coming, don't leave without me."

I went outside and watched him through the window. He kissed and hugged every girl in his circle. I wished I felt some jealousy, I should have, but I couldn't. I was upset with myself, 'Why I am not bothered when he touches other women? What is wrong with me?'

He came outside, tried to grab my hand and I didn't want to, so he offered me his arm and I held on him. When the street became narrow, he grabbed my hand again and hold it tight. He walked in front of me and I was following him. We stopped at a traffic light, he looked at me and smiled, "You are so beautiful. Every man in this town is jealous of me."

"You are so sweet, Adrian. You know how much I love compliments. It's frivolous, I know."

"This dress shows your perfect figure. Unbelievable how amazing you look. Everybody had their eyes on you." I felt like kissing him right there and right then, but I didn't. It was dangerous. Someone could have seen us, but when we passed under a bridge, I pushed him towards the wall, pressed my body against his and kissed him passionately. He was surprised but answered back right away. We were both breathing heavily. Our bodies wanted to feel one another right then, right there. "Let's go home." I whispered in his ear. He grabbed my hand and walked faster. I was wearing very high heels, but I was so used to them, it felt like wearing trainers. I was shorter than him and my steps were smaller, I was running, but I didn't complain. It was great exercise.

We've got home in less than five minutes, I opened the entrance door, let him in, closed the door and pushed him against the corridor wall. I was overwhelmed by desire. We kissed like teenagers for a few minutes. He wanted me, I wanted him so he pushed me towards the stairs and I started to climb them with uncertainty. He was behind me and his hand softly reached my bottom. My body was electrified and I froze. But he pushed me gently from behind. "A few more steps..." he murmured. I looked for the keys, he took them from my hand and opened the door. We were safe now. He took my shoes off and I ran upstairs to the toilet. I washed my intimate areas with cold water and patted them dry. I stood up and looked in the mirror, desire was written all over my face. I went into the bedroom where he was lying on the bed waiting for me. I jumped on top of him and he was ready.

He switched off the lamp, but we could still see due to the street lights. We'd made love like there was no tomorrow. "God, Tara, you're driving me insane."

He went to the bathroom, washed himself and came back all fresh and radiant. I kissed him softly on the lips, his hands were all over my body and we made love again, and again. "I cannot get enough of you," he whispered and I smiled. My mind and body were relaxed. I laid my head on his chest and fell asleep. I woke up when he went to the toilet, I followed and had a quick shower. He was already sleeping when I came back, I moved slowly and watched him sleep, 'I love you so much, Adrian. I want you to be mine.' I thought in my head. I lay next to him, his hands were looking for me and when he found my body, he grabbed it and got closer to it. I moaned and his hands rubbed my skin. "You're so wet," he murmured.

"That's because I ... "He didn't let me finish. He sealed my mouth with an endless kiss and we made love again. I moaned in ecstasy and cried from pleasure. We cuddled and slept until 9am.

"Please, don't go. Stay with me today... you don't go to work, do you?" I begged.

"I need to go, Tara."

I wanted to fight and scream, but I knew it was useless. I watched him walking away. He left without a kiss, without a hug and without saying goodbye, as every time. I didn't like it, I just had to accept it. Later in the evening, I sent him a text message, "Would you spend a weekend with me?" He replied "Sure," and I was fine with that answer. I knew he wouldn't have said yes without meaning it.

On Monday he sent me a text message, "Do you want to have dinner with me in town on Wednesday?"

I agreed, of course. I dressed very nicely, he was wearing a jumper. "You should have told me," he said, "I would have dressed up too."

"It's a dinner out, Adrian. I always dress nicely when I go out. You should have known that by now."

"And you should have known I don't do that. It's just dinner, not a date."

I was hurt and didn't say a word the whole evening. He seemed not to care, maybe he didn't even notice. He took me home and invited himself in. I didn't feel like it, but I said nothing. He wanted to make love and once again, I was not in the mood. "Why?" he asked with anger. I didn't want to lose him so I kissed him and let him do whatever he felt with my body. I participated absently, and he was happy with that. I am sure he thought that all was good. "Are you okay?" he asked when he finished.

"Sure," I replied softly. Tears were falling down my cheeks. He saw none as the light was off. One hour later he left without a word. I fell asleep crying and hating myself for betraying my body. I didn't want to leave a story like that.

AGONY

On Friday evening, I didn't go out, he sent me a text around 10:30pm, "Are you awake?"

I missed him so I replied, "Yes."

"Can I come to see you?" he asked.

"Sure," was my answer.

He was drunk and smelling heavily of beer and God only knows what else. We kissed and his hands wanted to make their way to my intimate areas. I was utterly terrified that he would give me something, like a disease, or a virus or... He clearly hadn't wash his hands. "I have my period," I lied. He didn't insist and fell into a very agitated sleep. I felt so sorry for him, I put my arms around his body and tried to make him feel safe. He left in the morning and I reached my arms to him, for a hug. He smiled and gave me one in a rush.

"What are you running away from, Adrian? You know I'll always be here for you, right? Today, tomorrow and in ten or forty years from now. No matter where I'll be, I would still be here," and I pointed to my heart, "for you."

"Yes, people told me this before and now they are gone."

"You're unfair, Adrian. You don't know me. I am not like that."

"Well, I cannot take any risk," he said with coldness.

"What do you mean? What risk?"

"Never mind." He refused to give me an explanation.

"You are not giving me what I need, Adrian."

"What do you need, Tara?"

"I need you to love me. I need you to play nice with me. The way I do with you. I want you to talk to me when you feel down... I would like you to come for dinner more often. Watch a movie with me. Spend weekends together. Go for walks or you could work on your computer and I could work on mine. Nothing major."

"We are not into a relationship, Tara. I can watch a movie with you, and come for dinner, but I have other things to do. I have friends I need to see."

"Why are you so cruel to me?"

"Why am I cruel, Tara? Because I am not doing what you ask? Well, I am the way I am. I can't change. I like myself."

"How can you like yourself? You're empty inside, Adrian. You're all alone in your world."

"Maybe I like it this way, Tara. Have you ever thought of that? I have thousands of friends anyway, I am never alone," he said.

"You are hurting me. Why? What have I ever done to you? You cannot punish me for things other people did to you. It is not my fault people left you. But you should know by now that people come and people go. It's normal life."

"I am troubled, you are right. Maybe I should let you be. Maybe you should look for someone more appropriate for yourself."

I felt a profound pain in my heart and both my hands reached to it in a desperate way to contain it. He completely ignored what he just witnessed. I could barely breathe, "Maybe you're right. We are not compatible. We have nothing in common. I need someone to make me feel loved," I agreed.

He said nothing, turned on his feet and left.

I fell ill for two days. On Sunday night I couldn't sleep, went online and made a profile on a dating website. I put some nice pictures of me and ten minutes later, I had forty-three new messages in my mail. I spent my time reading and replying to all. I liked no one.

That week I changed my working hours and said nothing to Adrian. I was to start at 8am and finish at 4pm. We would have never had the chance to meet again at the end of the day. I wanted to see him so much, but he hurt me. He wanted to be free, I had no right to fight.

Back in my country, I had been a blogger. I had had three blogs. It was a really demanding hobby; I used to work for twenty hours a day in the beginning. It got better with the years, but it was still a terribly time-consuming task. I had many followers who expressed their sorrow when I gave up on writing. It happened when I came here, my mind was occupied with several other things. I had no time for blogging. But I was good at it and I started to miss it. As a child, my mind developed a strategy to cope with the troubles from my childhood. I used to write down everything that made me feel unhappy, all the injustices, the pain, and the struggles put them in an envelope and send it to people I didn't know. I invented names and places, but my stories were real. Later in life, I found out that it was common for counsellors to ask their patient to write down their afflictions. It was a great and famous therapy technique, and I'd thought I'd invented that system. What a sad day for me discovering that. I got over it soon, I couldn't fight against studies and proof.

I decided to start a blog in English. I looked for a suitable template and wrote my first post, then many others followed. My colleagues were thrilled.

At the same time, I was replying to emails on the dating site.

I told Adrian about it, of course. He said he was happy for me moving on. I wanted to shout and scream that he was the only one I wanted, no one else. And I did tell him that and he coldly replied, "I cannot give you what you need, Tara. Send me a picture of you when you go on your first date." And I did... to make him jealous. He sent me an instant reply, "You're stunning. He's a lucky guy."

I cancelled the date and cried in despair. I wanted Adrian... with all his troubles.

The next day I sent him a text, "You could be that guy, Adrian if you want it. Please come to see me whenever you feel like it. I miss you."

"I miss you too. I could come tonight. Are you free?"

I wasn't, but I cancelled everything and cooked dinner. He came and placed his arms around my waist from behind. I burst in thousands of tears. "Adrian... you are the only one I want. Tell me you know that." And we've made love like there was no tomorrow. I moaned, he groaned, I screamed, he bit. When he started to get dressed, I didn't want to let him leave, I surrounded his neck with both arms, like an abandoned child to a big toy. He gently pushed me away asking me to let him go. He had things to do. He wiped out my tears and held me in his arms until I stopped sobbing. "You cry too often and too much."

"That's because I feel, Adrian. I would rather suffer than not feeling anything. Please, stay with me." But he didn't.

With tears in my eyes, I went online and fixed some dates. I met two guys in two days. Very nice people, but there was no chemistry. We were infinite miles away.

On Friday night he sent me a text, "Are you awake?" As I said I was, he came to see me. He was drunk and could barely speak.

"You're drunk," I murmured.

"I am not."

I let him inside my house and body. And I felt dirty, humiliated and used... by a boy. I swore it was going to be the last time. I told him to stay away, and I cancelled his number.

On Tuesday, I wrote him an email, "Please, forgive me. I shouldn't have said that. I miss you."

"I could come to see you tomorrow," he replied.

I agreed instantly and cancelled all my plans.

When he came inside my place, it was like seeing him for the first time. He'd just had a shower and was wearing a green t-shirt that highlighted the beautiful colour of his eyes, and a pair of blue jeans. He looked very handsome. I knew he did it for me and I loved him for that.

"Tara. Don't send me away again. We cannot keep doing this. It is not healthy," he begged.

"I know, I am sorry. I thought I could live without you, but I was wrong. Can you forgive me?" I stood up on my toes to kiss him and he smelled like soap. I loved men's perfumes, and I loved the fresh smell of soap. It drove me nuts. I pushed him onto the armchair, sat on his lap, and kissed his neck. I was sniffing him like a dog. It was mind-blowing. He pushed his hands under my blouse and started to softly stroke my skin, then he undid my bra and lifted my blouse over my head. I loved when he did that so I was moaning and pulsing with desire. He looked at me in a trance. He never ever actually saw me naked with the lights on. "You have a perfect body." He licked, sucked, bit, and kissed every inch of my skin countless times until I was writhing with pleasure.

I unzipped his jeans and whispered and his ear, "You drive me insane. How do you know these things? Who taught you how to kiss, and touch, and stroke or rub this way? You're a master of eroticism."

He was lusting for me and I gently guided him inside me. "You're exactly my size," I whispered.

We had dinner afterwards. He complimented my cooking skills and promised he would cook the next time, but when I remembered what he did to my kitchen last time he cooked, I said I am happy to cook for him anytime. We went into the bedroom, he lay on the bed and I lay next to him. I put my hands on both sides of his face and told him I missed him immensely and I wished the moment would never end.

"Tara, I cannot sleep. You're always in my mind. I walk in town, wandering every night, thinking of you, craving for you. Would you walk with me next time?" he asked in despair.

"Whenever you want, Adrian. I am always here for you. Just let me know, all right?"

But he thought I was pushing him away and I thought he was keeping me away. I should have said something, but he was leaving.

I went to bed full of hope. 'Maybe he will let me in now. Maybe he'll stop running. Poor child. He must be so confused. I have to stop this coming and going thing. But it's not my fault. He knows I love him.'

That evening I wrote about our story, 'Impossible love - age disparity.' Age is just a stupid mental obstacle I said (my old man told me this) and I meant it.

Someone left a comment, "Love is Chaos. Just a different kind. Unpredictable in all forms. You can guess what will work, and speculate what might not. But chaos is exactly what it is. It heals and burns us all."

***

Later on, Adrian admitted it was him. I was impressed. He was a man of moods, not of words.

Many times I wondered if he loved me for real, or if it was a just physical attraction. That comment proved that he loved me... at times, he just didn't know how to deal with it. He was afraid to let me in and I couldn't force him.

One day he invited me to a very curious party. I said I was not going as his plus one. He replied that there are not going to be people who knew us there and we didn't have to act as if we were together. I accepted as a favour to him. Two hours later he sent me a text cancelling the invitation. I've never known why as he didn't explain and I didn't ask. I once imposed myself not to ask questions if I was not ready to hear the answers.

Only two years after and only at the time I am writing this, I think that he might have invited his ex-girlfriend first, she said no, then changed her mind.

I was exasperated. My pride was hurt, but I am the one always affirming that we should not let our pride to destroy a love feeling. So I kept loving and dreaming about him. My mind disliked it very much, but my body... my body wanted him. Even for a few minutes. He was my size and he didn't hurt me. He was not the person who would experience new positions or moves. He wanted simple things and I am the same. I don't find it boring. I guess that is because I never have sex, I make love.

Even if there were many times when I didn't want to feel him inside, it was still making love to me. I loved him, that's why I lay down on my bed and allowed him to do whatever he wanted with me. It was better than not having him at all. How tragic is that? Why do we, women, let that happen? Don't we deserve something and someone better?

Every week he invited me to dinner, and every Friday evening he sent me a text with same words, "Are you awake?" I always answered and let him in, both inside my house and my body. At some point, I don't know if I enjoyed it or not. I thought about it and I decided I didn't. We always met on his terms. My body felt dirty and my mind was reproaching me every time I let him in without feeling the desire. I wanted to see him so much, even if it was humiliating. That was the only way. He stepped on my dignity, kept my self-esteem at the minimum, and ignored how much I was suffering.

He never changed, he never stayed when I asked or cried. He never spent a weekend with me. We never went for a walk at 5am in the morning to watch the sunrise as I so much dreamt about. He didn't spend a whole day with me, from morning to dawn. No, he had to go home. I felt used like a cloth. I wanted to scream and slap him in the face, to shake his body, to make him open his heart. But he wouldn't have listened. He knew better.

I always felt out of the world too, but I didn't want to fit. It was a choice. I didn't care, I loved being with myself. But we are not all the same. We are all lost soul to a degree.

I kept telling him about the men I went on a date with. He said he was hoping I will find someone to make me happy. I told him that he could make me happy if he wanted to.

"I have nothing to give," he confessed.

"You have a lot to give. Your kisses are magic. Your hugs calm me instantly down, no matter how dreadful I feel. That's what I need. It just has to be consistent. But you give and take. You make me rise to the top of Himalayas for a few minutes then you pushed me down without remorse. Then you watch me fall and crash, and cry, and twist in pain.

It's like you feel nothing for me. It is confusing Adrian. I really don't know what you feel inside."

"Why do you love me then?"

"Love has no reason, Adrian. My heart has chosen you from billions of people. It was destiny and I am happy, even when I cry in despair. You made me live emotions I never thought existed. Good and bad. For years, I thought I lost my capacity for feeling tenderness for a man. You proved me I had nothing to worry about. I am still human and I am grateful for that. I often wondered if it is better not to feel love or to lose the one you love. Now I can affirm with certainty that Alfred Lord Tennyson was right, *"'Tis better to have loved and lost than never to have loved at all"*. I sighed and kissed him on the cheek. He kissed my hand and left.

I kept seeing him in those circumstances only for at least six months. One hour in Paradise followed by countless days and nights in Hell. Every week, every time. I was drained. I didn't know if I loved or hated him. I knew I hated myself though. My brain hated my heart, and vice-versa. They were endlessly fighting. Night and day. When he sent a text message my heart made a jump and pumped blood faster, my mind would start mocking on it, ' You are thirty-eight! Stop fooling yourself, you're just some flesh. He doesn't love you, are you blind stupid? He just wants to get inside you and you have nothing against it. Just like those women you used to criticise and despise.

Remember? What do you have to say in your defence now? You're worse than them because you're not sixteen anymore. You didn't marry him and you don't have children together. You have no excuse to accept to be treated this way. You could just not open the door of your flat and keep your body out of his touches. Because yes, his touches would make anyone melt.'

**

My birthday was close. I didn't feel like celebrating. I never liked birthday parties. Why would you celebrate a lost year? I wondered and people told me it's exactly the opposite, you celebrate the arrival of a new one. Yes, I never thought of that before? Why? I don't know.

One evening I sent him a text message asking him if he wanted to spend a certain day with me, not mentioning it was my birthday. He didn't reply for several days. I felt like trash or less than that. I cried in despair. One evening he asked, "Why that day?"

"It is very important to me. I need to be with you that day," I replied with tears in my eyes.

He thought about it for many days again, then he said it was fine. I should have felt offended and hurt for the late reply. However, I realised it's been extremely difficult for him to take that decision. I knew he didn't love me the way I wanted, of course, but then again, he said yes when he didn't want to, so he must have cared for me in a way I couldn't understand. Or he was just afraid I'd close my body forever. I guess I'll never know for sure. Maybe he doesn't know either. Nothing was certain with him. No question had a clear answer. A real torture.

One day he asked if it was my birthday, somehow he realised it must have been a very special day for me and what else than my birthday? So I confirmed it.

"I thought you'd have a party. All your friends are talking about it. They must know your birthday is coming. You're famous for your parties," he said.

"I have nothing to celebrate. I just want you. No one else," I replied with sadness and wondered how the heck did he know what my friends were talking about.

"What do you want me to bring you?" he asked.

I never understood why people need to ask this question. 'Possible that you don't know anything about me by now? How is this acceptable? Bring me a box of Raffaello, a flower, a candle...'

Instead of that I said, "Just bring yourself." Women, wanting but not asking.

And he did come and brought nothing, as I told him. I was a little upset, but I couldn't allow that ruin my day, in the end, he did ask, I could have said I wanted something, but I didn't. I had no right to complain and felt guilty for feeling ungrateful. So I thanked him for accepting to spend that day with me. As it was some huge favour, a sacrifice which cost him a lot. He made me feel that, although I am not sure if he did it on purpose or it was just my high sensitivity that perceived the tension in the air.

We watched some movies, I wanted to eat junk food, chocolate, crisps... Yes, that was what I wanted to do on my birthday. To go wild on food I wouldn't normally eat. He didn't join me. Why I don't know, maybe because he didn't like the junk food I offered, or because he didn't want me to see him eating that. I knew he ate those types of unhealthy food and found it curious he refused to join me. But he never did anything he didn't want to. It didn't really matter to him if he hurt my feelings, ruined my day or made me feel uncomfortable. All he cared about was his own feelings. I guess he thought it was more than enough to spend the day with me. God, I so wanted to slap him in the face and throw him out, delete his number and never speak to him again. Instead, I rested my head on his chest and cried in silence. He didn't even notice. His body was there, but his mind was wandering, only God knows where and with whom as he never admitted that.

'I am such a liar, a hypocrite. We, women, always pretending from our men to read our minds, but they don't have these powers. They come from Mars. Men and women speak different languages. I should tell him how I feel, what I want.' But then again, I used to tell him what I wanted and he never gave it to me, he never, ever did something I asked, he never really cared and he told me that so many times, "I am the way I am and I'm okay with it. If I don't like something, I will not do it. My dignity is precious to me. I will never change and I am not asking you to change for me. Women always impose us to change. My ex never tried that."

His dignity or his pride? What about mine? His ex never tried to change him? But of course, when could she, in which context? They barely saw each other. He went out every night and got home in the morning, completely wasted. From what I came to understand, with no words though, they didn't even have sex for a very long time as he was extremely unskilled. He knew how to kiss, touch and stroke, God if he knew, he was a true master, but his body didn't respond right away. It was evident he didn't do that often. They maybe kissed from time to time, but she didn't make his body want her. How could you not feel the desire to get inside the woman you love? I found that strange and disturbing.

Maybe that's why I always let him in when he was craving for me. After the first two times, his body learned to lust for me in one instant. It was enough to look at him and he was ready. Even in public, his body was always ready for me even if I didn't look. It was enough for him to see me. I knew he could never resist me if I wanted. For God sake, I was emanating sex appeal from every pore of my body. Not on purpose, not ever. I knew I had that power since I was very young. Teachers, colleagues, professors, random people on the streets, fell for me all the time, but I never made use of it. "What a waste," I have often been told. And when I denied their advances they would start despising me. I didn't care. I didn't want any of them. I wanted this child who had no idea of how to love me. I was his slave and he used me whenever he pleased. I was grateful he had no weird desires at least.

Around 3pm he started to feel ill, one hour later I sent him home, although I didn't want to. He didn't even try to say he was fine, he just wanted to leave and he did it without looking back. 'Why wouldn't you stay with me? Why don't you want to sleep next to me?'

I cried when he closed the door... for hours after, and I hated my stupid heart so, so much. I knew he wanted to leave. He didn't really want to be there in the first place, he made me a favour, it was so clear, and he didn't even try to hide it. Another of his cold-blooded calculations to hold me in his power.

His mind was inconsistent, one day he couldn't live without me, another one he couldn't stand to look at me. And he accused me of doing the same. He fought against his feelings the way I did, or even more. I didn't know which one was more inconsistent than another.

**

I was thirty-nine now, and he was one year older too.

One Friday night he asked if he could come to visit again. He was in front of my building, going up and down he said. I opened the door and let him in. He was in distress and very drunk. I held him tight and let him fall asleep in my bed. He woke up a few hours later and went home, I begged him to stay. He didn't hear me. I got upset and swore it was over.

BROKEN

A Wednesday night, around 2 in the morning, I received a text message. I was asleep but the notification sound woke me up. If somebody sent me a message at that hour, it couldn't have been good. I grabbed my phone and read, "I could really use a friend right now." Adrian, of course.

I was sure something was terribly wrong so I told him I was always there for him. So he came over right away. He was completely wasted, smelled and looked horrible, totally out of his mind, "It's my ex. She told me that she met someone. We had a pact. She was not supposed to tell me this."

I was in shock and I wanted to slap him in the face and cry out loud, 'You selfish brute! It's always about you, isn't it? You and her, all the time. Why did you leave her if she's got this power over you? Just to screw me? Selfish, selfish brute! If she's your best friend, as you say all the time, why can't you just be happy for her? You don't want to give the exclusivity to anyone, but you want everyone to revolve around you only!' My heart was racing from anger and humiliation, I bit my lip and prayed hard not to say what I was really thinking. So I calmed down and said, "Adrian. I don't think she's done anything wrong. She's done well telling you that. What if you'd found out from different sources?"

"No! She didn't have to tell me that!" he shouted.

"Why are so upset, Adrian? Do you still love her? Are you jealous? What's the problem in here? I don't get it," I said starting to lose my patience.

"She broke our pact."

And I lost it. 'She broke a pact? Your pact? Your mind is so damn twisted! Everything has to happen how you plan it. No stepping outside the road.' "So you are free to go with other women, but she is not? How come?" I asked with anger.

"You don't understand. I never told her that I was seeing you," he mumbled.

"You were screwing me, Adrian. Not seeing me! You explored my body several times. You kissed and stroked every inch of my skin countless times!" I shouted. He completely ignored my statements. He was not listening to me. He was angry and hurt and that moment I didn't know who he was. I hated my heart for loving him. A monster of egotism, a different person. Cold, distant, deaf and calculated. His behaviour was so not right! I was terrified and didn't want to fight with him. I calmed down again and let him do his stuff, but I could not handle the pressure.

"How do you know about this anyway? Do you still see her?" I asked again.

"She lives with my father, she needed help with the rent. She's been my friend since we were children. My parents know her very well and my father accepted to take her in when she called in distress. We obviously see each other every day. We've always been and will be best friends," he said, like it was the most natural thing in the world.

The entire universe crashed over my head. I was in total disbelief. 'It isn't normal, you monster! No man lives with his ex outside a marriage. You have no children, you could live alone. She's an adult. She can take care of herself.' "She lives with your father? You live with your father! You see each other every day?" I started stammering, and I felt like a knife was crossing my chest from a side to the other several times. I could literally feel the blood coming out of my chest. It suddenly became all dark inside my room. My head was spinning, I was freefalling. I thought I'd die, I couldn't breathe. I needed water. He didn't even notice my reaction. I had the urge to kick him out, shut the door in his face, and never speak to him for the rest of my life. That was not normal. Nothing was normal about him, her, and me. I needed to know, so I asked, although I knew the answers were not going to be the ones I was ready to hear, "How long has she been living with your father?"

"Since we broke up. She was not well, her parents threw her out on the streets. She had no place to go. I couldn't let her sleep under a bridge," he said as it was the most natural thing in the world again.

"So you broke up, but you are living together in your father's house. With his family... Like a family. You and her. Don't tell me, you sleep in the same room... same bed maybe?! Did you really break up, or it was just to make me feel guilty?"

"Don't be ridiculous! I have my own room. My father's house is huge. You could live in there too," he mumbled again.

"And why don't I live in there then? Why is it your ex-girlfriend with you and not me? Which one are you sleeping with? Do you come to me after you had her, or you have her after you had me? Honestly, I had the feeling that you didn't have sex in years. Which one gives you more pleasure? How does that work? Do tell as I have never heard such an insane story in my whole damn life. Oh, wait, I just lied. My first man was sleeping in the same bed with his mother, that's why I left him. He also said it was nothing weird about that. Psycho!"

"Don't start your mumbo jumbo discussions with me. We are just friends. I couldn't let her sleeping on the streets, could I? I care about her. It's my responsibility to take care of her."

"Your responsibility? How old is she? Five? So that's the reason you always have to leave? Have you had a pact on this too? To never sleep in a different house?"

He looked at me with rage and considered I didn't deserve an answer. That was Adrian. Never doing anything he didn't want to.

"Answer me!" I shouted.

"You are overreacting out of jealousy. As usual. It is absolutely normal behaviour from my side. I am a good person, you know. I have a heart too. Although you think I don't," he said with loathing.

'The history repeats itself. That monster slept in the same bed with his mother, and this one with his ex-girlfriend and both accused me of being out of my mind. They despise me! I am the crazy one. It isn't normal, you brute. No man lives with his ex outside a marriage. You have no children; she's an adult; she could and should take care of herself.' My brain shouted inside my head over and over again. 'Do something, Tara! Kick him out as he deserves. He doesn't respect you at all. He cares for her, not for you. What more proof do you need? You're just a beautiful body, not a human being. He's got a heart… but it belongs to her. The fault is yours. You attract these weirdos into your life. Because you don't love yourself enough.'

I hoped he'll never have to find out that people use other people until the day they don't need them anymore, until the day they would have found someone else to take care of them.

In the end, why did I know about her? Maybe he was the one needing her, maybe he was the one who was using her. He didn't want to live alone; he couldn't cope with loneliness. That's why he always drank that much whenever he went out. He didn't know how to fit in, but when his mind was inebriated, he felt confident and worthy. They both took advantage one of another. An exchange. Isn't that what all relationship are all about? They had an understanding and he didn't consider me. How was I supposed to feel? Should I have given him a pat on the shoulder and congratulate his good nature? I am sorry, but I couldn't. I didn't need that; I didn't deserve that.

"How the hell have I managed to blindfold myself so tight? How did you manage to keep this from me for such a long time? You do realise that this is sick? Sick!... I feel sick..." I shouted, rushing to the toilet and vomiting. I hated throwing up so, so much. I heard the bathroom door opening. "Go away!" I shouted. "You're totally insane! You've made a fool of me!"

"Let me help you," he said while kneeling next to me to hold my hair. He somehow sobered up while I was in the bathroom.

"Such a cliché, Adrian. You're full of calculations, aren't you? You don't sense a thing, you cannot feel any emotions. Am I right? You want to feel emotions, you lie to yourself every day. You cannot give love because you don't know what that is. You're incapable of feeling anything. You're a monster! Leave my house immediately and never come back. I am done accepting all your eccentricities. This is too much. You took everything from me. Dignity, confidence, self-esteem."

"Oh, come on now. Don't do that. I know you love me. I didn't tell you about this because I didn't want to make you feel this way. You're so quick at getting angry. Please, take a moment to reflect on it. I will sleep on the couch."

"You want to sleep here? Now? Why? Is she screwing someone else in the room next to yours? Good for her! You deserve it. Shouldn't you be happy for her if she's your childhood friend? If you really care for her as you say!? What's the meaning of best friends for you, Adrian? You seem to use words without having a clue of the concept. Love, best friends, friends, and so on."

"I said I needed a friend, not a judge," he said with disappointment.

"So, I am the one who should feel guilty now, right? Is that what you expect? It is always me doing bad stuff to you...You're innocent, you never do anything wrong. Women are always the ones to blame, right? You brute."

"I didn't say that. Look, I don't want to fight with you too. I am going to call a friend and leave, okay? Just calm down. I am sick and tired of this."

I suddenly cooled down. I felt nothing more. He didn't count, I didn't count. There was no struggle, no pain, no nausea. Just dark and total peace.

I woke up in bed in the morning. I had no idea of how I got there, but I didn't care. I thought the shock of Adrian's confession made me wipe off what happened after that. I didn't care, to be honest. I was on holiday so I didn't need to go anywhere.

I went into the kitchen to make a coffee, and Adrian was on the couch, covered with his jumper.

I stood still and watched him sleeping. He was very agitated and was mumbling something... but I couldn't understand. I went into the spare bedroom, took a duvet and covered his trembling body. I couldn't stand watching him suffer and catch a cold. He twitched and opened his eyes. He looked so confused... his green eyes were big and beautiful. Tears started rolling down my cheeks when I realised how much it hurt seeing him in pain. I still very much loved him. 'Stupid heart!' I shouted in my head. 'I hate you, I hate you! Why do you keep doing this to me? After eight years, dammit! Couldn't you have chosen a normal person for once? He's clearly ill, broken, empty, incapable of feeling any emotions.' I kneeled in front of him and kissed his eyes with tenderness. I was suffering for him and for me. He had a problem and I had a bigger one. He couldn't feel a thing, I felt too much. But he tried, he tried hard, I was aware of that. He tried to be like me and others, I know he did. I loved him and I couldn't bear seeing him in that state. We are all broken and crazy to some degree. Who was I to decide that he was more insane than me or any other person? He raised the duvet to let me lay close to him. "I am sorry, Adrian. I was upset. You needed a friend and I let you down."

"Shh, I know. Calm down now, shh, calm down," he murmured. But I kept crying like never before. I was in big, big trouble and the pain was unbearable. I knew I was loving an empty soul, and

I needed to let it out. So I cried and cried and cried. He held me tight and I fell asleep. He stayed for the day, made me coffee and we watched a movie. Like a normal couple. Except nothing was normal about us. I was a thirty-nine-year-old woman, never married, utterly in love with a narcissistic child. 'How can I feel so peaceful in his arms? How can he give me so much joy when he doesn't know what joy is? Poor baby and poor me.'

I thought there was no way I could feel more pain than the last time, but that day I promised myself that I will never, ever, think there was no room in my heart for worse or for better. Because I was going to be wrong. There isn't only one breaking point in a man's life, there are thousands. But we don't know what they mean.

I was dying inside and I was afraid I would never recover. But never say never, right?

"Weren't you supposed to work today?" I asked.

"No. I've got some days off. I was intended to visit my mother this morning. I'll go tomorrow. What about you?" he said as if nothing had happened.

"I am on holiday."

"Perfect timing, isn't it?" he said smiling. I smiled back. It wasn't a happy feeling we had inside us. It was such an oppressive atmosphere in the house. We were both carrying a heavy burden on our shoulders. We were both in terrible pain. Too many conflicts between mind and heart. We were utterly exhausted. He left in the late afternoon. I wanted him to stay... but I said nothing and watched him leaving. He wasn't happy and put no mask on. He was suffering because of her, not me. I knew it, he knew it. I was just a friend to him. A friend with benefits. He needed to go to her. She always had the priority in his life. That's why he always had to leave, that's why he couldn't sleep next to me. He screwed me and ran to her. Double life. And I didn't know. I wondered if he slept with her too. Because he drank a lot and when you are inebriated you do stuff you wouldn't normally do. I guessed I would never know that and I didn't even want to know. I was torturing myself enough.

We took a break, I said I needed one. He didn't fight. He thought I was seeing someone else. I let him believe that and met with my friends whom I neglected for such a long time. I had a little party to ask for forgiveness. Lola came and just when I thought I couldn't take anymore, she asked me about Adrian. I said I didn't see him in a very long time. Which was part of the truth.

"Well, I have been seeing him quite a lot in the last three months."

I thought I'll go irremediably insane in that right second. It didn't happen. I cleared my voice and asked how come.

"It's rather curious, you know. He was with a black-haired girl at a pub where I was with some friends. He came to say hello. The girl was drunk and flirting with all the men inside. He let her do it and spent the time with me. He also had a lot to drink, but I didn't care. You know... I have butterflies in my stomach when he comes close. We talked about you a lot. He speaks so highly of you, Tara. If I didn't know better, I would say that he is in love with you," she said laughing.

I laughed too. "That's crazy," I almost shouted, but I realised it was too loud and said I wasn't feeling well and had the impression that my voice was fading. She handed me a glass of whisky. I drank it all in one go. "Oh, oh, oh... young lady, take it easy now. You know you can't handle alcoholic drinks."

I started laughing and said, "That's beer and cider you're talking about. I can easily drink a bottle of whisky and remain completely sober."

"Get out of here!" she cried out loud.

"Try me," I provoked her. So she poured me another glass. I drank it without blinking. I was grateful for that. I managed to hide my feelings. I was extremely drunk and my legs were weak, but I showed nothing on my face. We danced and laughed like crazy. At some point, Lola came to me and asked if she could invite Adrian to the party. They were often exchanging text messages, she said, that's why she thought of inviting him. He was free and had nothing planned for the evening. I hesitated only for a second; she noticed nothing. "Of course", I said laughing. "If he knows where I live."

"Everybody knows where you live, Tara. You're in the city centre. There is no place easier to find than yours. You, lucky bitch."

"Language, Lola, I do not like these nicknames."

"Sorry. I forgot you're an intellectual," she said sarcastically. I pretended I didn't hear. I knew she didn't mean to hurt me, she was just joking. Her face lit up instantly when Adrian came in, just half an hour later. It was clear that she was in love with him. It broke my heart. Not only because I still loved him too, but because I cared about Lola. She was a sweet girl, naïve and innocent. She had a terrible past, he's been trying to get better for years. I truly cared for her and knowing Adrian's narcissistic personality, it made me feel sad. I was drunk and in pain... 'and for what?!?' I shouted in my head. 'Lola is sweet, really sweet but she's just like him. She cannot feel emotions for other people... except Adrian. They are very similar, both narcissists, although in different ways, definitely a great match. They could live a perfect love story. I am sure she wouldn't mind sharing him with his ex. It's not my place to interfere, I will let them be.'

I completely ignored Adrian and moved around to speak with each of my guests. I was wasted, but I didn't care. I had to drink even more although I was feeling sick. I wanted to see if the pain goes away, the way people say. That's their excuse, 'I drink to forget, to stop suffering.'

'Really?' I thought, 'I still feel pain, I still remember. I still love and want him. This boy who likes drinking more than loving, this child who lives with his ex and thinks it's normal. This is bullshit. And I feel like shit too! Language, Tara!' I lectured myself. 'Even if people can't hear your thoughts, you should still behave with class. You're better than this.'

I turned around and felt Adrian's eyes on me. I pretended I didn't see anything and danced with my friends. I was walking with uncertainty on my high heels and I badly swayed. Someone put their hands on both sides of my waist to support my weight. "Ohohoho. You sure don't know how to walk in high heels." It was Adrian, of course. I felt offended and replied that weren't my heels, but my drinks. I took his hands off and said that he should never dare to touch me again. "I told you before." It was his turn to feel hurt. Lola stepped in, she didn't hear our conversation but witnessed the whole scene.

"I see that you finally said hello. It was a long time, Adrian, since you last saw Tara. Isn't she looking stunning?" asked Lola.

"Yes, she is," he said, "it seems years since I saw her and I completely forgot her charm."

I was already burning hot from the alcohol levels in my blood, but those words made me feel like I was about to explode in thousands of tiny pieces. I looked at both and excused myself, I needed to go to the toilet. I washed my face with cold water, looked in a mirror and I felt disgusted with myself. My body was lusting for Adrian, it was all written on my face. My heart was pumping fire in my veins. I felt the urge to slap my face and shake my body, to make it see, understand, and stay away. But I wasn't blind, nor deaf or stupid, I knew all that, I just couldn't fight against my heart. Couldn't or wouldn't? I saw my reflection in the mirror, 'Damn, I look good. I would want to sleep with me if I was a man.' I thought. 'Mercy. I am as narcissistic as those two. I should feel ashamed.' But I didn't. It was true, I was just beautiful.

I opened the door to go back in the living room. In front of the door was standing Adrian. He was completely wasted, but he looked good. I felt my body melting... Our eyes met for a moment and I was his and I knew he was mine. He grabbed me and kissed my lips with incredible passion. I felt both bodies filling up with pure fire. I pushed him away. "What's wrong with you?" I meant to shout that he can't do that in public, but I saw some of my friends staring at us on the corridor. I left him standing there and I went to talk to them while Adrian went inside the toilet. "He's drunk, he doesn't know what he's doing."

"We thought he was with Lola," said someone. "But who stands a chance when you are around?"

"There is nothing between us. He's helped me with things, I owe him a great debt of gratitude. That's our relationship, nothing else. I don't know what's gotten into him this evening."

I asked them to forget what they saw and keep it for themselves, "Lola is so much into him. I don't want to break her heart and you don't want that either. Right?" They all agreed and we went back in the living room.

Everybody was very much wasted and we started dancing, only Lola was sitting on the couch, next to Adrian. She was eating from his palm. He put his gaze on me and didn't let me go. I went to the dance floor, and if I turned around, Adrian's eyes were still on me. It felt good. I knew he wanted me, and I was drunk. I felt extremely guilty and sorry for Lola, and I hoped he didn't sleep with her too. 'I knew him first. I am not doing anything on purpose. I am actually ignoring him, everybody knows that. She wouldn't step back if she knew he was sleeping with me. She wouldn't let him in my arms if she knew I loved him. She doesn't have room in her heart for anything other than her pain and Adrian. Understandable. Some people cannot give what they don't have.' I hated myself for thinking all those terrible things. I was such a bad human, a horrible friend. 'I did warn her though. She doesn't want to listen. It's not my fault. She's an adult. I did what I could.' I lied to myself but still felt disgusted with myself, body and stupid heart.

Lola was looking into his eyes, utterly lost. He didn't try to escape... it was clear that he was playing with her. I wanted to shout and slap him in the face, 'You, egocentric brute! Stop playing with people's feelings. It has grave consequences!' But I said nothing and kept dancing. When Lola tried to kiss him again, he suddenly stood up and brought her to dance. She was over the moon. When she went to the toilet, he came to me and said, "You're irresistible. Would you dance with me? You drive me insane."

"No. I will not dance with you and stop messing with Lola!"

"Are you jealous?"

"I wish it was that. She's been through a lot. She doesn't need your dirty games."

"Who said I am playing?"

"Don't play dumb and dumber with me, Adrian."

"She's a good friend of mine. There is nothing between us. Don't worry, I am not trying to seduce your friend. What do you think of me?" he said offended.

"How the heck do you manage to find all these troubled creatures? Do you have some kind of radar that helps you recognise the most distressed souls in town? Let her be, please."

"Are you her lawyer, by chance?"

I almost said the f-word. Instead, I turned around and hugged one of my friends. He hugged me back and tried to kiss me. "Hey, I thought you were gay, man! Really!"

"I am gay, Tara, relax. But you're hot and I thought it was cool to kiss you."

I was in disbelief, I thought for a second, poured another glass of whisky and drank it all up. I then turned around and passionately kissed my gay friend. Everybody stopped whatever they were doing. Lola was standing in the door with the mouth wide opened. Someone went to switch off the music. They were in shock, some for the second time that evening. Total silence in the house. Adrian's face was blank, he wasn't breathing. I looked at my friend, he looked at me and we both started laughing like crazy.

"What is wrong with you guys? We were only playing. He's just a boy."

"So what, he's a boy, Tara? Love has no age. What the heck, you wrote a post about it, remember?" said Lola. "We thought he liked men though. That's why we are in shock."

My gay friend was dying from laughing. "Quit it!" I said, but I started laughing too. Whisky's fault.

"He fancies men and we are not screwing one another, if it's what you all think. We just had some fun. Oh, come on, keep dancing! You, silly people."

Lola was fixing me and had a very weird smile on her face. I went to ask her what was she thinking about.

"Tara, you have sex appeal to sell. I don't think there is a man who wouldn't like to have you and I know some women who fancy you too. God, I would want to make you mine if I was a man. You keep talking about age disparity and so, but how old are you in the end? Thirty-two maybe? What's five years' difference? Especially when it's not apparent? You preach well but act badly. Who is this guy you wrote about? If you really love him, you should go and fight for him."

Adrian couldn't take his eyes off me and I really wanted to kiss him, Lola's words reminded me of how much I loved him and tried to deny my feelings. I looked at Lola and said it wasn't that simple.

"Why? Is he married? In a relationship? A Catholic priest maybe?"

"God, no!" I said, "He said he's free, but I think he's lying to himself. It's really complicated, Lola. Drop it, please. Let's have some fun." It was 3:30am, all my other friends were preparing to leave. Lola looked at Adrian and asked him if he would take her home. He said he was meeting someone else in town later on.

"It's almost 4am. Who goes to meet people at this hour?" asked Lola surprised. I was surprised too.

"Lola, I cannot take you home tonight, another time, all right?" he said with power.

She looked at him and smiled. She didn't need much to feel happy. She could not understand men at all. She could not understand anyone, for that matter. Not even herself. Poor girl.

When they left I closed the door and started to clean up when my phone rang, a text message sound. I thought some of my friends left something behind so I checked to see who it was. "I am outside." I started shivering. I seriously didn't expect that. I knew he didn't want to take Lola home, but I had no idea he lied just to meet up with me. I thought he went home to his girlfriend, or ex-girlfriend, or whatever she was. I hesitated to press the button, but I did it in the end. I wanted to see him, I really deeply wanted that. And I felt ashamed, guilty and extremely disgusted. I had been trying to resist, but I was too weak. I needed to feel loved... even if only for a few minutes. My heart and soul were in abstinence, so was my body. I wanted to feel Adrian on and inside me. I was dependent of his touches. I knew it was wrong, I knew I was going to pay for a couple of hours of bliss, but I decided it was all worth it. I really, deeply loved that cruel boy. I drank another glass of whisky to force my mind to shut up.

The flat door was locked, I went downstairs to open it. I heard him running down the corridor, so he rushed inside where I was waiting for him. He took me into his arms, held me tight and whispered how much he missed me and that was killing him. I placed my hands on both sides of his face, looked him in the eyes to see if it was another of his calculations. But they were filled with pure love. 'Eyes are the soul's mirror. They cannot lie.' I lied to myself instead, deliberately. He was lusting for me and I was lusting for him. He put his hands on me and crushed my body with his powerful hands. He was so hungry, we were both hungry. Insatiable. "I am not lying to you or myself, I am a free man, free to make love to you. Do you hear me, woman?!" His husky voice rolled over my skin, making my body shivering from extreme excitement.

And he had me right there, standing, with my dress on, leaning against the wall. He didn't even try to take it off. He didn't do it with his clothes either. We couldn't waste time getting naked. "You are so damn sexy!" he whispered several times while inside me.

'He is so my size. I didn't have a man inside my body for eight years. I never enjoyed having intercourse. It hurt so much. I had no sexual life. I am made of flesh too. I am just human. I deserve this.' I kept repeating in my head... like I needed a reason for all that turpitude.

Barely breathing, we looked into each other eyes and defeated I said, "What's going to happen with us, Adrian? Someone put a twisted love spell on us. We cannot be together, but we cannot stay apart. We are doomed. Cursed." He sealed my mouth with the most tender kiss I ever felt. My body felt electrified and I screamed in ecstasy again. "You are my weakness. I cannot say no to you. Ever." He took my hand and kissed the palm, licking and biting on it softly.

"Oh, Adrian... what are you doing to me?" He kept kissing my palm until I couldn't bear anymore. He knew it was something I was crazy about. Another erogenous area of my body... I had many others, not sure he managed to discover all of them. I took his hand and went into the bedroom. I let my dress fall on the floor. I stood in front of him in a red lace thong and bra, and a pair of black holds up. He remained in adoration. "You have a perfect, absolutely perfect figure. No wonder so many people feel the urge to kiss you. I couldn't take my eyes off you since I first saw you."

I pushed him on the bed and his hand went to switch off the light. "Leave it. Women are used to switching the light off because they are bashful or ashamed of their body. I am none of these things. I don't think my body is flawless, the cellulite is a very bad intruder, I am aware of that, but I can't do anything about it. I accepted it." He said he couldn't see any on my body and I loved him for lying to me. I kissed his lips avidly. I licked them, bit them softly, and pushed my tongue inside his mouth. They fought and embraced one another with infinite pathos. He stroked my arms and whispered, "I wanted to do this for the whole evening." He moved his lips on my back, "and this," my thighs, "and this," and he sprinkled countless tiny bites and kisses on every inch of my skin. My body was utterly consumed by desire. I was all shaking, moaning in delirium. He put his teeth around my thong and slowly slid them over my legs. I thought I was going to faint. His hands were everywhere and none of us could wait any longer. I dug my nails into his skin and abandoned myself into a frantic dance of mind-blowing emotions.

'He is my size.' I thought again. 'Where would I find another one to drive me on this edge? He makes me cry and burn in hell, but he also gives my body so much pleasure. I am sure he cannot do this with any other woman. His body pulses only when he's with me. These moments wipe away all the struggles. It is all worth it.'

"I dreamt of you being naked in front of me like you are right now so many, many times. And I felt you around my body every night. But dreams are nothing compared to this reality. I never felt this way," his husky voice murmured.

I screamed and cried in ecstasy, again and again, and again. We rested out of breath for a few minutes. I went to wash myself with cold water, he copied me... I loved when he cleaned himself for me. It was a sign of respect. Respect aroused me like nothing else. And I kissed him and we started it all over again, then again. We were both utterly insatiable. It was psychedelic.

We slept until midday. I woke him up with a kiss, he looked at the phone, jumped out of bed, dressed up in a few seconds and rushed out without a word. My eyes filled with tears, 'What did you expect? He doesn't love you, his body wants you. That's all. Animal instinct! You're a pathetic woman. You could have anyone and instead, you are humiliating yourself every time he touches you. Maybe he comes to see you only when she says no. Think, Tara, think. It would explain why he's so hooked to his phone and rushes away when he gets a text message. They are a family, you're just a beautiful body under a curse. Stop this vicious circle, Tara! Stop making a fool of women's category. He's going to her. She's the one he really cares for. The only woman in his life. You deserve a man who gives you the priority. You deserve so much better. You know you can have it. Fight!' I knew that my brain was right and I promised myself once more, that I won't be falling into his trap ever again.

How many times I swore that before?! I lost count. I felt terribly ashamed and impotent.

POISON

That afternoon I went on a date with another guy from the website. He was short, petite if you want, and bold. Definitely not my type. But then I wondered who my type was? Was Adrian my type? 'Do I even have a type?' I never asked myself, but short and bold was clearly out of discussion. Except that I liked him.

It was instant chemistry between us and I hated my heart for liking someone that my brain refused to consider. Same old story, my heart says yes, my mind shouts no, or the other way around. A constant fracas, just to make everything so damn harder. 'Why can't you work together? Why can't you reach to an agreement? Yes, you two, mind and body. It is you I am talking to. You are sabotaging one another. Can't you realise that you are one?'

We spent the whole afternoon together and I was happy and at peace in a very strange way. He invited me to go on a trip the next day and we went to have a walk in a forest. The view was breathtaking, and at some point I stopped and observed the greatness of Mother Nature in silence. Overwhelmed by the beauty of it, a few random tears dropped out of my eyes. 'Adrian and I went nowhere together. We've never seen or shared anything, except body fluids.' It hurt. He was looking at me with profound admiration. "You're an amazing person. I've never met anyone like you. The people I know don't see what you see. Tara, I will be out of town for the next three weeks, but I would very much like to see you when I come back. What do you say?"

"Yes. I'd like to see you too." I didn't tell him that it wasn't only nature's beauty that made me cry. It wasn't right.

"Come, let's have lunch in here and maybe dinner in town tonight." And we went to look for a suitable place. Unfortunately, it was out of season and only one was open but was full. I was starving and he was too. I had a chocolate bar and an apple in my bag, we sat on a bench and shared. It was the best lunch I had in months. We kept walking and when he grabbed my hand, I didn't show resistance. Back in town, he took me to his favourite restaurant. It was a rustic place, very intimate. I loved it. And I loved the food too, except it was too expensive and I had to tell him I didn't fancy places like that. I couldn't tell him that I earned less in a day of work than we paid for a dinner in there. And although he didn't allow me to pay, I felt guilty for letting him spend that much. We went for another walk in town, he wasn't able to let me go. Just before midnight, I was in a desperate need of a toilet and I saw my chance to escape. He hugged me tight and I left in a rush.

I thought of him a lot and I was truly grateful that I could take my mind off Adrian. That week I decided to set my phone to switch off at 9pm. I needed to rest more and avoid being bothered. On Saturday morning at 5, when it was set up to turn on, my phone informed me I had a text. I was afraid it was from home, maybe something happened, but I read, "Are you awake?" and I felt like I was in Heaven. Adrian was thinking of me at 5 in the morning. It was clear he was missing me and I was always in his mind. I answered back that I was. No other text came through that day or the following one. I was very confused but didn't ask. On Tuesday morning at 5, I got another text and when I checked, it was from Lola, "I need to talk to you."

'Lola writes me at 5am? Something must have happened.' I called her right away, but she didn't pick up. I worried. Three hours later she sent me a text asking me what was wrong. Something was not quite right indeed so I checked the date and hour of the text from 5am. It was sent at 9:27 of the night before, but because my phone was off, I only got the notification first thing in the morning. I didn't consider that at all. That meant that Adrian wrote me in the evening or night of Friday, as always. I felt stupid. I wanted to make sure, but the text was gone. Same as the number.

When he didn't reply, I got upset and deleted all the conversations with him along with the number. And that wasn't the first time. I have been trying to get over him, to fight and resist the temptation of contacting him right from the start. And if I didn't write, he didn't either, except for Fridays. When he was drunk and horny. He must have thought I was crazy to send him a text at that hour in the morning. He didn't know I had decided to set my phone to switch off at 9 of every evening, just to avoid falling into his regular sex traps. On Saturday he didn't reply because he wasn't free anymore, he was with his family and her... 'Tara, you're pathetic.'

Lola and I agreed to meet in a week after I explained her the misunderstanding.

I thought enough was enough and for the first in my life, I understood what a sick love feels like. I understood how easy is to become one of those women who cry and shout never again, and the next day are on their knees praying God to make him come back to them. Emptied of dignity and self-esteem. Destructive relationships that never end.

And I used to judge these women, even deride them for their weakness. 'There are so many men in this world, you don't have to humiliate themselves like that. You don't have to accept this treatment. Close the door, huddle up and move on.' As if it was that easy. I was dead wrong again. I realised with infinite shame that you have no right to judge a situation you've never lived. Not ever. And even if you live a similar experience, don't criticise those who don't act like you. We are all unique. Our minds work in different ways, our feelings are almost never the same. Our reactions, instincts, decisions could be extremely different. It depends on so many factors.

I was one of those poor women now... except my situation was infinitely worse. I had many more reasons to be blamed and despised for. I was almost forty and in love with a boy who was twelve years younger than me. He wasn't' my husband, I had no children of his. I was independent and incredibly beautiful. I could have anyone and I should have learned something about love and men by now. I was supposed to be wiser and smarter. But I acted like a teenager, in love for the first time with the only man on Earth. I honestly hated myself. It was like having two minds inside my head, one knew it was wrong to allow this situation to continue, and the other one didn't give a damn about anything. In the end, it was just the mind fighting against the heart. They both knew it was not healthy, but my heart decided to pay the price because it was all worth it. One hour of happiness was better than nothing. Not matter how many reasons the brain brought on the table, the heart always won. Stupid heart.

The petit guy stayed away for three weeks, a period in which I saw Adrian once to tell him I couldn't go on like this. I sent him an email, as I didn't have his number anymore, "Would you please come to see me?" He came over the very next evening. He didn't look happy, I was devastated. "We can't keep doing this. You cannot give me what I need."

"What do you need, Tara?"

"Love. I need to be loved."

"You know my feelings for you."

"What feelings? Love? Do you love me? Do you have any idea of what that means... how it feels? You don't even love yourself. How could you give me something you don't have?"

He said I was right, "It was not healthy. This is the last time, Tara. I won't be coming back next time you call."

"I never called you!" I shouted.

"No, you sent emails."

He blamed it all on me. I was the one playing. I was the one pushing him away. I was the one wanting to keep it a secret. I was the one abusing him.

"What do I keep it a secret, Adrian? What would you call what's between us? Friends with benefits? We are not friends. Sex mates? Yes, that's more like it. I don't want people to think I need a younger boy to screw me. It's humiliating."

"I thought we made love."

"I made love, you had sex."

"Isn't the same thing?"

There was no point replying.

We both loved each other in a way none of us could understand. Our minds were antipodal. We spoke different languages, I was from Venus, he was from Mars. There was no secret. It's science, like Maths, but then again, Maths is a perfect science, you cannot argue with the fact that two plus two equals four, but a human can learn a different language. Everybody can change if they wanted. I wondered myself if I tried to understand him...I have tried, so, so very hard... but he didn't speak the language of other men either. He spoke a language only he could comprehend. I looked at him with infinite pain, "We were not destined to be together. We both knew that..."

"I didn't know that. I am not God. Are you?"

"You know what I mean," I said.

"No, Tara, I never know what you mean. One minute you tell me you love me, the next one you say we should not see each other anymore. You're very inconsistent."

"*I* am inconsistent? What about you? You only contact me when your body needs another body! And if I want to see you again, I have to accept that and pretend I am okay with it. Well, I am not, and you know it. I told you so many times."

"That's not true. I invited you out, we went for dinners. I wanted to stay close to you when we met outside by chance, but you never allowed me to touch you in public. Like you felt ashamed."

"I wanted to kiss you in public, I was never ashamed! I was proud if something. So many times I wanted to shout and let everyone know you were mine! I thought of you... I didn't want to risk your reputation."

"You thought of me?! What reputation? What are you talking about?"

I was sobbing. My heart was fighting again. My mind was trying to stick with the decision I took so many times, 'For the love of God, stop this. It is not healthy. You deserve someone to love you. Let him be. Act like a woman. He is destroying you. You are simply wrong one for another.' "I met someone." I said all of a sudden.

He looked at me in shock. "Why are you telling me this?"

"I don't know."

"Well, I am happy for you." I was lying in the bed and he was sitting on the border of it. He stood up to leave. I grabbed his hand. I was utterly desperate. My heart shut the brain down. I couldn't let him go.

"What do you want?" he asked with a fainted voice.

"I don't want you to go. I am sorry. I know it's wrong and I know I am crazy... crazy for you." I said while thousands of enormous tears were falling down my cheeks. Adrian sat back and wiped my tears off with his thumb. That gesture always made me think he loved me. 'No person would do that if they were not loving.' I ignored his ex-thing. We both did that, it was a tacit understanding.

"Tara... how can you say you love me and meet other people?"

"You are living under the same roof with your ex."

"It's not the same thing. She's my oldest friend. My family is used having her around. I owe her a lot."

I hated hearing those words. 'It is not right, not normal. How could he not realise that? You cannot live with your ex-boyfriend or girlfriend in your parents' house. You were not married, there is no excuse. Unless they are ill, or something. She was perfectly sane.' I wanted to shout and shake his body... to make him understand, instead I kissed him on the lips. He was surprised, but didn't pull back. I kissed him again. He put his hands on the sides of my face and looked into my eyes, "I hate when you meet other men."

I was shocked. He never ever showed any jealousy signs before. "What? I thought you didn't care."

"I never, ever, could stand anyone looking at you. I can't control myself. It makes me go crazy. I cannot think or reason. I fell ill so many times because of that. Do you remember when I met you in that pub on South Street?"

I moved my head side to side.

"You were with some colleagues. There weren't many chairs, so you were sharing the chair with one of these colleagues. I waved at you, but you pretended not to see me, as usual. I sat in front of you for fifteen minutes when you raised your head to look at me and still didn't say hello. Your colleague went to grab some food, when he came back, there was a free chair, but he sat on your chair again. Now, why would he do that if he wasn't hitting on you? I thought I'll go insane. I left and you sent me a text to ask me why. I told you I didn't feel well. Remember now?"

"Yes. I remember you didn't look well."

"I thought I'd die that night. I went home and started to work with my mind. It wasn't me. I never felt that way. I couldn't allow my brain to go there again. I can't feel this way. I never, ever, felt jealous in all my life before I met you."

'Omg, he loves me... he really loved me.' I thought in that instance. It was the only time when his actions proved that.

"Adrian, you fought against your feelings for me. You talked yourself out of love. How could you do that? Why didn't you tell me? You never speak to me! It's okay to feel jealousy when you love someone."

"Do you?! Feel jealousy, I mean?" he asked.

"No... but..." I tried to explain.

"You don't love me then?" he enquired.

"I trust you. Your heart belongs to me. You couldn't kiss me when you were with your girlfriend. I know you wouldn't do this to me," I said in a low voice.

"I trust you too... I just don't trust others, you are so beautiful and sexy."

And here we were again. Doubting and questioning everything. I felt so guilty... my heart was overwhelmed by pain, 'I hurt him. I left him alone. Why haven't I noticed that? How can I say I am intuitive, sensitive, or smart? I stepped on his dignity as much as he stepped on mine's. We are even. I am so arrogant!' I hugged him tight and murmured, "I had no idea you thought this way. I am really sorry. It was never my intention to do you any harm. Forgive me, please, forgive me." I looked into his eyes... there was such a mix of feelings, love, pain, anger, desperation, confusion. I didn't like it. "Come to bed with me. I want to feel you close. Please."

"You said you met someone."

"I don't love him."

I took his jacket off. He hesitated for a second. I was still crying so he wiped my tears off. I kissed his beautiful lips with pathos.

"I missed you so much," he murmured kissing my neck. "You are becoming more and more beautiful with every passing day." He didn't pay me compliments as often as I wanted, but when he did, they made me feel like he loved me. He used to say that compliments should be rare, otherwise they'll lose the meaning. I disagreed. Totally. I never had enough of kind remarks.

He stroked my back, I pulled his hair. We kissed like we were fighting. Our breaths exhaled fire... I felt his body pulsing, I was lusting for him and he made me wait. I think that the moment he finally realised the immensity of the power he had over me.

His lips had to touch every inch of my body first. He stopped in a few places more and made me groan and scream in pleasure. I watched him caressing my body with his hands and lips.

"Your skin is softer than silk, and your scent is pure bliss," he said in a rasping voice. That compliment was my favourite. I dug my nails deep into his skin, "You drive me crazy." He bit my neck with strength. I screamed in real pain. "You left marks on my skin. Jesus! Why did you do that for?"

"You're mine. Only and forever mine," he whispered under some sort of spell.

Unbelievable how much pleasure that crazy statement gave me. I should have been scared, but I was happy. Absolutely ridiculous. It wasn't real. 'He wants everybody to know I am taken. He loves me. Did you hear that mind? He loves me.' My mind didn't reply. It was switched off. As always when I was with Adrian.

His hands were everywhere. Every kiss, every single touch, every word, or murmur charged my body with electricity. I left the earth and reached the paradise.

"Can I have you?" he asked me timidly.

"Always," I murmured in his ear. I felt the weight of his body on mine. I held my breath. He sealed my mouth with a lascivious kiss. In ecstasy, I screamed, "Oh, Adrian, you're just my size. Please don't ever stop making love to me." Our bodies, minds, and souls were one. There was no tomorrow. His body pulsed and I cried. He held me tight until I fell asleep. Then he left and I wanted to shout and beg him to stay. I knew he was going to her. 'Where are you going? Why? Does she give you more than I do? Why can't you stay with me? I live alone, you're free in here. We are both free people. Nobody will disturb us. How can you not appreciate that? Love has all the answers. Please stay with me, I beg you.' But I stood in silence and wondered if I will survive without him.

I promised myself I would never speak about his ex with him, and he never did that either. But he used to check his phone very often. I hated that so much. I told him right away, but he didn't care. He cared only for her. He needed to be present in her life. He needed to have someone to take care of. He needed to feel that he was needed. To make him feel good about himself. 'Why doesn't he take care of me then? I need him more than her. She's English, she's got a family in here. I am all alone.' The truth is that I was a very independent woman and never asked for help. I didn't fit in his world, I didn't make him feel useful. And that made me be just a passenger in his life. She was the one he was convinced will never leave him because she needed him. They had a pact and he was sticking to it. I thought they were really meant one for another. An absolute match. In all and for all. They didn't have a sexual life, but that was easy to fix as long as I was always there, ready to let him in. Even begged him never to stop. And I was sure that bodies like mine were everywhere. He would help her pay the bills, and screw someone else. A perfect relationship to last a lifetime. She had what she needed and he had the same. Plus me. I honestly felt disgusted by me, him and all that sick situation.

I wondered if they ever thought of all these things, if they realised it was a very twisted situation. Were they only best friends, or they screwed each other every time they were drunk? Maybe even convinced themselves it was perfectly normal. What are friends for? Right?

What if they were often doing that? In the end, he drank a lot... You don't control yourself when you're drunk. But what if he had told me? Would I still have opened my legs when he wanted me? I hope I didn't.

I guess I'll never know that for sure. I was grateful he never mentioned any of that.

What you don't know can't hurt you, right?

LOLA

That evening, at 7, I met Lola. She was in obvious distress. I didn't ask, I waited for her to start. At some point, she burst into tears, "Tara. I am in love with Adrian. I cannot stop thinking about him. I am dying."

I knew that already. I looked at her and saw me. I felt the urge to shake her, to shout and kick, 'Stay away from him. He'll make you go insane.' Instead, I coldly asked, "Have you told him?"

"No. I am too afraid. But he can't possibly not know."

"Has he made a move on you? Did he give you any hope?"

"No, but we are seeing each other twice a week, sometimes even more."

I forced my heart to slow down its beats. Lola was saying things I was not aware of. "How come you two meet so often?"

"We have friends in common."

"So you meet with other friends?" I asked trying to understand the real situation. I was under the impression that Lola had misinterpreted everything. It wouldn't have been the first time.

"No, just the two of us. He adores bowling. We meet in a place near the University, twice a week. He's the one asking me to go. I sometimes invite other people. I used to, at least. Not anymore. I want him just for myself and he doesn't seem to be bothered."

I was stabbed directly in the heart. I didn't expect that. He never mentioned Lola.

"Do you think he feels the same for you?"

"Why else would he spend so much time with me? All my friends say it's pretty clear."

It hadn't been Lola misinterpreting everything, I was. My heart started to bleed. I was feeling the blood coming out in cascades out of my chest. I looked down to make sure it wasn't real. Lola didn't notice.

"Why don't you ask him then? I would do that if I was you," I tried to sound normal.

"It's easy for you to say. You're different. Who'd say no to you?"

I felt like crying, 'If only... ' "Lola, what are you planning to do?"

"I don't know. That's why I came to you. You're the expert," she said.

"Are you kidding me? I am almost forty and I have never been married. I didn't have a relationship in eight years!" I shouted exhausted. I couldn't bear any more. It was too much.

Lola looked at me surprised, "Are you okay, Tara? You don't look so well."

'Thank God you noticed,' I thought with anger. 'You don't see anything except your pain.' I wasn't going to tell her that, of course. Lola was a sweet girl. She wouldn't hurt a fly. I thought I should feel guilty for having those thoughts about her, but it was all true. She wasn't mean, but she was a very selfish person. She never really cared for anyone. I was happy she had no sisters or brothers, but I was sad because she had no one really. That's why I cared for her, unconditionally. I felt she needed it. She was raised by her aunt because her parents had a very weird relationship. They never got married and her mother couldn't afford to raise her. Her father wasn't blessed with fatherly instincts. Lola didn't love her parents. Why would she anyway? For what? They only conceived her... who knows in what context they left her live with her aunt. On the other hand, her aunt was a very delicate woman. I met her a few times. She went to church daily and was a true believer. She loved her niece with all her heart. Lola was not able to exchange the feeling. I guess her family's story made her become insensitive. She moved out of her aunt's house to go to University and never went back. She preferred sharing the house with colleagues or random people. That's how we met. She felt very alone and needed to be surrounded by humans all the time. Animals were not her thing. Too much responsibility, too much work and no actual reward. She needed words and human contact. She had countless friends... She calls them that, I wouldn't. But I am different. Lola told me everything about her life, although she forgot to mention that she was incapable of loving. Of course, she was completely unaware of that. I noticed her cold heart right from the start. Her personality was no secret for me while I was living with her. Things had changed and I was shocked to hear her saying that she was so deeply in love with the man I was loving. What a miserable situation. What twisted mind's planned this? But Adrian wasn't mine, nobody knew about us. And we said *Adios* the day before. She was free to have him. They were very much alike.

"I am fine, don't worry about me. I am sorry I yelled at you. I am just tired, didn't sleep much last night," I said in the end.

"Were you with someone?"

"No. Just with my books. Lola, I don't know what would you want to hear from me. As I said, if I were you, I would bluntly ask him. Or send him a text. The technology is an amazing invention. Use it."

"This is very important to me. I wouldn't write it in a text. It's too cold. By the way, do you want to come with us this Friday evening?"

"Whatever you think it's best, just ask him, all right? Dialogue is always the way. Come where?"

"Dancing. All of our friends will be there. Adrian too."

"Right... some people sent me a text, now that you mention it. I have completely forgotten to reply to them. No, thank you, I won't be joining you."

"Tara, you never go out. You should. It's not good being always alone."

"I am a solitary person, that's why I moved here. I want to be alone. I love peace and quiet. Going out is such a waste of time for me. Sorry."

"That's fine, we are all different. But you'll come for dinner once. All your ex-housemates asked about you, they will be happy to see you," she said with a sweet voice.

"Lola, by the way, you've said something about Adrian's ex. Are you sure they are not back together? What do you know about that? Don't reveal him your feelings before making sure they are not together."

"Have I? Don't remember that." She hadn't, I just wanted to make her aware.

Lola continued, very sure of herself, "He's sworn they are not together, just childhood friends. Did he tell you that she lives with his father's family? I mean, they are all living under the same roof. It's a weird story. But it's quite common in the modern society. I know some other people living under the same roof with their exes. You know, they are in a relationship, move together in the same house. The love burns out, they fell in love with other people but don't want to look for a different house. So they agree to hang around in the same places, living separate lives. It doesn't worry me. I heard this so many times. They are friends since they were children, are like brother and sister."

That brother and sister statement made me feel sick. "I didn't know they were dividing a house," I lied. "Doesn't this make you think there is something complicated going on?" I tried to raise doubt. As crazy and false does this sound, I truly didn't want her to live the same nightmare I was living. Maybe I deserved that, but she didn't. I didn't know what else to do. I couldn't just tell her about him and me. Tell her what? That he had a great power over me? That he was my size and screwed me whenever he pleased? I just couldn't.

"What do you mean when you say you're not worried as it's pretty common? I never heard of such a situation. I find it abnormal. And I thought Italian men were crazy living with their parents until they die. I couldn't get my mind around that style of life. But this is infinite times more insane. I understand living under the same roof when you were married or have children together. There are good reasons to keep living together, but they were never married. Or were they? Maybe they have children together. What do you know about that? I would be worried if I were you." I realised my mind was going crazy and doubted every single thing. It was not good.

"Well, it's good you are not me then. No, they were not married, Tara! Why would you think that? He wouldn't keep that a secret. I went to visit a few times. We had dinner with all his family, and she was there too. They did seem pretty close, now that you make me think about it. I don't know. I saw no children around. Nah, Adrian doesn't have children. He would tell me if he had, don't you think? Anyway, he said they are childhood friends. I trust him. Why would he lie about it? I trust him," she concluded with confidence.

'Why would he indeed? She went to visit? He'd never asked me to visit him! What a player. He made such a fool of me... I made a fool of myself. He didn't lie, he just omitted to tell me. That's how men think, if they don't mention, it's not a sin. I am so damn pathetic.' "Lola, I don't know what to think, you saw them together, you know better. Just be careful, all right? The guy is troubled. That's the only thing I can tell you for sure," I said defeated.

"I am troubled too, you know. We have a lot in common. I am positive he likes me, and I am in a very good position. If I was to listen to my friends, he's definitely in love with me."

'Sure he is. Just like I thought. This boy is the devil himself. Lola was easy to play, but I have never been fooled in my whole life. Until now. And by whom? The same man she loves. Something to be proud of, Tara. Well done, very well done.' I thought with sarcasm and profound disgust.

"A lot in common? Like what?" I asked ironically; I really failed to see what things they had in common, except for the incapability of loving others.

Lola didn't pick up on my tone of voice. As I said, she wasn't good at understanding people, tones, or signs. She needed concrete words or facts. Just like Adrian.

"Well, I like going to the cinema and we went together several times. We like going out, we like spending time together, we like food, bowling... there are many things we both like."

'Do you like breathing?' I almost shouted. But that was mean and Lola didn't deserve that. She had no idea I was crazy about Adrian. It was not right punishing her for something she was not guilty of. "I didn't know you like bowling," I said with a forced smiled on my face.

"To be honest, I didn't use to. I started going when he asked me to join him... Now I like it very much. It's a lot of fun. He laughs all the time. He's a very happy person. How can you say he's troubled?"

'You just do whatever he wants, because you love him. You don't like bowling, you like spending time with him. You need people around, just like him. That's what you have in common. He laughs and he's happy? Are we talking about the same person in here?' It was a ridiculous question to ask myself. 'He might have a double personality. It would all make sense. I know he's got several issues. Dear lord. He could be a serial killer!' I thought, but discharged the idea immediately. Everything, but that. I was mean, too mean. I had no right. All of us have issues. No one is completely sane. What's sane and what's insane in the end? Who decided that? I shook my head with power to make that dreadful thought to go away. It was nonsense. 'What if he is truly happy with her?

What if she makes him laugh? I never considered that. Maybe she's the one he really loves.' That last idea hurt even more, but I knew you couldn't force someone to love you. 'If he loves her, then be it.'

"I am glad to hear that you are both having fun. Adrian gave me the impression of a very unhappy person. I almost never saw him laughing. Maybe it's me who makes him feel that way."

"Hmm… now that you mentioned it, I did notice that he's different when you are present. Take your party, for example, he was upset and his behaviour wasn't like the one I knew. You might be right, Tara. It is you who makes him be different. That's really, really weird. He might feel intimidated by you. I know a lot of people who feel that way in your presence."

"What are you talking about? Why would they feel intimidated?"

"Well, you have like an aura around you. You dress and walk like someone very important. It's like you're from a very high social class. Blue blood or something."

I looked at her in disbelief. I didn't like what she was saying. I never intended to make people feeling that way about me. It made me feel terrible. "Are you saying that people think I am arrogant? That I somehow try to make them feel inferior? God!"

"No, no I didn't mean that. You are a very friendly person, everybody likes you. Nobody thinks you're arrogant! It's the way they perceive your presence. You're like a queen. High heels, always so elegant, great figure. It's good, trust me."

"It doesn't sound good to me, Lola. I am really hurt. I am a simple person, just like you."

"Oh, you're a person, all right, but nothing like me or other people I know. You remind me of a teacher of mine... Yeah, I thought about that when I first saw you. She looked like a queen too. Maybe you are related."

"Was she from Eastern Europe too? Maybe we are spies!"

Lola didn't start laughing as I was expecting. She looked at me carefully as to make sure I wasn't crazy or something.

"Oh, come on. I was joking! You didn't believe that, did you?"

"Jesus, Tara! I did think that for a second. You need to work on your expressions when you are messing around. You, being a spy, not such an absurd idea in the end. You could easily be one. Hmmm...Are you?"

I burst into laughter and Lola joined in. To be honest, I always wanted to be a spy. For years, I hoped that I would receive an email one day, with a secret destination and offered that sort of job. I would have earned enough money to go on a holiday at least once in my life!

I asked Lola if she had dinner, she shook her head, "No" so I said I'll make something quick. I opened the cupboards, looked inside, and decided I would make *pasta e fagioli*. It was a basic Italian dish with small pasta shapes and beans. This recipe was a personal interpretation. I knew she would like that dish. Everybody loved my pasta e fagioli.

Lola went to the toilet. I took an onion, peeled the skin off, and minced it. I placed a saucepan on the hob and turned it on. I then took a pack of smoked bacon from the fridge, cut some small pieces with a lot of fat on them and threw them in the pan. I stirred for a minute and added the minced onion. I closed the door and opened the window to avoid filling the whole house with the smell of food. Couldn't stand that. I put the kettle on. From the cupboard, I took a can of chickpeas and one of kidney beans, opened them both and dumped the contents inside a drain basket water, rinsed well and thrown everything into the saucepan, added hot water from the kettle and covered it with a lid.

When Lola came back, I offered her a hot tea and said it would be ready in ten minutes. She said it smelled delicious and was starving. I was too. She looked at me with profound admiration, "Earlier on you said you are a regular person, just like me. Tara, you are everything, but regular. I don't know what you're cooking, but you are the fastest cook I ever saw in action. In less than three minutes you prepared food for two people and made me a tea. It would take me forty minutes just to decide what to cook. Other one hour - if I am lucky - to gather all I need, then maybe hours to cook. You are unbelievable."

"You are exaggerating. First, you don't know what I am cooking or if it's good. Secondly, it is canned food. Nothing extraordinary about that. Everyone can do it."

"You're too modest. I couldn't do that. Let's wait and see and I'll be honest. Either way, you are fast."

I continued cooking. Took the lid off, added half of a pack of small shaped pasta, seasoned with my special herb from my country - similar to thyme - put the lid on and announced, "Five minutes."

"That's not canned food! You're lying!"

I didn't reply, I didn't think it was a big deal. I learned to cook when I was seven. It was a joke for me.

Lola put the cutlery on the table. I took some cheese from the fridge, opened a jar of Kalamata olives and put everything on the table. I had no bread or crackers, but the pasta e fagioli didn't need that. Too many carbohydrates.

She started eating cheese and olives. I loved olives, but I couldn't stand cheese. Nevertheless, I always had these two in the house. Just in case. I learned that from my mother. Always have food stored, especially cans. I guess it was a war lesson.

I turned off the hob, took two white bowls from the shelf and filled them with the food. It smelled divine. It was a long time since I last cooked that. I was famished and couldn't wait to try it.

I placed a bowl in front of Lola and said, "Bon appétit!"

Lola looked at the steaming bowl, then at me and shouted, "You're crazy. You know that, right? This is a proper meal and it looks utterly delicious! Thank you so, so much!!!"

I thought of Adrian. I always wanted to cook for him... every evening. My eyes filled with tears.

"I am sorry, I didn't mean to hurt you," said Lola thinking it was because of her statement.

"No, it's not you Lola. Don't be silly. This food reminds me of someone."

"Is it your family? It's a Romanian dish, right?"

"Yes, family. But no, it's not Romanian. It's a combination of two recipes, one Romanian and one Italian. A personal interpretation, like most of my recipes; I added other stuff that was not supposed to be in this dish. I hope you like it."

Lola blew on her spoon, I didn't. I love hot food. It's bad for your teeth though, don't do that.

She chewed the food, "My goodness, it is magnificent! I have never tried anything like this before. I have no idea of what I am eating. I want the recipe. I am so in love!!"

"What, with me?" I joked.

"If I didn't like men, I would totally be in love with you. Who wouldn't? But I was referring to your cooking skills and this dish. I cannot believe you made something so tasty in less than fifteen minutes. What are you? A witch?"

"Indeed I am. You got me! By the way, you cannot love someone just because they are good cooks. That's a heart decision. And your heart could decide to love a serial killer," I said with sadness.

"Jesus! Are you in love with a person like that? I truly hope not."

"No, thank God for that! That would be the ultimate punishment and I don't deserve that."

We laughed and joked about many things. I cared for Lola, I really did, although I knew she didn't. I am sure she believed she cared for me too. It wasn't her fault. You cannot force your heart to feel love for someone. She had no room in her heart. Too much pain. She forgot about Adrian. I didn't. I would have loved him to be there and eat with us. I was maybe sicker than he was. Still loving him after all those things Lola's told me. I knew he felt alone... but then again, what did I know about him? He seemed to have shown me an entirely different side of him.

She hugged me tight when she left. I felt sorry for her. She was in love with the most unsettled individual I ever met until that day. She was putting herself in trouble. Exactly like me. I was not angry, I was not jealous, I was just sad.

I went to bed straight away. I didn't need the hot water bottle anymore. It was warm enough.

THE PLAGUE

It was July. At the end of it, my petit admirer came back. He called me right away. We went for a long walk on the riverside.

"I talked about you continuously. All my friends know you and everybody wants to meet you. I am not going to present you to them."

"Why not? You just said they want to meet me."

"I am afraid they will take you from me. They are taller and more handsome than me. I cannot take that risk."

I laughed. He complimented me often. I loved it and I needed it more than anything. It was dark when we sat on a bench and he asked me if he could kiss me. I said it was all right. I didn't know what to expect. Part of me wanted to find a reason to reject him. My heart belonged to someone else. But when his lips touched mine, they fitted to perfection. He was a great kisser and I was impressed. We couldn't take our mouths away one from another. We kissed for hours, then he asked me if I wanted to go home with him. I declined and said I was tired.

He accompanied me home and we kissed goodnight. He sent me a beautiful text when he got to his place. I turned my phone on like I had a feeling he was going to text me. It made me feel loved, appreciated, desired, and finally understood. He was delivering what I was needing. I was thrilled. We'd seen each other five times in two weeks. I still didn't go home with him. I never invited him to mine either. I didn't want to make love to him. My body felt no attraction. I loved his kisses though. Immensely. I knew it couldn't last forever. He was a man, different expectations.

Things were going well with my job. My working hours made it easy to avoid Adrian. One evening, Lola send me a desperate text, "I made a move on him and he said he's in love with someone else."

"I am sorry Lola. It must be his ex. I am truly sorry."

"No, it's not his ex, but didn't want to say who."

I felt a sudden pain in my heart. I knew it was me, I sensed it. A woman always feels when she's loved or not. When she's betrayed or mocked on. We are aware of this power, but we don't trust our instincts. Maybe we got it wrong in the past and we just chose to ignore and shut it off. Our sixth sense is sometimes unreliable, we think. But how can we tell when someone gives us so much love and happiness, and two minutes after they leave us the floor, crying and begging. It is not our instinct that malfunctions, it's people who don't know how to love. Selfish and narcissistic humans. The world is full of these creatures. Most of them are completely unaware of that side of them. And they struggle so much without knowing why. And they make other people cry. So much unhappiness around them. But they cannot control themselves, they don't even want to be that way. They were born this way, it's not their fault.

I couldn't hold my tears back. I started sobbing. I missed him so much. I wanted to feel his arms around me. Nothing's changed. My heart was never going to be free. I was cursed. There was no point in lying to myself. I sent a text to my admirer, "I am sorry. I cannot see you anymore. I am a dreadful person. My heart belongs to someone else. I shouldn't have accepted to go out with you. Please, forgive me."

"Are you with him?" he replied right away.

"No. I cannot be with that guy."

"Then we should talk. I won't let you escape."

"It's a waste of time. My heart is stupid and works against me."

"Tara, I won't give up on you. Please, let's meet and discuss. Let me know when you're free."

We've met for dinner, I said I didn't like the place. He got upset and we fought. "You never like the places I chose. Why don't you choose then?" he said with anger.

It was a great opportunity. I didn't want to explain, there was no point. It didn't take much to say it was over. He gave me what my brain wanted, but my heart was deaf, blind, insensitive, and stupid. "Don't call me again. Delete my number."

"You're a very complicated and fussy human being," he replied. "But I still like you, please, let's calm down and talk."

"There is nothing to talk about. I am not in love with you."

"But you like me. You kissed me and your body responded to my touches."

"I love kissing you. I won't lie about that," I honestly admitted.

"There is hope then," he said with a sigh.

"No. I won't be meeting you again. I am not worth it," I replied.

"You are worth it and I will fight if I have to. I can't and won't let you go that easily. I never met anyone like you."

I left, there was no point discussing any longer. He would have never understood. I didn't understand. I wanted to cry and I cried for hours.

At 3am I wrote a very long email to Adrian. I told him that I was still loving him like the first day. I wrote that I knew we couldn't be together, but I couldn't command my heart. I asked for forgiveness and I begged for a sign. He replied the next morning and said that he knew that but I had a very weird way of showing it. He was missing me too. I wrote him another one and said I had something important to tell him. We agreed to meet on Thursday evening. I didn't know if I should cook or not. I didn't.

When he got in, my heart started racing. I planned on speaking about Lola. But my heart didn't allow me to stick to the plan. 'My job is to pump blood and feel for you. You think of you. Lola can take care of herself. You were here first. Stop trying to fix things which are not in your power. You are not God.'

'He lied to me,' my brain said.

'Did he? He didn't tell you, but he didn't lie. Did you tell him everything?' my heart responded.

'He left me crying on the floor,' the brain insisted.

'He was confused. He's got a strong conscience. He felt guilty for living her and you didn't want a relationship. He didn't know what to do,' the heart murmured.

The usual fight inside any woman in love with the wrong person. The heart inundated by pure love craves for his kisses and finds excuses for everything. The brain pretends to know better and brings on the table strong arguments to prove he doesn't love you. They are both right. Always. There is a battle for survival and each side has its own theories and fights with all the necessary means. They never rest, they never sleep, they are always alert. But the heart, somehow, always wins. Nevertheless, there is no happily ever after, no peace, no victory. One hour of pure bliss when the brain is forced to step back and don't interfere, followed by days, weeks, months, or years of struggling in which the brain is sovereign, and the heart can only feel pain. That's the price so many people pay every day. No matter the colour of the skin, the education, the country of birth, the age, or gender. Love has no barriers.

He looked handsome and mature. When his arms surrounded my body, my brain shut down. The fight was over. I hugged him and he smelled so good. Fresh soap... old hard soap. So erotic. It instantly turned me on. I kissed his lips with tenderness. I drank a glass of red wine and kissed him again. That smell drove me insane. I couldn't control myself. He sat on the couch and I sat on his lap. He looked into my eyes and saw the infinite love I was feeling for him. His breath became heavy and his hands got under my blouse. "I missed you so much Tara... so much," he admitted while kissing me everywhere his lips could go. "Stop pushing me away. I cannot take this any longer. Stay with me."

I was wearing a red mini dress and no tights. I sat on his lap, both of us still dressed, and made love like there was no tomorrow. As every single time. Because we both knew that was for the last time. We always felt the same. Our bodies were in perfect harmony and our hearts belonged to one another, defying all human boundaries and common sense. We were utterly crazy one for another, but we couldn't be together. We both fought. We pushed and pulled, grabbed and let go, we stood and we sat, again and again, and again. Our hearts were always racing. It wasn't healthy. We were both perfectly aware of that. It was a curse. We were overwhelmed and exhausted. So much passion, too much. I wanted him in, but I wanted him out. I didn't want to have a relationship, but I couldn't live without him. A constant fight.

"I want to cook for you, Adrian. I want you to come home to me every evening. I want to walk with you on the street holding hands. I want to fall asleep in your arms. I want you to be the first thing I see in the morning and I want to make love to you like we did now. I am dying without you."

"You said you didn't want a relationship. You want to keep it a secret. You are ashamed of me."

"I said so many things, but never that I am ashamed. Why would I be ashamed?"

"I always knew I couldn't have you. You're out of my league, you're out of anyone's league."

"What are you talking about? What do you mean? You cannot possibly think that. Can't you feel that I am crazy about you?"

"Yes, I know you are crazy about me, but your mind doesn't want to accept it. I am not good enough for you. You deserve someone better."

"I only want you," I said with tears in my eyes.

"You want me only when we are alone. In public, I mean nothing to you. You don't even see me."

"You're the only one I see. There is no one else in this world for me. I now know that you'll always be in my heart. No matter where I'll be." My heart was torn apart.

"Do you hear yourself? You always say that, *no matter where I'll be.* You don't want to be with me, you know you'll go away."

"But Adrian, this is not my country. I will go away one day. Anything could happen."

"But you are here now. Even when we are one, you push me away. This passion of yours... it overpowers my entire being. It's a desperate battle. You love me and you fight me."

"I never thought it this way.... I am sorry I hurt you. I promise I have never wanted to harm you. I wanted to make you feel alive. Besides, it seems to me you are doing the same," I murmured desperately.

"I've learned from the best, didn't I? You make me feel alive and very angry when you ignore me after we made love and after you told me how much I mean to you. You don't know what you want."

I had no answer to that. I was completely overwhelmed. I thought I knew myself. I was so proud. He proved me wrong. His allegations made sense. I humiliated him in public and I never saw his point of view. In this room, I was his slave, but in the world, he didn't exist for me. It was insane. How could I have been so blind? What sort of monster was I? Was I really in love with him or... 'Maybe I am crazy. Maybe this is a nightmare. Oh, God, please, let it be a nightmare.' He held me tight. I was out of my mind. "I am sorry, I am sorry. Please, forgive me. I didn't realise. I didn't know.

You've never told me. I am so ashamed. Why didn't you tell me this before? Why?"

"You never wanted to listen. You always said you knew you so well... "

"But you never speak! What can I do to make this right? Please, let me try at least."

Adrian's eyes were incredibly sad. There was no life in them. Just the colour. Green. He was miles away. I felt so desperate. In the end he said, "Come to a party with me. There are going to be some of your friends in there."

I knew I couldn't do that. It was too late for a public admission. Lola was in love with him and I didn't tell her I was there first. I didn't want to tear her heart apart. "I can't," I murmured hopelessly.

"I know," he said with a fainted voice.

He took my dress off and kissed my entire body countless times. His hands touched me everywhere bringing my body on the edge of insanity again. He made me fly in Heaven until I screamed for mercy. I went to have a shower just to put some distance between us. I thought my heart would explode if I didn't. I came back with a bottle of baby oil in my hands. He didn't need to be asked, took the bottle from my hands and started to spread it on my trembling body.

"So that's why your skin feels like silk," his husky voice rolled over my skin. He placed the bottle on the table and started to sprinkle kisses and bites onto every inch of it. Then the tenderness became wildness and we could hardly breathe. We were both groaning and moaning with lust. We were exhaling and inhaling fire. He knew he had the power to make me melt like the butter under the sun... He just needed one second and I was under his control. He explored every fibre of my body and soul. He ate me with his eyes. He stroked and bit and touched, he caressed and squeezed tender or with pathos observing my every reaction. I guess he wanted to fill his entire being with the image of me. More like a movie, actually. He wanted me on the edge again and I screamed once more, "You are my size. Don't stop, don't stop." And he looked into my eyes and didn't stop. Then he did and was his turn to need a shower. I fell asleep naked, without a blanket to cover me as I needed to cool myself down. His wet body pulsing with desire woke me up with a bite on my neck. His thumb stroked my upper lip, his eyes were devouring me. I instantly got aroused and let him in, no questions asked. We flew to Heaven again. Desperately.

When he dressed to leave, I knew it was over. I knew that every time. And my eyes blurred with tears. I didn't want him to leave, I needed him, he was my size. I wanted to cry out loud, 'Don't go, I beg you! Make me yours again.' How many times I felt that before? How many times did I swear I was not going to see him again? Was he the one using me, or was it me using him? I wasn't sure anymore. I hated him and I adored him. I knew he was undergoing the same terrible struggle and I hated myself even more. 'I should have never told him I had a crush on him. It's all my fault. He would have never had the courage to make me his.' But then I remembered that I have never encouraged him in any way. I ran and hid. He was the one looking for me, asking, offering to help. 'As he does now with Lola.'

"Adrian," I said when he turned around to leave, "do you know that Lola's in love with you?"

"Really? I think I kind of knew. Who told you this?" he asked, without showing surprise.

'He knew, of course he knew. He played her the way he played me!' I tried to stay calm and replied, "Lola and I are close friends, you know that very well. She tells me everything. You let her fall in love with you? Why? Do you love her too?"

He said nothing for a few seconds. It seemed an eternity for me. "She's my best friend."

"Is she now? I thought your ex was your best friend. Anyway, have you told her about me, about us? If I had a best friend, I'd told them everything. That's friendship to me," I said with superiority.

"You made me promise to keep it a secret," he replied innocently.

I didn't know who was he lying to, himself or me. Both maybe. "But do you love her? Because if you do, you have to do something about it or let her be."

"What do you mean?" he asked again like he didn't follow.

"If you have feelings for her, you have a chance to be together. But if you don't, you shouldn't see her anymore."

"She's very important to me. I won't give up on her friendship."

There was something in that statement... It didn't feel right. 'He can't be so selfish. He cannot use her to fill his emptiness inside. He cares for her. I can tell. Maybe it's more than that, and he doesn't know it.' All of a sudden I knew, 'Oh, Jesus! He loves her.' I couldn't stand the thought. I couldn't breathe. I needed to be alone.

"Adrian, go to Lola. Clear things up. Maybe you are in love and you don't know it. It happens when two people spend so much time together."

"You can't be serious."

"I am dead serious. If you love her, I am happy for you. She's a good person. She's not like me. We couldn't have been together anyway," I said with such coldness in my voice... it frightened me. 'How can I do that? I love him. How can I send him in her arms? We just made love. He is my size and we are so compatible. It took me eight years to find him. Why am I doing this? What's wrong with me? I am as crazy as he is. Maybe even more."

He was so confused, "She is great and nothing like you indeed. You have a fire within you, she's got water. When you walk, you turn all heads around you, she is invisible. You smile when your heart is crying, she cries when her heart is happy."

"Don't say that. It's very offensive."

"You can keep your head up in any situation."

"What's that supposed to mean?"

"You can get out of a deadly situation without a scratch. You're like a robot."

"How can you say that? Why are you doing this? You are hurting me. You know I put body and soul in everything I do. I am not a machine. I feel everything... even things that don't exist..."

"You told me that you love me like you never loved before, and ten minutes later you send me to Lola, your friend. How is this consistent?"

"I am doing this for you. Both of you. How can you not understand that?" I said with sincerity.

"Do me a favour, will you? Stop telling me how I feel and what I should do. I can think for myself. I know you consider me a child, but I am not," he replied with pain in his voice.

"I am sorry. I didn't mean that. I know you're not a child. But you forgot one thing, Adrian. You knew Lola was my friend. You were aware of the fact that she was single and desperately looking for someone to love. And you spent so much time with her. She tried to kiss you the first time she met you, for God's sake! What did you expect? It was unavoidable, a matter of time. Don't put this on me. You've done it to yourself. Do you even realise that? You've played with her heart. And if you behave with her the way you behaved with me at the beginning, of course she couldn't help but fell in love with you. You give so much... Maybe you love her too... otherwise, why would you spend so much time with her? Her words exactly. She's a woman; she can feel when a man is attracted to her. If your feelings for her are genuine, you'll do the right thing. Go."

I couldn't look into his eyes. I was dying inside and I had the feeling he felt the same. He stood up, put his close on, took my hand and placed a goodbye kiss on to it. I didn't move a muscle. The pain was unbearable. 'He blames me because Lola fell in love with him? This boy has no heart. He doesn't know what he's doing. Maybe he is ill. He does show all the symptoms.'

FROM HEAVEN TO HELL, AGAIN AND AGAIN AND AGAIN

When the entrance door slammed, I started shaking and I was convinced I won't come out of it alive. 'He's the only man I ever really loved until now. He made me feel emotions I had no idea existed. He made me fly in Heaven and burn in Hell. He's peace and chaos. I am nothing without him, but if he loves her, I cannot be in his life anymore. He needs some peace. I want him to be happy.'

In that moment I understood why people let go to those who they love most. I always thought that you couldn't let go when you truly love, you have to fight! But you cannot force someone to love you. You cannot keep someone close just because you love them. The feeling, the desire must be mutual. Adrian was oscillating between Lola and me now, and I realised that he did the same when he broke up with his girlfriend. He didn't know what to do and I pushed and pulled so many times. 'Lola would never push him. She's such a sweet girl. She doesn't fight with passion. She doesn't know what that is. She's quiet and accommodating. They have a chance to a normal relationship.'

I bit my lips and held my tears back, 'I won't cry. I won't beg. It's too late. It's my fault. I want to sleep, I need to sleep now. I'll think about it tomorrow.' I hugged my pillow and fell into oblivion. I was utterly exhausted.

The next day I went to work like nothing had happened. I laughed and smiled as always. Just like Adrian said, a robot. I complimented people on their clothing. A pleasant word makes people feel better. It doesn't cost a thing to be nice. I wished someone told me some words of hope. Anything. But people have their lives, different issues, various strategies to cope with things. I was a dead body moving without a direction. And I was so bad with orientation.

One day I went to visit my old man's tomb. I couldn't stand cemeteries, but I missed him so much. Drefan told me where the tomb was, but I couldn't find it. I had to ask a person who worked there. They checked on the computer and pointed me in the right direction. As I said, I was bad with directions. I got lost and wandered for a while when I saw his picture smiling at me. I fell on my knees and asked for forgiveness. Then I got upset, "Why did you leave me? How could you leave me alone in here? I needed you more than you needed me." I was desperately sobbing when I heard a women's voice saying, "Don't cry, child, don't you know he's in a better place now?"

I raised my head to see if she was talking to me. She was. A tiny old woman, with white hair and trembling hands in which she was holding a bunch of yellow chrysanthemums.

I couldn't speak. She came closer and wiped some of my tears off with a colourful paper tissue.

"Was he your father?"

I shook my head "No." My tears didn't stop falling. I wasn't able to stand up, so I remained on my knees, immobile, like a statue, staring at the flowers.

"Do you like them? They are for my baby. I don't even know if he likes them. He left this world way before he could speak."

My heart felt for her. She's lost a child, but she was still able to smile. I admired her strengths. "I am so sorry," I murmured.

"Don't be. It was a long time ago. Sometimes I think it didn't happen to me. So I come here and check. It's my name on the grave. I cannot deny the proof." Her blue eyes became a little cloudy and I didn't want her to start crying. There was no way I could bear her pain. No more room in my heart for that. I was afraid I'd go insane. I stood up, gave her a hug, and thanked for the kindness. She smiled. I held on to that and walked away, adagio.

I never went back. The old man will always be in my heart, there was no need to see his grave. I could just open my heart and find him there, waiting for me. It's what I do when I miss him. He always says he doesn't want me to be sad. He's with his wife. But I still cry and miss him so much. I am just human.

Three weeks after that, I sent Adrian an email to ask how he was. He told me he was lost again. I asked him to come and talk to me about it if he wanted. The truth is I needed to see him. My body craved for him and I felt like the most dreadful human in the entire world. 'I sent him to Lola and now I want him back.' My heart was consumed by jealousy. For the very first time since I met him, the thought of him touching another woman, Lola in this case, made me go insane. 'He wouldn't touch her, he loves me. He couldn't kiss me when he was with his ex, I am sure he couldn't kiss her either. I don't care about Lola, I don't care about him, I only care about me. Who am I trying to fool? I want him to kiss only me, not Lola and not his ex. I need him! He's my size and he doesn't have pervert desires. Just simple, plain, pure sex. Sex?!? I thought I made love to him?! Jesus Christ, have mercy on my soul, I am utterly insane. I despise myself. I am no human, I am a monster. I am a wolf in sheep's clothing. A devil playing the angel's part. How can you allow someone like me to walk among humans?' I cried out in my mind looking at the sky above.

He came on a Thursday night. I gave him a short hug and we sat on the couch. His eyes looked greener somehow. His lips were bigger and so sensual. He looked so handsome, so clean. I tried to act nicely. He was in pain, I could see that.

"How are things with you and Lola?" I asked.

He looked away and didn't reply. So I told him how I was feeling. I told him I was utterly consumed by jealousy. The devil's confession. Then I started crying, of course, the angel's part. He looked at me with anger, and how could anyone blame him?

"Why have you sent me to her?!" he shouted. "Why? If you really love me that much. Do you have any idea of what you've done?"

I was surprised by his reaction. He never shouted at me after that first time. He never lost control since then. I hated his calmness every time I shouted and screamed. I used to tell him it was an incontestable prove he didn't care and I wished he slapped me on the face instead of going away. The devil stepped in again. "What happened Adrian? What did you do?" I asked with fear.

"It is you who did it, not me! I didn't want to. You put me up to this. I listened because you are wiser, you know better," he shouted again.

Now I was really afraid. "What happened, for the love of God?"

"I kissed her, all right? I kissed her just to realise I still have feelings for you! Are you happy now? I lost her friendship, she'll never forgive me for this."

I felt the urge to slap him so hard! 'A minute before I blamed it all on me. Forget about that! This guy is totally nuts!' "Why the hell did you do that for? I didn't tell you to kiss her! I told you to clear things up. To speak, discuss. Do you know what that means, Adrian? Speaking? Present continuous tense? *'The action of conveying information or expressing one's feelings in speech'* as Google says? Have you ever heard of this verb before? Eh? No? It's in your language! Don't put this on me, I wasn't there. I never had any power over you, you've never done anything I asked and all of I sudden I can make you kiss your best friend, my friend? Against your will? Give me a break. Take responsibility for your actions. For once in your life. You always do whatever makes you happy. You care about no one, but you. And you know it. All of us have a degree of selfishness. I am selfish too. No one is immune. You wanted to kiss her and now you are afraid of losing her? It's exactly what you deserve for playing with people's feelings. Luckily, Lola is not like that. You didn't lose her friendship. She'll forgive you, just wait and see. When someone's in love, they forgive everything."

"Did you hear that I said I still love you?" he asked with anger again.

"All I heard is that you are afraid you lost her."

"It's what you women do, no? Focusing on the negative just to screw our minds up," he shouted again.

"How dare you to blame me?! You are the one screwing me, Lola, your ex and God knows how many others. How many women you've slept with since you met me? Tell me the truth. Don't lie or I swear to God I would never speak to you, ever, ever again!"

"Just who do you think I am? I slept only with you," he said, obviously hurt in his pride.

"And why I can't believe you?"

"You believe what you want. I am sick and tired of this. My ex wasn't like that at all. I had such an easy life with her. She never complained, she never asked why I am not home or where I am going, she never pretended anything."

"No, because she didn't give a damn about you. None of you knows what's love all about. When was the last time you slept with her before meeting me? Look into my eyes and tell me the truth."

"Love is not all about sex. You can love someone without wanting to have sex. That's love if you ask me. Do you think what happens between us is real love? This pulling and letting go? This is just an insanity. I don't know what I want anymore."

"Do you like men perhaps?" I asked in all seriousness. "Maybe you are bisexual. It's nothing wrong with that. We are what we are." I don't know why I said that. It made no sense. He was right, it wasn't love between us, it was war. It has always been war.

He reached out to my face and put a thumb on my lip, stroke it and tears in cascades started rolling down my face. I melted. That power he had over me. It took him one single gesture to transform a lion into a baby cat. "I only want you. My body doesn't react in any way when I am with other people. You've changed me. I don't know what and how you did it, but you completely shattered my life. For better and for worse. I didn't know what burning with desire felt like. It's a pure drug. You make me feel high every time you kiss me."

I didn't know if that was love, what he or I felt at that point, but I wanted to kiss him. I didn't care if he kissed Lola... 'poor girl. Or poor me? Poor Adrian? Poor all of us! We are insane.' I didn't know who was crazier than whom. I just let my body take action. So I put my hands on both sides of his face and asked, "Do you really love me?"

"Yes. How can you not know that?" he replied.

"Because I don't know what's the truth and what's a mask anymore. You never tell me what you feel, what you want. I have to guess and make assumptions. I cannot tell what's anything for sure. Except that my body wants you. Only that." And I kissed him and he responded with infinite pathos. We made love, but it didn't feel like before. The magic was gone. I was on earth now. I wasn't making love, I was having sex and I didn't like it. I knew I was not going to do that again. Both of us knew. He was consumed by guilt. He lost two of his best friends over a kiss. But no matter how much I tried to put a part of the blame on me, I couldn't. I didn't ask him to break up with his girlfriend and I didn't ask him to kiss Lola. Those were his free decisions. I ran away from him from the start, I only dreamt of him. I only wanted him to kiss me. I hid, he came for me. He lured me with infinite tenderness. He lied and played me from the start. But I was aware of it. I allowed him to play me.

There was something I felt terribly guilty for, keeping it a secret from Lola. But I had an excuse. It was already too late when they met. At first, I didn't want to hurt her. At least it's what I told myself. It was just part of the truth. My story with Adrian was an underground story and I wanted to remain that way. She would have told everyone. And in all honesty, I think I would have been the one to pay the price. 'Look at her... a middle-aged woman screwed by a boy. With all these older men around. Pathetic.' Yes. I was selfish, I didn't want people to mock on me. I deserved to be loved, even by a boy. I needed it. But at that point, I thought of Lola. I didn't want her to lose all her trust in the human race. I was sincere. She considered me a good friend. God, she even asked me what to do, how to act with him. She told me everything about her past and present. She trusted me and I am sure she trusted him even more.

I made him promise that he won't say anything to her. Not ever. Under no circumstances. "If you really care for her, you're going to spare her this horrible story. She doesn't need to know. Some people think the truth is always the way, I completely disagree with that. Truth should be always said, except for things that will hurt more knowing. Nobody knows about us, besides you and me, she will never find out unless you want to free your soul. I hope you're not that selfish. You take this secret with you in the ground. I'll do the same."

And that was it. Over. *Kaput. Finito.* I felt relieved. But was it really over? I prayed to God it was, for both our sakes. We deserved some peace.

I cancelled his number and tried to get him out of my head... or heart? Body? I couldn't really tell.

I stopped going out all at once. I closed the curtains, I only saw my closest friends, seldom. It was just work and house. I was still thinking of him often, but it didn't hurt as much as before. I was sure I was cured. What a happy life. I was so grateful. I felt proud of myself. I was starting to gain some self-respect and confidence.... But I was missing him so much. I haven't seen him in two months or more. I sent him an email telling him I was not well. He replied a week after, apologising for the late reply. "I made a folder where your emails would automatically go. I checked every day to see if you wrote me, but I forgot about this folder."

I thought he didn't know the meaning of the word "Sorry". I never, ever heard him using that word or any other synonym before. I was touched. So damn easy!

"Anything I can do?" he asked.

"Spend some time with me?" I replied with hope. 'Stupid heart!'

He came to dinner. We watched a movie and I felt like kissing him. I asked for permission. He gave his consent by reaching out to my mouth with his lips.

I then asked a very stupid question. He gave me a reply I wasn't prepared to hear. It was just a rhetorical question for me... I already had the answer in my mind, except it was completely different. "Have you slept with someone else in this period?"

"Yes," he replied without hesitation. Not only a second he had to think. He didn't hide, he didn't lie, he was honest. After we had that discussion about some things are better kept hidden.

I've got upset, of course. I was convinced his body reacted only when he saw me. I moved aside.

It was his turn to get upset, "You didn't want to see me anymore. I felt rejected, it hurt. When a different woman showed interest in me, I had sex with her. It's no big deal."

"Why did you have to tell me? Couldn't you just lie?" I said in tears.

"You've asked me. You're never happy, are you? If I lie, you feel hurt, if I tell the truth, you feel hurt. What am I supposed to do, or say? I thought the truth is always the way."

"You're wrong. But you cannot understand that," I replied.

"What do you want from me, Tara? I never knew," he asked annoyed.

"I always told you want I want, always. You never gave me anything I asked. Not ever. You didn't spend an entire weekend with me, we didn't go for walks, we didn't watch the sunrise or the dawn, you refused to stay for the night after making love for hours, we didn't go on a holiday or any day trip. You never brought me a single flower, you don't know anything about me, you don't even know what chocolate I like. We never spoke. Ever!" I said in tears.

"You don't like chocolate," He replied upset. "I didn't stay for the night because you told me you can't sleep with someone in your bed, and you complained about my snoring. For your information, I do not always snore."

"I do like chocolate, just not any. I do not eat it often, that's true. And you do snore, you just don't know it. You can't hear yourself," I replied.

He laughed, I laughed too. It was true that I couldn't sleep with someone in my bed, not even in the same room and a different bed. I couldn't hear another person breathing the same air while I was sleeping. I couldn't stand that, ever. He stayed one night, I didn't close one eye. I liked it that he stayed, but I told him I wasn't sure I could do that very often. I guess that's one thing he remembered very well. I completely forgot about telling him that. I've always been fairly honest with my feelings and thoughts. My directness hurt him many times. Just like his hurt me know.

And he was right about another thing, we fell out so many times, this time he had another woman ready to take him. What man would have said no? It was unfair to feel upset for that. He was there, I was aroused, so was he. We've kissed. There was no more passion in the air, just animal instinct. He asked if I had a condom. Luckily, I had, so I handed him one. Then he had me. I didn't shiver, my body didn't feel electrified. No more fireworks, no flying in the sky, no mount Everest. I wasn't sure if I even felt his size. I didn't scream, I didn't groan, not once. He made no effort, I made even less. But I felt something after that, dirtiness. Both morally and physically.

I realised that I taught him to make love... or sex.

I had a long shower and rubbed my skin until it almost started to bleed. I also cleaned my body internally. I haven't done that in years. I didn't like it, was not healthy. 'That was it. Pure sex, animal instinct is not my thing. I need to feel loved.'

It was not going to happen again.

LADY IN RED

One evening, I went to a friend's birthday party. I didn't expect to see Adrian. But I should have, as I knew Lola was going to be there too. How stupid of me to ignore that. I was already there when he came in. As usual, I felt his presence, but I didn't want to look. At some point, someone called my name, so I turned my head and stared directly into his eyes like someone compelled me to do that. It was one nanosecond only, but I was furious. 'You cannot do this to me, you stupid heart. I won't let you. He's just a troubled man. Stay away from him. Don't you dare or I swear I will reap you from my chest with my hands. I am dead serious. I cannot go through that again. He sleeps with random women without sentiment. He's an animal. Aren't we much better without him? Please, I beg you, be strong.' My eyes blurred with tears. There was such a battle inside me. I almost stood up and left, like I did so many times in the past. But I couldn't. Everybody was happy that I was out, like they cared. I knew all were just pleasantries. I promised myself that I wasn't going to stay long. Lola was eating from his palm again. It was painful to see her in that state. She looked so desperate.

A friend of both of us told me that she was crying every day. I called her a few times and invited her to dinner. But she was in such a mess. Poor girl. I knew exactly how she felt, except that I was a very passionate person and highly sensitive, she was just the opposite. I had faith she'll come out of it as soon as he dumped her. But was he ready to let her go?

Adrian always wanted to have the exclusive in everyone's life, but he was not ready to do the same. He surrounded himself with thousands of people and called everyone friends. Exactly like Lola. They couldn't stay alone not even for a day. But Lola gave up on everyone else in her life for him. And he was over the moon. He was the only man in her life. She was his, except he didn't want that. He wanted to be free. He was not the man of a single woman. He was nobody's property. He was single and loved that life. Drunk or sober, he flirted with every woman he met. All the time. I even told him that a few times, he strongly denied. "I am just a nice guy. You are only jealous."

I wasn't sure if he imposed himself to believe that, or simply was not aware of it.

The whole time I was at the party, our gaze crossed several times. I never, ever, did it on purpose, and I guess he didn't do that either, except he couldn't take his eyes off me. I was wearing a red midi wet-looking dress. Bodycon style. High heels. Ignoring me was impossible. I felt everybody's eyes on me, but Adrian's gaze penetrated me to the bones. Lola was orbiting around him, and he felt like a king. I felt disgusted with both, but mostly with myself.

A friend came and asked me to go with her to order a drink. I found it a sign of the destiny, a perfect moment to leave without drawing attention to me. With that red dress, I couldn't avoid it unless I had the excuse of going to the bar which was in front of the door.

Adrian came to me, I ignored him as much as I could. I was about to leave, I laughed and refused to talk to him pretending I didn't care. He was such a mess, so drunk and so hurt in his pride. When everybody was busy speaking with one another, I slid my body out the door. A man made a very nice remark on my looks. I said thank you and run away. Another one shouted I was insanely hot and I should stop to talk to him. I ignored all that and kept walking. I was out of Adrian's sight and I sighed in relief. I was safe. I checked if my phone was off so if he felt the urge to send me a text I couldn't have seen until the next day and I wouldn't have replied when he was with her. He wouldn't have cared.

I heard someone running behind me, my heart told me it was him, but I tried not to worry as the town was pulsing with people. It was Friday night. "Why did you leave?" he asked and mumbled other things which made no sense to me. There was no more doubt, it was Adrian. He looked dirty and smelled even worse. I couldn't stand that. I looked at him with disgust. Yes, he told me he read it in my eyes, it was all over my face. He didn't feel compelled to look good for Lola. She didn't care if he was a drug addict, a killer, or a saint. She didn't care if his hair was shiny from a good wash, or if he smelled like a dead fish. She was in love, completely blind, deaf and with no olfaction.

He used to take care of himself while he was... screwing me. But he wasn't always very keen on that. When I met him, he gave me the impression that wasn't very fond of his washing machine. Maybe he didn't have one, neither a shower. But once we've started to meet, he seemed to have discovered the hot water miracle. That's why I found the soap scent on him being utterly inebriating for me. That clean smell turned me on instantly. But not that night. My heart acknowledged him all right, but my body rejected him. He looked nothing like the man I slept with until a few months back. He was shouting at me, and I was not able to understand much. I have never seen him that drunk in my life. It was disturbing. His pride was even higher when he was in that state. He was utterly arrogant and aggressive. I had the impulse to leave him standing alone in the middle of the street. He would have totally deserved that, but I didn't have the strength to humiliate him like that. I didn't say much, my feet were sore, so I took my shoes off and said I needed to leave, I was tired. He offered, more imposed really, to take me home to speak and discuss some things. "Don't tell me I didn't try," he shouted. "You've always complained that I never speak with you. Here I am, speak!" It was an order from a king I didn't respect anymore.

He was making a lot of fuss, and I was afraid that would draw attention to us, so I accepted to be accompanied home. "Let me carry your shoes," he said with a voice that didn't allow a denial.

I had nothing to discuss with him. "We said everything, Adrian. There is nothing left for us to speak about." He moved his head side to side with anger and started to walk very fast. I asked him to wait for me, I was bare feet, it was painful.

"You shouldn't have taken your shoes off then!" he said with... revenge. Yes, he enjoyed the fact my feet hurt and didn't hide it. 'Just how much I don't know about this boy?'

He used to be kind and sweet. I guessed he gives that to Lola now, doesn't have anything else left for others.' He most definitely didn't show that in public, but I was certain he treated her well in privacy. Why else would she be so hooked by him otherwise? And all of a sudden I realised that was the exact copy of the relationship we had not long ago. Lola was playing Adrian's role, and he was playing mine. Cold, distant, inaccessible in public, and a slave in privacy. I felt sick. But, somehow I just couldn't imagine Adrian kissing and caressing Lola the way I did with him. But what did I know about him anyway? I was discovering another side of him every day. It was frightening. 'Who did I love?'

I sighed in relief when we got in front of my building, I grabbed my shoes, thanked him for the company, unlocked the door and got in. He kept walking still very fast, and I couldn't help but notice he was swaying on his feet. 'Just how much did he have to drink?!' I worried he might fall.

He was used to offering drinks to everyone every time he was out. I guessed he thought it was a friendly gesture and people appreciated him for that. He spent a real fortune those evenings. His father had a family and asked for a rent. I would have done that too, especially if I had known how much he spent on random people who couldn't care less about him. I often wondered how the hell did he manage to pay his bills, hers too. But it wasn't my business. I shouldn't have asked myself that. He never asked me for money and offered me a drink, twice. I offered back, but I knew most of his friends, didn't follow that rule. But if that made him feel good about himself, who was I to judge? What did I know about friends? Or best friends and twisted relationships?

I moved on by inertia. I read and wrote a lot, trying to fight against his memory. I was completely and utterly alone. I saw him a few times, my heart still acknowledged his somehow, like it had a mind of itself. I knew he felt the same. How? I just sensed it.

I had to admit that I still loved him, but my body didn't feel any sort of attraction for him anymore. He stopped looking shiny like before. But

I was also sure I could have kissed him anytime. I always loved kissing. I said that already.

Months went by like that, between memories of him and my war against them. Christmas was near. I used to love this day. It was the most magnificent period of the year. Not since I left my country though. Nothing felt the same. It became a regular day for me. And I remember that Adrian had the same idea about it. So I thought it would be nice to spend that day together. Like old friends. Thing we've never actually been. I imagined him all alone in his room when everybody else was having fun. Just like me. I felt sorry for both of us. So I sent him an email and invited him over for Christmas Day, "We could watch some comedies, eat some nice homemade food, going for a walk maybe, or whatever we might feel like doing. No plans."

Three weeks later, two days before Christmas, he replied declining my invitation. With no excuse. Apparently, I didn't deserve one. 'He's got better things to do.' I thought. 'He's got her to take care of, and his family, he doesn't need me. How stupid of me to come up with such an idea.'

I cried. I don't know why. Maybe because I didn't want to be alone, or because he still had a place in my heart, most likely because I missed him. I was sad, but Christmas came and passed. I sobbed for hours, watched silly movies, ate crisps, and went to bed. New Year's Eve came too. The year before I gave a big party, this year I was invited to several parties. I declined all of them. I spent the night in bed, with a glass of whisky. I hoped I'd see the snow. It didn't happen. It wasn't Romania.

I asked every person I knew not to send me wishes, texts messages, emails, or cards. I didn't like that. It would have made me feel sadder and lonelier. He knew about this request, I told him so many times. So he didn't send me one either. Neither did I.

The months went by on the same note. I saw old friends, spent time with new ones. Things were pretty normal.

One day I was speaking with some colleagues when they told me a strange story about another colleague of ours. They said that he broke with his girlfriend a few weeks after they moved together in the same house, and decided to continue living under the same roof because they were best friends. They all thought was weird, however, admitted that it was pretty common behaviour in England. They knew about many stories like that. I was shocked, and although I used to like that guy, I decided I will never speak to him again.

Later that evening, at home, I went online to do a research about that bizarre phenomenon and read about thousands of cases. But the worst part for me was when I discovered that in every country of the world best friends often end up having sex, and it's considered normal behaviour. I felt sick. That was far from normal for me. I don't know why I cannot conceive any of that. It is not because of my education or nationality, I heard it's pretty common in Romania too. I must be the one who's not normal then because I always thought that sex is not included in the friends/best friends package. How the hell are we supposed to make a distinction between love stories, or friendship stories? I swear I am confused. Am I the one who's absurd?

***

One day, I met Lola. She was desperately crying. I hugged her tight. I knew the reason, of course. She told me everything... everything I already knew. The way he treated her in public and in private. The things he didn't do and she craved for.

I asked her if they were having a relationship. She said they didn't. They were only friends. She told me about the kiss and his confession about loving another one again.

"Have you found out who that woman is? Are you sure is not his ex?" I asked. I knew he didn't tell her about us, at least I hoped.

"It could be, I don't know why is he keeping me away. He knows I love him and I am dying without him. He keeps searching for me all the time. It is very confusing. Sometimes he sends me texts after midnight telling me how much he misses me, some days he doesn't even know I exist. We spend many days a week together. Evenings, weekends, we go for trips, we even go shopping together. We do things as a couple. He is always so tender and careful, he hugs me all the time. We fell asleep in each other arms. I can feel he likes my company and me. But he doesn't want to consider me more than a friend," she's confessed in thousands of tears.

Adrian didn't do any of those things with me. I had to admit that maybe he cared for Lola infinitely more than he cared for me. It was so painful; my heart was heavily bleeding. I think I already knew, I just refused to accept it. Lola was twenty I think. So, so many years younger than me. Maybe three, four or five years younger than Adrian too. I couldn't tell as she didn't look that young at all. She was the complete opposite of me. In everything. It's extremely mean of me to say, but I never found her attractive. Obviously, I wasn't Adrian. He loved her. He must have seen her with different eyes. Beauty is subjective, isn't it? What I find irresistible, someone finds unattractive, and vice-versa. We are all unique, with different tastes, ideas, opinions. What a blessing though. Can you imagine a world where everybody thinks the same way? Very disturbing.

I wished I felt some jealousy. But no, I was genuinely sorry for her. It was like seeing me. She broke my heart. I had a lump in my throat. I wished I could help her, but I knew I didn't have that power. Adrian had it. I tried to encourage her saying that he wasn't the only man on earth. She didn't want to listen. I told those things to myself, and I didn't listen either. When you are in love you don't listen, you don't even hear, you just feel. Stupid heart!

I hugged her tight again, praying she'll come out of it if only he will let her go. I understood that he didn't want to be with her, but didn't want let her free either. It was that pulling and pushing thing he did with me and he blamed me for doing it. Selfish brute!

But that meant he loved me too? What a twisted love it was then.

***

Have you ever asked yourself the reason you are crying when you witness at a sad scene? A person crying, a catastrophe, a loss, a death, etc.

Sometimes is because it reminds you of your past, of someone you knew and cared for. Sometimes we put ourselves in their shoes and we feel their pain like it was ours. There is also empathy or sympathy. I used to think I am a very empathetic person, but after what happened with Adrian, I thought I just lied to myself for all those years.

***

Before she left, she said something I found extremely confusing, although it was pretty clear,

"We... we've been very intimate. Friends don't do those things."

Ah, she didn't think it was normal behaviour either. I wasn't the only one who thought that. 'Not in your world, no, and not in mine, apparently it's a regular thing to do in his though.' I almost shouted. 'That animal shagged her!' I was in shock. I knew about the kiss, he's told me about it. But he never mentioned anything about being inside the body of his best friend. After the kiss and the fear he'd lost her, he made a promise in front of me that he will never, ever do anything to risk that friendship, not again. He was utterly terrified of the thought of losing her. What the hell is wrong with him? Does he ever think straight?'

Like I was better. Haven't I always done the same?

HE LOVED ME, HE LOVED ME NOT, HE...

I went home and sent an email to Adrian. I felt I had the duty to intervene at that point. It's what I told myself at least, truth is, I was furious.

He came over to mine, for dinner. He didn't wash his hair as he used to, he didn't smell like soap. He didn't care anymore if I liked him or not. He was screwing his best friend who wasn't that demanding. I kept my heart on a leash because she wanted to betray me again anyway. 'Stupid, stupid heart.'

With no further delays, I told him about Lola and asked him to do things right. She was in a lot of pain, it wasn't fair to do that to her.

He looked at me with so much rage. "How dare you to tell me what to do, what and how to feel? Just who the hell do you think you are?" he shouted.

I should have expected that. I knew him very well. I would have thought and done the same. He was right, I had no right to do that. I hated my impulsivity.

I dropped it and tried to have a different conversation with him. But he was too upset, hurt. That's when I lost it.

"Do you sleep with all your friends, Adrian?"

"How can you say that? You know I don't," he replied.

"Actually, I don't know. You slept with me, with two of your best friends and God knows with how many others. And I remember when you said with such conviction that there was no way that you and Lola will end up sleeping together. No way! You were terrified at the thought of losing her. How do you explain that? Is this normal in your world? Sleeping with friends, best friends?"

"Things have changed, you know..."

"In what way, Adrian? Have you fallen in love with her?"

An imperceptible pause, "You don't know everything."

"Of course I don't. I don't know *anything* about you, I never knew anything because you never talked to me! You must love her to some degree, otherwise, you wouldn't spend so much time with her. But it cannot be real love if you screw her once then ignore her for weeks. I also imagine that she's somehow forced you into this. She is deeply in love with you. I know you just wanted to make her happy. Because it's your speciality, making people happy at the beginning, right? At least, it's what you are telling yourself to can sleep at nights. But you don't sleep, Adrian, do you? Because you didn't want to have sex with her, not from desire at least. However, you've convinced yourself it was desire, isn't it? What's in your head?"

I looked at him with anger, he didn't reply. I think he agreed with me, he knew I was right. I was hurt, so hurt and angry that I couldn't breathe. "How could you? I cannot believe this. How could you do this to her, your best friend?! What are you? I am suffering for Lola too, that's right, because Lola is me, Goddammit! She's told me everything. I know both sides of the story. I knew it was just a matter of time, but I believed you when you promised you won't risk that friendship again. What the hell made you change your mind? Were you drunk, did she put something in your food, what did she lure you with? Were you feeling lonely, horny, desperate. Just tell me why? Why did you do it? Because, most definitely, this is not about beauty, perfect body, irresistibleness."

We both looked at one another with anger and pain, we both had reasons for that. He didn't give me any answer. He got up and left. I didn't try to stop him. I knew he was in pain I couldn't understand. I knew I couldn't help him in any way. Just as I couldn't help me or Lola. Nobody can help a soul who suffers from a sick love.

I felt the urge to send him an email asking for forgiveness, he was right, I shouldn't have told him what to do. I promised I will delete his number and never contact him again. I said I wished we could be friends, real friends, no interests. I still cared for him, not with so much intensity as almost two years ago, but enough to make me feel sorry for seeing him suffering. In the end, he did make me feel emotions I didn't know existed. I owed him.

He begged me to keep the number. He confessed he missed me and not only because what we've shared, but because he missed the time spent with me. I wasn't sure what he meant with that. My heart told me that he missed making love to me, my brain said he missed screwing me. I was confused again, 'does he love Lola or not!?'

I thought that he knew he's lost me forever when I found out he slept with Lola, my friend, and played another card of his twisted mind game.

I cried for hours in despair. I knew there was no going back. I didn't even want that, I was fighting with all my strengths not to go back.

We had something beautiful, in a way, but wasn't meant to be easy or forever. He fought against his weakness which made me fought against mine.

One day he sent me a text, "Let me take you out for dinner, make things right. Catch up properly."

I agreed, I still cared for him. That night I looked ravishing and I knew it. High heels, maxi black dress, easy makeup, on my shoulders I was wearing the scarf he gave me as a Christmas gift after he declined my invitation a year ago. It was black and pink with roses and hearts.

"Why pink?" I asked.

"Because you like it?" he replied with a question.

The truth is I didn't use to like pink until I moved to England. In my country, a woman of my age has no unwritten right to wear that colour. I loved that scarf though. My lipstick was matching its colour to perfection. He was not able to take his eyes off me. "You look breathtaking," he said at some point.

"I know, thank you." I replied with no false modesty. "I've changed, you know? I have been working on my self-esteem. I am getting better day by day. Last year I wouldn't have been able to take a compliment this easily."

"I have noticed," he replied.

It was obvious he felt uncomfortable in my presence, and when he walked me home, he saw how people were looking at me. I think he thought again that he was right to think I was out of his league. But I never thought that. We were a great match physically.

I wished I told him that he didn't help me with my confidence, quite the contrary. Every time he refused to pay me rightful compliments, every time he ignored my emails, my invitations, every time he left me crying in despair, every time he flirted and opened doors in front of other women, but never in front of me, he destroyed every millimetre of confidence I managed to build during the time I fought to keep him away. Every time he ran home after I begged him to stay, I felt that I didn't deserve to be loved. He made me feel ugly, unattractive, ignorant, not good enough, inferior to his ex. I told him all these many times, so he knew, but didn't care. I was a body, his best friend was waiting for him in the his father or parents' house. Now that I think about, I don't know if it was only his father's house. It's not important anyway.

Our story reminded me of a movie I watched many years ago. A man lost his wife in a car accident, fell in love with another, but was not a free man. The woman alive, present and tangible, deeply in love with him, felt like competing with a ghost, and knew she had no chance of winning. I felt terribly sorry for her. I now related to that dreadful story.

I hoped he'll start giving me what I needed one day. I hoped he will let go to the ghost. Love changes people completely. Because I believe at the very beginning it was love what he felt for me, but he fought against that feeling because it was hurting him and made him unable to think straight. He was not comfortable with losing control.

I am not sure if he knew what he was doing to me, but I have mentioned that many times, and he kept playing the same cards over and over again.

He must have known because he's reproached me a few times that I was too demanding. "I won't change because you feel hurt by my behaviour. I am a nice guy, I have loads of friends, they care for me. I won't pay you compliments if I don't feel like it. I'll come when I want and I leave when I feel like it. I've never done anything I didn't like in my life, for anyone, except for my mother, once. It's who I am and I am fine with it." He knew and didn't give a damn. What I think is that he didn't pay me compliments on purpose to make me feel I wasn't beautiful enough for him; he held me in his power stepping on my dignity, destroying every shred of confidence I had, with no remorse.

I sometimes thought he loved Lola, as I thought he loved me, but what man does those cruel things to the people he loves without blinking?

No man flirts with every single woman on Earth if his heart belongs to one woman only.

Nobody watches a woman in free falling because of him and walks away one minute after he told her I love you.

Nobody makes love to a woman like there is no tomorrow, and five minutes after runs to sleep with his ex.

No man who loves for real refuses to spend Christmas with his woman who's all alone in an empty house, in a country that is not hers.

***

To this day, I don't really know why he had sex with Lola. I made many assumptions, of course. I thought he slept with her because she insisted, he could have been drunk or sober. I didn't think it was his idea, I really believed he wouldn't have risked that friendship. He is very loyal to his friends.

I thought she promised him that he will not lose her if they had sex because she must have believed he would fall in love with her after that. Why would she believe that, I don't know. Maybe because he was always with her, playing the role of the nice guy who cares?

I guessed she truly believed they could be best friends and have a love relationship at the same time. He must have felt so alone that he wanted to believe her, so he let his animal instinct to act. But as soon as she started to pretend exclusivity, more dating, more time in bed, more things to share, he pulled back because he already had another one to do those things with.

I think Lola wanted to tell people about them being together, but he didn't want that. He wanted to screw her anytime he pleased, and keep his status of single so he could move to another body at any time with no guilt, remorse, or shame. Then to another one and so on.

He treated her with tenderness at first, he was always available when she asked for help, he listened, talked, spend time together. But the closer she got, the farther he ran into the opposite direction.

I think Adrian is utterly incapable of loving anyone, including himself. He is so terrified of exposing his feelings to others that he talks himself out of love all the time he starts to feel consumed by desire and jealousy. For the fear of being abandoned. I often wondered if he realises how much harm does that fear to himself and to any possible woman who really likes him.

He acts like the nicest guy in the world until you start asking him to stay with you. He gives immensely at first and gets tired in a short time, especially if another woman begins to show interest in him. He doesn't fight the fear, he fights the love. He closed his heart because someone hurt him in the past, so now he hurts whoever comes in his way.

I think he needs to feel useful to someone so he could find a purpose in his life. But that someone must be needy and has to abstain from questioning his methods, and his ex-girlfriend is that person. As long as she doesn't find another man to do that for her, he feels accomplished and in peace. "She's always here, we'll always be and remain best friends." They could share the same roof for the rest of their life. They might even think that love is what keeps them together, even if there is no sexual desire; unless they are inebriated by litres of alcohol or other stuff I do not know about. None of them will ever know that Love is something else, the most wonderful feeling from all.

Adrian will never belong to another woman except for the woman with whom he shares the roof in this moment. The one he left to be with me. Is she doomed or is she lucky? As long is she's fine with it, who am I to judge? But I am entitled to an opinion as I am trying to understand why did I have to live this story. He could be a cold-blooded murderer of souls, or he could just be afraid. He could be anything, just like me, you and everyone else. The human mind is not a perfect science. God have mercy of those poor souls who fell into his trap. Like Lola and me.

I am not sure of any of these things, of course, mostly are only empty allegations. Adrian made so many efforts to transform my body into a ball of fire, at first. He stroked, caressed, kissed for hours. I was just a passionate receiver. I tried to do the same for him, but he was very uncomfortable, he didn't know what to do and I gave up. I used to ask him why, he said, "I am a giver, that's why." The truth is that he had lured me with that infinite tenderness, making me believe he did it for me, when he only did what made him feel good. He made sure I was in his power, and when he had nothing else to give, he moved to another needy body, and he'll do that until the end of time. I guessed he wanted me for a while when I didn't question. But if he's happy and at peace, who am I to judge? Am I happy and at peace? Not even close, but I am working on it.

The question is: was he a Casanova or a Don Juan?

There have been many moments in which I thought Adrian loved me, and there were infinite more that proved me wrong. He made me reach the peak of Everest, watched me in freefall, and let me crush on sharp rocks. He didn't reach a hand to help me getting up, bind my wounds, or wipe my tears of an unbearable pain. He let me twist and shudder all alone, and ran to pay his ex's bills and buy her gifts. And I knew what he was doing, but I didn't really know why.

Was he still in love with her? That sense of responsibility was an excuse or was it for real? If they had been married, would he still have taken her to live with his family, sharing the same roof defying all the rules of common sense?

And when I would finally manage to get up and shut my mind off, when the river of tears was all dried out, I would ask him to come to me with so damn humbleness, blaming it all on me, desperately hoping he won't do the same. He would come when he wanted, and he would take me to that edge of absolute blissfulness, then pushed me down without blinking, one hour later. And my heart will still beat only for him.

> *"A word, a murmur of reply*
> *How often did I pray!*
> *What matters then if I should die,*
> *Enough to live that day;*
>
> *To know one hour of tenderness,*
> *One hour of lover's night;*
> *To hear you whisper soft caress*
> *One hour, then come what might!"*

This fragment of the poem *Down Where The Lonely Poplars Grow* from a great, The Great, Romanian poet, Mihai Eminescu, translated by

Corneliu M. Popescu, had been on my mind for those two years in which we both pulled and pushed, stood and sat.

***

Love has never been blind to me. I've always seen everything, and I wished so much to fall in love and be blind at least once in my life... like other people. I don't know how that feels and I envy those who cannot see. I envy them so badly! I knew Adrian was going to give me one hour of lust and several days, weeks, months of unbearable pain. And I still let him inside my house and inside my body. I thought that hour was better than nothing.

But have I loved Adrian? What were those doubts, accusations, assumptions, struggles, the pushing and the pulling, the flying and the falling, the kissing with insatiability, the fighting with rage?

The day he gave me that black and pink scarf, he put his feelings on the table, and I didn't even notice. I was so deep into my pain that I totally ignored that prove of love. Months later, a friend of mine took the scarf in her hands and noticed the hearts and the flowers. It was the first time I saw those too. And I cried and felt so guilty. Why didn't he tell me?!

But then again, his behaviour never changed in my regards, was that scarf enough to conclude that he loved me? Wasn't another move in his twisted mind game?

How do we measure love?

My heart will recognise his until the end of time, I know that now, and I am okay with it.

One day I asked him if he ever really loved me, he said yes, but I couldn't believe him.

"Believe what you want," he told me as usual.

We loved each other in different languages. Not because of the age disparity, or because of different background, culture, no; it was because we were not right one for another. We were antipodal.

I never trusted him, as I said. I wanted to trust him, but how can you trust someone who's in a relationship and courts random women in the streets? If he did that to his girlfriend, it means he will do that to you too. Because that's the way he operates.

But has he treated me worse than I treated him?

I stepped on his dignity, he stepped on mine's. I didn't do it on purpose, I like to believe he didn't either. Unfortunately, his behaviour proved that he wanted to punish me for the times I hurt him. He was the vindictive type. I guess he would have loved showing off with me. I was and still am a great catch.

Have I given him more than he gave me?

I guess I have. From my perspective, clearly. Countless times. I gave him my body when I didn't feel like it, and I did many other things for him which I didn't like. I resented him for all that because he has never done anything for me against his will. When he kissed and caressed my body for hours, it was for his own pleasure, not mine. The fact I loved it was just a bonus. If I didn't feel love for him, I guess I would have never felt satisfied. I must admit though that he never really forced me to do anything I didn't want to. Everything I've done, gladly or not, was my free choice. So I cannot really blame him for my choices.

Which one was more insane, he or me?

Well, that's difficult to say. He never cried, he almost never got angry, he never tried to assure me he loved me, he ran to his ex-girlfriend after sleeping with me, etc. It was like he never felt anything at all. For some people, these are signs of a very stable person. Not for me though. Cold-blooded humans are capable of anything.

On the other hand, I cried, shouted, insulted, went crazy, ignored him in public, etc. I knew it was not good, and I hated being like that. I kept trying to change, fought against my impulses to avoid hurting him. I almost always blamed everything on me, because I was older and I should have been emotionally more stable.

He couldn't care less about what and how I felt. He never ever thought twice, he always did what was best for him. Hell, he left me all alone when I was very, very ill, and never called to ask if I was still alive. What human would do that to another human? Girlfriend, best friend, sex partner, or a perfect stranger?

I knew his behaviour was off, I noticed it right from the start, you don't need a degree in medicine, psychology, psychiatry or whatever to realise he was not an ordinary human being. I should have stayed away, but it was like I wanted to suffer. I felt attracted to him like a mouse to a cat. If a woman would stand completely naked in front of him, begging him to have sex with her because she might die if not, I believe he would not do it if he didn't consider it was good for him. How many men could say the same? Most males think with their wieners, but not Adrian.

He convinced himself that it is a matter of discipline, strong will, principles and all that sort of stuff. For me, it is just lack of empathy for others.

I often wondered if he would help a random person in need on the street, and based on how he treated Lola and me, I concluded that he wouldn't. Unless he had something to gain from it.

Lola told me that she spoke about him with some of his colleagues (mostly women), and some friends. All of them said that Adrian was an extraordinary human being. Always ready to help. Very loyal and trustworthy.

He helped me at first too, because he wanted me to fall for him. As soon as I became addictive to him, and he was sure of my feelings, he changed completely. So yes, I can imagine him being a superhero in front of others, but they were all cold-blooded calculations.

I used to be terrified of him, especially when he was drunk. I disliked his personality and my weakness. I was happy I didn't work with him as I often thought that he could have had me fired at any point.

What did he do for a living? I've never asked him. Maybe he was a hitman, he surely had the perfect character for that.

Sometimes I really envied him. I wished I felt nothing for anyone. Just for a few minutes though.

I would rather die from pain than live without feeling anything. But it's my choice.

Love is the most thrilling feeling ever.

Isn't love about giving with the only intent to make the other one happy?

If any person is able to do that forever, not for a short period of time, I truly admire them. We are not made of the same flesh, with the same stamp. Someone must have messed things up in that Creation day. Maybe God was looking at the first people he just created in his image and fell in adoration. And the Devil took advantage of that moment and used his image to create other creatures. Like me and Adrian, and many, many others. We are all humans... to some degree. There used to be Gods, but are all extinct now, we've killed them with our flesh desires. With the desperate search for lust and pleasure.

If I have to be honest with myself, keeping in mind that Adrian always did what he wanted, I would have to admit that he never ever loved me.

Or Lola. And I don't believe he loved or loves his ex, present and forever girlfriend, because he only does what makes him content, no matter what. He needs to feel useful and irreplaceable. He lives with her in his parents' house, helps her with everything and they both act like they are a couple. Nothing wrong with that. Except he has sex with other women. How is this fair towards her? Does she know about his behaviour? What does she think he does when he's out until 4am every weekend? However, who am I to judge? They love one another and agree to be a couple without a sex life. I wouldn't want a relationship like that. But again, it's their choice. Nevertheless, I always envied those who can remain best friends after breaking up. I never wanted to hear anything from my exes again. But we were never best friends.

To be honest, although he always says that he doesn't love himself, his narcissistic behaviour proves him wrong. And he's got no idea or he doesn't want to. You don't need a doctor to diagnose you, just be honest with yourself and do a research.

We all have narcissistic traits in our personality, and it's very difficult to fight against them.

I used to think that love can make you want to change completely, and I still believe that.

Love can transform any devil into an angel, and vice-versa.

What about me though? Haven't I kept telling him and myself that he wasn't the one, and I didn't want a relationship for the future with him? I expected him to listen to me and fight to change my mind. But my mind was already set, *he was not the one*. I felt it deep inside me. He couldn't fight for me because I didn't want him to.

I made a final revision of that twisted story and when I arrived at the moment in which he slept with Lola, and said nothing to me, I remembered the day he told me that he had sex with a woman. "You've rejected me. I was hurt and a woman showed interest in me."

That brute omitted to mention Lola's name because he knew I would have never, ever, let him inside my body if I knew. That was the only thing I couldn't or wouldn't fight to overcome. From all the countless humiliations I had to endure, that was the worst. And that was what killed the incredible lust my body used to feel for him. I guess I should be happy, but I am not. Because I really never thought he could be so diabolic.

Adrian and I have lived a real nightmare and many people live the same every day.

There is a simple explanation of why your partner treats you with disregard and doesn't care you suffer, *they don't love you*. You're not on the same page. Utterly incompatible. People always say respect the differences in your partner, and if your partner behaviour makes you suffer, then you have no other choice than setting them free. You are not meant one for each other.

I don't think there was a single thing I liked in Adrian, it was clear we would live a war, but I just chose to do it. That was my frequency, looking for men to treat me wrong. Like I was addicted to suffering. I should have stopped seeing him the first time he disrespected me, but I didn't. He didn't force me to stay with him, I forced myself. It was my choice.

Are we women always that weak or we are just craving for someone to make us feel something, anything?

***

With all this in mind, will I ever be able to love again? Trust another human being, after being under the power of a bizarre individual, and knowing the gods are all extinct?

I might spend the rest of my days and nights alone, with my hot water bottle, random books and with a glass of whisky from time to time. Unless I will break free and want to learn to respect myself, start believing again and change my vibration. Love is all we need and I have never felt loved. I don't know what loves is.

Fundamentally, we are all born angels but we lose our purity when people hurt us. We chose to bury the God side of us so we could survive among evils.

I looked in a mirror and swore I would never beg for love again. 'Do you hear me, body? You won't have another man inside you unless he is a god. Because you'll talk yourself into a god state again so you can deserve him. You are not a child anymore, you have the power of discernment, you can be whatever you want.'

That's what I decided that last time I saw Adrian and closed another chapter of my life, the one who took everything from me, the dignity of being human.

Adrian was gone. He was never mine. After crying a sea of tears, after so much hate and disgust towards myself, two years of unbearable torture, and just hours of walking on air, I was finally free. Despite all the crying, struggles, and fights, he will always have a place in my heart.

***

The house was full of dust, I cleaned it all up. I washed and rubbed every surface and object so nothing could bring him to my memory again. No fingerprints, no odours, no images. I changed the bed lining and put everything in the washing machine, along with my clothes.

I had a bath, rubbed every inch of my skin, patted it dry and spread a very generous amount of baby oil on it. Then I went to bed and slept for less than one hour. My alarm went off at 6am. *'Every day is a new beginning,'* I murmured.

ABOUT THE AUTHOR

Born in Romania during the oppressive communist regime of Nicolae Ceausescu, Cristina G. is uniquely qualified to address topics encompassing communism, immigration, abuse and exploitation. Her novels face those obstacles head-on, but are accounts of love and survival that weave together fact and fiction into stories for the soul.

A farmer's daughter, Cristina was the eleventh child and a seventh daughter. She thought her life path was sealed until she read *"Les Misérables"* by Victor Hugo and decided to be a writer.

She immigrated to Italy in 2000 to follow her dream, but quickly discovered that Romanian heritage there marked her by society as someone of inferior birth.

Soul weary, the author returned to her native Romania with few options. "Freedom without opportunities is just another kind of prison," says Cristina. With the encouragement of her brother, Sebastian, she blogged for many years and owns two highly popular blogs in Romanian and two in English.

With the aid of a British friend, in 2014, Cristina G. moved to the UK where her expectations were not great. Here, against all odds and despite the Brexit Referendum, she has finally managed to fulfil a dream she never dared to dream before: becoming a registered author.

Cristina's writing endeavours have been very well received. Her memoir, "Three Weeks a Human: A Memoir," garnered rave reviews from readers with the suggestion that it be made into a film, exposing the slavery that still exists in the world.

With an astonishing background, outstanding determination, and remarkable passion, Cristina G. is a perfect candidate to greatness.

If you want to know more about Cristina G. and keep up to date with her work, please visit: https://authorcristinag.blogspot.com

If you liked this book, why not review it on Amazon or Goodreads?

OTHER BOOKS BY CRISTINA G. ON AMAZON

Oranges at Christmas in a Communist Country – A Memoir – True to Fact book that chronicles her personal experiences during one of the most oppressive regimes in Eastern Europe

Ten Years in Italy: Three Weeks a Human – A Memoir – Another True to Fact book that addresses bigotry, exploitation and slavery in the 20th century

Humans Cursed by Geography in the Pursuit of Happiness – True to Fact Stories – Publication that gathers the previous memoirs set in Romania and Italy

It's Never Game Over – A Self-Help book – A highly motivational and inspirational publication about self-discipline, self-growth, and dreams come true

iLive – Stories From the Prison Called Life – A psychological thriller set behind walls

God is Weary – Tragic and Witty Short Tales – A collection of stories that explores the harm that mankind inflicts upon each other but not only

Half My Age Plus Seven – The Sequel – Too Good to be True? – A story of love, sacrifice and hope

Îmi Curg Mucii, Deci Exist – A Collection of Ironic Poetry in Romanian

EXCERPT FROM GOD IS WEARY

A Mile Away

It's a Tuesday night in March 2017. I can't sleep, so I am walking on a dark pavement on the outskirts of the city. It has rained, the roads are wet. In front of a couple of buildings with large eaves, a few homeless people are sleeping on cupboards beds. I feel sorry for them and speculate about what brought them in that situation, but mostly, how can they sleep when it rains?

Besides them, the city is all deserted. If it were a Friday, you wouldn't be able to have a peaceful walk among the crowd of people out until morning. The contrast makes me reflect on people's behaviour, interests, and priorities. But it's not my business what others do, I have enough on my plate.

"Out of the way, mate!" shouts a voice behind me.

I jump and move on the other side of the pavement by instinct. A second later, a bicycle knocks me down. I fell on my knees into a puddle. Unsure of a wound, I wonder if I should laugh, cry, curse or all three at the same time.

"Bloody hell!" imprecates the voice. "I said out of the way!" The voice belonged to a middle-aged man.

"Yes, it's what I've done, and look at me now, all wet like an otter's pocket," I say in all seriousness.

"Wet like what?!" asks the man confused.

"Otters... they live in the water and... oh, never mind," I reply while getting up.

The man drops the bicycle to give me a hand.

"Don't touch me, you've done enough already, mate!" I say with sarcasm.

"Don't be stubborn, you might have a broken bone."

I push his hands away and check my legs, the bones seem fine, but the muscles are all aching. I am sure I'll have a huge purple mark on the right thigh tomorrow.

"Are you all right? Should I call an ambulance? A friend of mine is a nurse, maybe I could call her."

"At 3 on a Tuesday morning?! Don't be silly, I am fine. Stay away from me though."

"Oh, come on now. I didn't mean to crash into you. It's not my fault," defends himself the middle-aged man.

"Of course not. You have all the legal equipment on your bike... lights, bell, helmet.... Is this dodgy object even yours? Should I call the police?"

"You may if you really have nothing better to do. But I can assure you this stuff is mine. It belonged to me for the last ten years. The last time I used it, four years ago, I almost killed myself and gave up the lessons."

"What?! You are learning to cycle at this age and hour? You're a danger to all things and beings!"

"I have been doing this for two weeks now, nobody walks on these streets at 3 on a Tuesday morning. Has your husband thrown you out?" he asks in a cheeky tone.

"Right... because I am a bad woman and deserve that, right? All women are mean to their innocent partners... Give me a break, you chauvinist."

"I am sorry, I was only teasing," says the man with a guilty voice.

"Teasing? How long have we known each other for? Five, six minutes? Why all this confidence with a complete stranger? Are you even British?" I ask with fake fury.

"What's that supposed to mean?"

"British people take a long time before befriending outsiders; years, sometimes even decades," I explain.

"Not all Brits are so stiff. Where are you from?"

"And why would you ask me that? Because my English is not perfect and my pronunciation sucks? Or because you've voted *Leave* at the referendum?"

"Wait now, I am not a racist..."

"I didn't say you were. It's your country, you are free to hang pigs and dogs at your own desire."

"What?!" asked the man perplexed. "I am vegetarian, I don't eat meat."

I burst into laughter, "People don't eat dogs! It's an expression in my language."

The man looks at me thinking I must be insane. His expression, a mix of bewilderment and annoyance, is priceless; I laugh even harder. Cannot stop. He doesn't join me, and after a few seconds, it becomes dissonant. I feel guilty and terribly ashamed. I take a deep breath, clear my throat, and ask for forgiveness. He ignores my sincere apologies and says, "Well, it sounded like you were accusing me of bigotry. The reason I asked is that you brought it up. I would have never dared otherwise. And for your information, people eat dogs in several countries around the Globe, and I voted *Stay*. Bloody Brexit!"

He was vexed. 'I really exaggerated this time. I am a guest in this country; I should be more considerate,' I am thinking in my head. Tears start to flow suddenly from my eyes. I try to hide them, but I soon sob like a child.

"I am so sorry," he says. "I didn't mean to be rude. You must be very upset and in terrible pain for this incident. Let me take you home."

I can't speak, so I start walking in the opposite direction. The man grabs the bike and follows me running next to it. Ten minutes later, I stop and take the keys out of my pocket.

"You live right in the city centre! What a luxury!" the man exclaims with admiration.

I don't reply, just step inside the corridor slightly illuminated by the lampposts.

A noise makes me turn my head. The bike is down again. The man is behind me. He grabs my hand and pushes me against the wall. I should be scared and afraid, but I am not, my life worth nothing anyway. I prayed for this moment for so many years. 'I am not going to scream, I am not going to cry like a coward. I am a strong woman.' I close my eyes and pray not to suffer. His lips barely touch mine. A dazed sound comes out of my mouth. 'I was wrong, he doesn't want to kill me, he's trying to rape me! I heard of stories like this but never thought it could happen to me. No, no, no!' I shout in my head. 'Fight, Scarlett, fight!' I gather all my strengths and prepare for the attack.

"I am so sorry," he murmurs all of a sudden.

I stop and stare into his eyes, they are not filled with criminal intentions.

"I don't know what's got into me… Forgive me. I scared you to death, I know. You… I am sorry. You must think I'm a horrible man, and you're right, I am, but I hadn't planned any of this. An invisible powerful force attracts me towards you, like a magnet. I can't fight it," he explains startling. "Your husband will provoke me to a duel. I deserve it, I dared to…."

"I am not married," I murmur overwhelmed. 'Shut up, Scarlett! Are you nuts? Maybe he's testing you. Psychos are everywhere, you know?'

The man looks at me in a trance, his heart beats are visible in the large jugular vein. We are both breathing heavily. There is a war inside my head, memories of horrifying real and imaginary stories clash into one another; *Jack the Ripper,* a movie in which a woman is saved from a rapist by another rapist who seemed such a cool guy, *Criminal Minds*. In nanoseconds, the scary speculations reach a deafening crescendo; I don't know what to do. 'Maybe I should scream. We are in the city centre, people will hear. What people though? It's 3 in the morning.' I feel like fainting. 'I never fainted before! Now is not the right time for foolish behaviours, Scarlett! You're a grown woman. Tell him to leave you alone, go inside and never, ever walk on the streets at this hour again.'

"I don't even know your name…" I murmur. 'Really?! You want to know his name?! You're crazier than him!'

"Jack…"

"Oh, come on now! That's not helping!" I shout exasperated.

"What do you mean? I do…don't…," the man is baffled.

"Jack? The Ripper?! And why in hell would you write his name in capital letters? He was a cold-blood murderer, not a celebrity!"

Jack starts laughing, "Oh… you thought I was a criminal! Ha, ha, ha."

I look at him and wonder if we are both mad or just overwhelmed by these strange events. 'It's clear that the destiny wanted us to meet. Why? I don't know yet, but I will soon find out,' I think in my head.

Suddenly the light from the street disappears, it's all dark and can't see anything. My heart makes a jump. I am worried sick. Too much tension, I cannot breathe. "Help," I murmur.

"Shh... shh...," whispers Jack.

So weak... I struggle and slide down the wall. Oblivion.

***

To read more go to
https://www.amazon.com/God-Weary-Tragic-Witty-Short-ebook/dp/B074415WXL.